. . . For every man I killed, another stepped forward. I was reminded of a great wind that brushes over with ease the trees at the edge of a forest, yet loses its strength as it goes deeper in and the wood closes thickly about it.

Thus far I had not been touched, for I kept my wits and my shield close about me and wielded my sword with a savage dexterity. But I could feel myself rapidly tiring; I was sweating profusely in my iron cocoon, a great, numbing weight that now tried to pull me down. My sword was so pitted and gouged that I weened it would be useless after this fight, whatever the outcome. And with weariness came doubt. *This is madness. What are we doing here? Has all my philosophy brought me only to this?* . . .

Belatedly, for Jennifer

THE BOOK OF MORDRED

Peter Hanratty

Cover painting by David Cherry

New Infinities Productions, Inc.
P.O. Box 127
Lake Geneva WI 53147

THE BOOK OF MORDRED

First Printing, January 1988

Printed in the United States of America

Distributed by the Berkley Publishing Group, 200 Madison Avenue, New York NY 10016

9 8 7 6 5 4 3 2 1

ISBN: 0-441-07018-3

New Infinities Productions, Inc.
P.O. Box 127
Lake Geneva WI 53147

PART ONE

1

AT NIGHT EVERYTHING WAS ODDLY DIFFERENT.

To his few confidants he had often joked that he could make the journey blindfolded, yet when he came to the spot where he usually dismounted, he almost rode straight past. It was only because his courser slowed down at the bend in the road out of habit that he realized where he was. He patted the animal for its astuteness, then dismounted carefully, for the ground was wet after a full day's rain and he did not want to slip in his armor. There should have been a fallen tree near where he stood, but that too had shifted in the dark. After some seconds of blind, puzzled groping he found it, just a few feet away from where it was in the daytime. Then, after tying the horse, he began making his way on foot into the wood.

In front of him, some distance off still, he could see the pinpoint of light, so tiny that only someone who knew it was there would look for and notice it. The only other illumination came from the watery moon that showed its face now and then through the treetops.

When he had followed this path in daylight, the sun had always shone, penetrating the thick-leaved forest and peppering his face with its mottled warmth, putting him in a receptive mood for the pleasures that awaited him. Those had been golden afternoons.

But in the darkness, everything changed. Tonight he

was drawn not by desire, but by the voice that had plagued his sleep — soft and unintelligible, but clearly recognizable, and insistent enough to wake him and then drive him from his bed. He had donned his armor hastily — but thoroughly — and galloped past the astonished sentries into the cold night. Now, as he plunged almost blindly through the undergrowth, noisily crushing it underfoot, the darkness enfolded him like a damp, scented veil. But he was aware of none of this. All he cared about was the voice.

Was it making sounds of ecstasy, or pain, or both? Whichever, it was louder now — though still only in his mind, for surely he was still too far from the hut to hear noises from within it. He stopped for a moment. Yes, there was a clear difference. The faint, nervous scurryings of small animals, yesterday's rain dripping from sodden leaves: these were the real sounds.

But the other sound was real, too, in its way. Had it not brought him here? He had taken no precautions against discovery, had prepared no alibi. There would be a lot of explaining to do when he returned home.

For a moment the light vanished from the single window, blocked by a thicket of silver birches. He walked on, and then he was standing in the moonlight, in the clearing with the daub-and-wattle hut in front of him.

It seemed there were the three of them: the heavy moon, a sailing cloud, and he in his armor that sparkled like the dark sea. Then the cloud passed in front of the moon and he was standing alone in his armor, black and coarse.

He was no longer sure about the voice. It could still be coming from his head, or from inside the hut. Whatever its source, the owner of the voice was clearly in pain now; her heavy and rapid breathing was punctuated by ragged gasps. Amid the surrounding silence it was sharply clear, and it shocked him to hear it even though he had spent so much of his life inflicting pain on others.

He did not know what to do next, so he just stood there, treading the grass like a restless horse. Go on or turn back? The voice did not help much. It had drawn him all the way, but now that he was here it would not tell him what to do next.

I can do no good here. I am a man, of no use here. I can only take life, not the other thing.

He thought those words, then spoke them. His voice, like a stone in water, shocked the silence. The words, like ripples, encircled him, then vanished into the hungry recesses of the forest.

He wanted to turn back then, but something stopped him. An awareness, perhaps, that in that ghostly and silvery stillness something quite remarkable was about to happen — and that he, wavering uncertainly amidst the dense, uncanny beauty of the night, should be there to witness it.

Another light appeared in the doorway as an unseen hand pulled aside the curtain that hung across it. Hesitantly, wondering why he should have to summon so much courage now when he had done this countless times before, he stepped forward.

And stopped dead.

The thin scream that rent the air was not a woman's, nor a man's. . . . Some animal?

Almost immediately it died away, leaving in its wake a shocked and expectant silence. But still the knight remained frozen in horror. He was staring incredulously at the ground in front of the hut, at what must surely be a trick of the light. Something was lapping out of the doorway and oozing gently toward him. At first it was a trickle, but soon it became a dark, viscous flood, spreading in all directions. It moved slowly but his mind, striving to comprehend, moved slower still, and when he finally decided he had seen enough the cloying liquid was already swirling thickly about his feet. The warmth of it penetrated his thick-stockinged soles and the smell, horribly familiar, made him want to retch. He gave a cry of horror and disgust that became one of panic when, turning, he realized he could no longer remember the way out of the wood; the trees seemed suddenly much denser, and the illumination from both the moon and the hut had vanished.

Still shouting, he stumbled toward the edge of the clearing. No matter that it seemed impenetrable, no matter if he was lost — any direction would do. But his armor had become inexplicably heavier; either that, or he had suddenly become much weaker. Every footstep in the dark pool that now surrounded him seemed to require so much effort, as if the liquid were alive and reluctant to let him go.

With a scream that owed as much to fury at his clumsiness as it did to fear, he slipped and fell heavily on his back, jarring himself painfully in spite of the thick padding he wore inside his mail. In his frantic haste to get up, he rolled over and over so that his face and body became covered, and he spat and snorted heavily to free his mouth and nostrils. The moon returned and in its light his writhing body glistened; he was like some curious, armor-plated animal wallowing in a thick crimson mud. From a sufficient distance it might even have looked as if he was enjoying the experience.

Sometimes, with much effort, he might rise as far as his knees, but his scrabbling hands and feet could find no purchase on the slippery ground, and he would soon slide helplessly down again.

At length his struggles subsided; he was too exhausted even to panic now. He knew he was slowly drowning in this seemingly endless tide, but as his mouth and nostrils became once more clogged with the sweet stickiness, he could only splutter and choke helplessly. He had not the strength to do any more, and soon he would not even have the will.

As he lay there, face down, still incredulous but willing now to submit to this improbable and not very dignified end, he thought he heard the light, pleasant sound of laughter. It sounded quite far away and like a woman's laugh. She sounded politely but genuinely amused. Then another voice joined in, a baby's this time. No, not a baby; it was a child's laughter he could hear.

But that was impossible. Surely it could not be. . . .

* * *

"What is it? What's the matter?"

Arthur looked up. His whole body was covered with sweat; the bedclothes were soaked. He felt sticky and uncomfortable, and inside he was still shaking with fear and apprehension. But what struck him most vividly at that moment was the expression on Guinevere's face.

She looks so concerned, he said to himself. She is worried about me. See how it shows. She really cares.

He could not remember the last time she had shown her feelings like this. It softened her face too, making it young again. She looked suddenly, invitingly lovely, and Arthur felt a confusing intermingling of desire and guilt.

When he had woken her with his struggles and muffled shouts, she had hastily lit a candle — it really had sounded as if a demon was in the room with them. Now as she bent frowning over him her hair, in the light, glowed like a halo, framing her pale worried face.

I don't deserve her, Arthur thought. I really don't.

"You've been having a nightmare." She sounded almost disappointed. "You never have nightmares."

Slowly, unsteadily, as if he were still a little unsure of his footing, he pulled himself to a sitting position. When his face was on a level with hers he said, "It was no dream. It was more real than any other dream I can remember."

That was true. He did not feel as if he had been asleep. He really feared that if he looked down he would see not harmless perspiration but glistening blood and dark-stained sheets. He could still feel the chill of the woodland's dank night air penetrating the bedclothes.

Guinevere tried to look interested and bemused, even though she had a shrewd idea of what was coming next. What her expression really said was, You do not have to say any more; in fact, I would much rather that you did not.

Arthur did not notice."It was a message, I think," he said. "From her. From Morgause."

Guinevere sighed. It sounded like tired forbearance. It did not sound like surprise.

Arthur too was tired, and he was breathing heavily. The simple act of sitting up in bed had quite exhausted him. "I think her time has arrived."

Guinevere's lips became tight. She knew how he disliked this matronly expression of hers. It made her look older, less desirable. She did not care any more. "I'm surprised the whole palace hasn't fallen about our ears, then."

Arthur, though saddened and disappointed at the hardness in her face, knew also that he was largely to blame for it. "Please don't be like this. It isn't like you. How many more times must I tell you how sorry I am?"

Oh, but these days it *was* like her. And it would get worse, she knew. There would be many more occasions like this, when he would turn his melancholy eyes to hers and look genuinely, boyishly contrite.

And he was sorry, she believed. Not for destroying their short happiness and her faith in him, nor really for the gulf that was now so unbridgeable that it was hard for her to remember a time when it had been otherwise. He was sorry because he felt guilty; and then his remorse, so thoroughgoing, so candid, assuaged his guilt and prepared the way for the next indiscretion.

That there would be others she was certain. Arthur had made a monumental blunder, and it would chasten him for a while. For a few months he would be on his best behavior while Merlin and poor Sir Ector scurried frantically behind the scenes to repair the damage as best they could. He might even show her some of the old affection. For a while.

Two years ago she had not thought like this. She had been in her teens then; naive and newly wed. And in love.

It did not take me long to grow up, Guinevere thought. She sighed again, and in the sad whisper of her breath the candle flame briefly trembled, stirring the shadows that rested in the room's dim light. Is this what it means to be a woman? To lose your youth in a matter of months and become bitter and cynical while learning not to care that none of your husband's children will be yours also? . . .

She realized that Arthur was speaking to her. "Yes, what is it?" she snapped.

"I said, what should I do?" He was too agitated to notice the sharpness in her voice.

Guinevere gazed abstractedly at the tapestry hanging from the end of the bed. It was more functional than decorative; heavy enough to keep out most of the fierce draughts that howled through the unglazed window. But when she had first come to this bed, she had often sat up in the still hours while her lord slept and she could not. In the candle's flickering light she could sometimes imagine the figures in the tapestry moving. That sort of thing just did not happen any more. Still, Arthur would insist on these trysts, these fumbling attempts at reconciliation and closeness. But the bed was so large now, and the space between them was a cold and sterile desert. It could never be like it was. She turned toward him fiercely. "She's a witch, isn't she? Burn her. The brat too."

She did not mean it. She rarely blamed the women. What chance did they have against the King of Albion?

Even for an enchantress it would be at best an even match. She was simply tired; of his bleating, his childish yearning for forgiveness; of the slow, wearing tedium that her life had become.

She had wanted to shock him, though, and it had worked. Arthur said nothing more that night. She felt him turn away, and after a decent interval she blew out the candle and shifted nearer to the edge of the bed. It was colder there, and the draughts whistled like arctic gales. But at least it was dry.

* * *

Things could have turned out differently. Life, I know, is full of might-have-beens, and it is mostly idle to speculate upon them. I never sought the opprobrium so savagely — and unjustly — heaped on my head by all but the more perceptive commentators. It was never my intention to depose Arthur, most emphatically not. Why, as a child I doted on the man. Even when I became aware of his lack of foresight, his flawed vision and fatal self-aggrandizement, it did not greatly diminish my affection. This only vanished, together with my sense of filial duty, when I learned of the dark truth. Yet even then I could not strike the first blow.

But Arthur could, and did so many times.

The first was when I was about four years old.

2

THE BOY DID NOT THINK IT EVEN A BIT STRANGE that his mother should send him out of the hut whenever one of his uncles came to visit. He liked to play on his own anyway and wander through the forest as if it were his. And when he grew tired of being alone, there were his friends. But he did want to stay long enough to say hello — and perhaps receive a small gift also.

"Is it Uncle Kay?" His small mouth gaped unself-consciously wide as he lifted his moon face to hers in an expression both of polite entreaty and frank incredulity. He had only lately become aware of his mother's beauty, and these days he was quite in awe of her.

For she was flawless; ageless and unlined. When she laughed or, more rarely, became angry, no creases ever marked her moods. Even on his own face — which was to him so revoltingly fat — he could make smile-lines and thought-lines appear. He was sure that if he practiced in the mirror long enough, he could make himself look old. But he would never do that, in case the lines did not go away afterward.

His mother would never look old. Her face was like the pool in the forest that always looked so still that it was not like water at all, but like a flat, polished stone. His friends said it was so dark because it had no bottom, but they could not explain why the surface never moved.

Morgause laughed and pretended to poke a finger into his still-gaping mouth. "Catching flies, are we? No, it's not Uncle Kay." Uncle Kay did not like children.

"Is it Father, then?" (Sometimes she would push him out of the house early, saying something like, "I don't think I shall let your father speak to you today. He has neglected us lately. He does not deserve to see his fine son.")

She had just begun to shake her head "no" when she stopped. The laughter had died from her face. She looked sad and anxious, and just for a second there was a crease or two in her forehead.

Oh, he thought. *Oh*. . . .

His mouth fell open again, in horror this time. It was a terrible shock for him; a reminder of mortality. Not of his — he knew about that; that was not important — but of hers.

It surprised him too, the suddenness with which she took him into her arms and hugged him fiercely, almost painfully. He could feel the warmth of her body and that soothing motion her breasts made against his face. But was it she who was trembling, or he?

"Who is coming?" he whispered as his supple bones bent and the breath was squeezed out of his body. "Who is it?"

She always knew who was coming, when they would arrive, how long they would be staying, and whether or not it would be appropriate for him to stay and say hello. She always told him. . . .

Morgause relaxed her grip a little, but only so that she could pull his little face closer to her own. "Now. Listen to me."

But he could only stare, in growing dismay, as slowly his flawless mother began to age before his eyes.

To anyone else it would have seemed barely noticeable; she was still a great beauty. But to Mordred, who could not bear these imperfections, she was suddenly transformed into an old crone, and it surprised him to realize that he could love her still. In truth it was nothing more than simple anxiety. In the past, largely out of vanity, Morgause would never let him see her worried or unhappy. Now she was beginning to lose control just a little.

"Listen," she repeated while Mordred tried hard to conceal his distaste and suppressed an urge to struggle free. "You must go far into the forest today; quite out of sight of the house. And you must stay away. You must not come back until"— she paused —"dusk. Come back before it gets dark."

"I'm not afraid of the dark."

"I know. You're my brave darling. You're not afraid of anything. But there is no need to stay out after dark. And . . ." She fixed him with a searching gaze from which he quickly turned away. At times he could not bear to look into her eyes. He did not like the things he sometimes saw there.

"Mummy, what is it?" he asked, fixing his eyes instead on the graceful curve of her neck. "What's wrong?"

"If I am not here when you get back, there will be food for you. Be sure to eat it, even if you don't feel hungry. After a day or so somebody will come for you. I cannot be certain of this, but I am almost sure." She paused, staring thoughtfully at nothing in particular. "Yes, someone will come. You must not be afraid. They are kind and will look after you."

He wanted to cry, "Where are you going? Why can't you be here?" But before the words could come, she had taken his chin firmly between her thumb and fingers and was pulling his face up so that he could look nowhere except into those deep, green eyes. There was silence for a while. Then he ventured, "Shall I go to the pool?" His unvoiced protest was quite forgotten.

"Yes," she said quietly. "That is quite far enough."

It was the farthest he had ever been. In that part of

the forest even the animals seemed to hold their breath. He only dared go so far because, if the forest was indeed his, then he had to prove title.

"I could play with my friends."

Morgause nodded. She never referred to them in that way. Nor did she call them by their proper name. Whenever she spoke of them at all, she called them "those people." And she said it in such a way as to make it impossible to confuse them with the other people — the ones who came to visit, who lived outside the forest or on its harmless fringes. She did not have much time for his friends; she called them idlers, and sometimes much worse things. They always kept well clear of the hut.

But today she said, "That sounds like a good idea."

She gave him another fierce embrace, then pushed him away — but so gently that he hardly felt it. He was in a sort of daze anyway, and as he stumbled out of the doorway toward the trees he had the curious sensation of seeing not through his own eyes but through hers. There was that same green, shifting mist, slightly luminous, that he had seen when she had so roughly pulled his face up to hers. But in a moment it had vanished, and in another he had forgotten everything except that he was free to do what he liked for the rest of the day. Oh, yes . . . and that she might be out when he returned.

The pool would be a nice place to go, he told himself, without any of the foreboding that usually accompanied such thoughts.

To his small eyes it was more like a lake. Once he had tried to throw a stone across, but it had only flown halfway before dropping into the water, soundlessly, leaving no ripple. He had not tried again. Standing now in the cold light of that sunless glade, his imagination found it easy enough to summon forth horrors from beneath its surface of the pool, so still that it must be waiting for something.

He had asked his friends about it. "Oh, yes," they had

answered at once. "There is a creature down there. A true horror."

"What's it like?" he had asked.

"Oh, ugly, ugly," they had said.

But for the moment he was alone except for a hoodie-crow, a huge, unkempt tramp of a bird with feathers askew, noisily feeding on a dead sparrow nearby. Mordred threw a stone at it. The bird turned to face him with a large and shapeless piece of flesh dangling from its beak, its head slightly cocked as if considering whether or not this impertinence was worth troubling over. Then it turned again to feed.

Mordred knew all about "nature's way." That is what his mother called it whenever the cat brought in something that was still alive and he, loudly protesting, tried to set it free. He supposed that this too was "nature's way." He did not agree with it.

The next time his aim was considerably better. With a loud squawk of outrage and surprise, the crow dropped the food from its beak and turned, red eyes glaring balefully at its adversary. It took a few steps forward, cawing fiercely, and Mordred suddenly realized just what a huge animal this was.

"Wicked boy!"

He jumped with fright — but it was not the crow that had spoken those cackling words. For one thing, the voice had come from behind him. But it was a clever imitation and as he turned round, grinning, he clapped in appreciation and some relief.

The Oakapple Elf, a clumsy, ungainly creature slightly larger than Mordred, pulled itself from behind a thin screen of branches and waddled into the clearing on legs so impossibly small they were almost hidden beneath the folds of his enormous torso. He was laughing with far more gusto than the joke warranted and was making rather disagreeable snuffling noises through his flat and warty nose.

"Ssh!" said Mordred, but the elf had few manners and no idea at all about how to control the obnoxious noises he continued to make.

"Dead meat is fair game!" he bellowed hollowly. The hoddie-crow, oblivious to all this, was patiently dragging its catch beyond the reach of intrusive fairies and small boys with stones. "What do you want with that anyway?" The elf bent his bald and bulbous head closer so that Mordred could smell his woody odor, pungent and sticky-sweet like resin. "I can get you something much tastier. Oh my, yes." And he launched into another series of inexplicable and vulgar guffaws. Mordred smiled uncomfortably and moved away slightly. Sometimes the elf was not all that funny. He hoped somebody else would come along soon.

Another stone, not thrown by him this time, landed on the elf's head with a curious effect. It made a soft, pulpy sound as if it were landing in dough and did not bounce off but lodged itself in one of the deep wrinkles of flesh that covered his white scalp. The elf's eyes, growing wider as comprehension slowly dawned, gazed first at Mordred, then swiveled searchingly upward before their owner let out a howl of distress and pain so loud that Mordred, though greatly amused, had to cover his ears.

"Stop your howling, testicle-face!"

They both looked up. From the dense cluster of the treetops something jumped. There was a blur of movement and a whisper of sound. Then the Baobhan was among them, crouching and sniffing, her black, membranous wings vibrating soundlessly as she turned her head this way and that about the clearing.

Then, satisfied, she stood upright and her wings gathered themselves neatly into the deep hollow between her shoulders. At this point the crow, deciding that enough was enough, gave a bitter cry of frustration and rage and, abandoning its catch, flew heavily away.

The elf rubbed his head ruefully and grinned at the

Baobhan. Had it been anyone else, he probably would have reached for his club — but then nobody else would dare, would they? He judged it best to treat the whole thing as a joke. He laughed sheepishly, obscenely.

The Baobhan bared her yellow, jagged teeth. "Fetch the others!" she ordered.

As the elf scampered off, Mordred went up to her and began gently caressing the dark folds of her wings. He was not disturbed by her nakedness. He had seen his mother naked once, and that had shocked him, but this sight was really no comparison. With her black, sagging breasts, her sharp, protruding bones and pale, hungry eyes, the Baobhan was probably the least appealing of all his friends — but her wings fascinated him so. They possessed the texture of skin but not its warmth. They felt alive but terribly old. And dusty, like a moth's. When he touched them, they quivered slightly. Once she had unfolded them for him and, lifting him onto her back, had risen high above the vast and primitive forest so that he could see it stretching on three sides to the world's end.

Not today, though. With a brief downward glance she pushed him to one side, distractedly, not unkindly, and began to pace about the pool's edge, muttering to herself things like, "You are in trouble, young man. Now, the thing is, what's to be done with you?"

Like the others, she was a Fomor — one of the race of demons and monsters that had ravaged and terrorized Ireland for centuries. In her guise as a beautiful and carnal woman, the Baobhan had lured many unwary travelers to their deaths. With her irresistible and mesmerizing gaze she would imprison them and render them senseless. Then, using her sharp, unwholesome teeth, she would bite and drink.

After the men of Ireland had made an alliance with their gods and finally defeated the Fomor at the Battle of Moytura, some of the survivors had fled across the water to Albion and had come at length to the great forest, where they now resided together but apart, sulking and quarreling among themselves, feeding on their bitterness.

And on other things.

They brought their customs and habits with them, some of which were particularly repellent. For instance, every year at the feast of Samain, which is also called Hallowe'en, they would claim their entitlement to a tithe of corn and blood — fully two-thirds of the produce of the land of Ireland and two-thirds of its children.

Morgause had only the one child, but the Fomor had been quite prepared to be flexible. By their own standards they were even being quite reasonable when they visited the hut one day to explain all this to her. She was the only person living within a day's travel of their lair; otherwise, they said, they might have spared her. As it was, they were quite prepared to take the child only and leave her with her livestock and gardens. Until next year, at any rate.

Morgause had listened attentively, smiled, and nodded. Then, with an almost imperceptible motion of her hand, she had sent them screaming from the hut pursued by a swarm of invisible and implacable wasps that harried them for days afterward until, creeping pathetically back to the hut, they promised never to harm either her or her son.

Several times after that Morgause had tried to recruit them for her own ends. "You could be very useful to me," she told them. "And you could also make something of yourselves."

But the Fomor had had enough. That terrible battle against the wild Gaels and their gods, the flight across the cold sea, and the long years of festering exile in the forest had dampened their enthusiasm for earthly kingdoms and glories. The food here was not what they were used to, but at least it did not fight back. No, they politely declined, we do not care to make something of ourselves. But we will look after little Mordred, perhaps make something of him.

Now things were quite changed around.

They were all here; the small clearing was rapidly filling with curiously shaped bodies — the goat-man, the sow, the satyr and the cyclops, tree elves and sprites. Some were beautiful, most were hideous. Most comely was the ogre Ruadan, son of Bres — a word that in some parts of Ireland means beautiful. But though fair, he was not a pleasant fellow. What he loved most to do was to place a live rabbit or two into his enormous mouth and delight in their squeals and helpless, frantic wrigglings as he slowly crushed them between his hungry jaws. Even that was not as much fun as eating humans had been, but nowadays he was content enough to take his pleasures where he could find them.

Some were shapeshifters, others had different tricks of their own. They eyed Mordred in various ways, all of which made him feel suddenly, deeply uneasy — a sensation he had never felt in their presence before.

"The boy is in trouble," the Baobhan announced when she had finally stopped their eager chattering.

"It's his mummy who's in trouble," pronounced the cyclops in his thickly slurred voice. "Up to here." Grinning to his companions, he indicated a spot just below his knee. His name was Finn; he was one of the sons of Balor, who had been the most formidable of the Fomor. Like his father, he had in fact two eyes, but one was kept shut because when open it had the power to kill all within its view. He had kept this eye closed for so long now that he had forgotten how to open it, and so he was more or less harmless.

"Shut up, fish-features," snapped the satyr as it landed him a resounding kick in the head with one of its hooves. *It is true,* Mordred thought. *With that eye, he does look a bit like a fish.* But he had a special affection for Finn, who was always particularly solicitous of Mordred's comfort. "The old bitch isn't dead yet," continued the satyr in a low, savage, grating voice. "She might hear you."

That made them all think. Some of them looked quite frightened for a moment. The Baobhan turned to Mordred. "We grownups need to have a little talk," she said in a friendly but firm way. "Why don't you go and play on the other side of the pool? I think I saw a frog over there. . . ."

This did not excite Mordred at all.

". . . And afterward I'll fly you home."

Mordred hurried across to the other side of the glade, and as he went he wondered in a distracted, casual manner what it was that was worrying him so. He remembered something about staying out late and getting his own supper. He might even have to fend for himself for a day or two. Everything else had been forgotten.

His forgetfulness, unbeknownst to the boy, was the effect of what had been Morgause's last spell. In view of the state she was in at the time and the sheer difficulty of working magic where close relatives are concerned, she had done very well. Mordred's lack of recall was not complete — that would have been disconcerting, even alarming, to the boy — but neither did he remember enough to be really troubled by the memories.

At the moment he could not understand why his friends had sent him away. Their voices carried so clear and loud across the water that he could hear quite well enough whenever he wanted to listen.

"A promise should not last that long. Especially when it has been exacted under duress."

"Yes, but what if she sees? What if she finds out?"

"It doesn't matter. She will go to Tir na Nog. She will forget everything there."

"They will not have her. She will be sent to the other place — where we shall go."

A series of low, pathetic whimpers reverberated about the clearing. Though long-lived, the Fomor were not immortal, and they had heard rumors of that "other place." No one wanted to go there.

"Wherever she goes, she can't harm us," cried the Oakapple Elf in a voice that betrayed more fear than certainty. "Dead is dead is dead!" The flesh on his distended belly rippled in time to each emphatic syllable.

"But where does that leave the bastard?" asked the Baobhan.

"Aah!" they chorused, and a thoughtful silence followed. Mordred, searching desultorily among the undergrowth, wondered vaguely who these horrid people were that his friends were so afraid of. So far he had disturbed a viper and almost caught a lizard. But he had not seen a frog.

"I think we should carry on as before," the Baobhan continued. "The lad trusts us. Why, he even likes us. When has anyone else treated us with affection? He deserves something in return."

There were some nods of agreement to this, also a few angry and disappointed growls — but more of the former than of the latter. Ruadan, who was longing to sample some real meat again, suggested, "Let us ask the monster."

"She cannot tell us what is best to do."

"No, but she can show us things. She can show us if the bastard is worth keeping alive." He glared at them all. "And she can tell us if the bitch is dead."

A discordant chorus of approval and a stamping of various malformed limbs followed this. Ruadan picked up the fallen tree trunk on which he and some of the others had been sitting and hurled it into the middle of the pool. Mordred dropped the lizard he had finally succeeded in catching — though he was overweight, his hands and his brain were quick enough — and stared open-mouthed. The water's surface did not break with a heavy splash but seemed to bow inward, forming a huge and unbroken hollow into which the tree, its dead roots uppermost, could be seen plunging deeper and deeper. For a moment he thought it might come springing back like a missile from an enormous catapult, but instead it simply vanished from sight. The water closed soundlessly over the hole it had made, and the pool resumed its normal air of placid menace.

The Fomor were surprised too, but once they realized that the pool was not going to fight back they set to with a will and began hurling all manner of objects into the unprotesting waters, screaming obscenities and capering wildly close about the edge.

Too close, as it happened.

There was no warning, no rush of sound or even a subtle change of texture on the water's surface, as something rushed toward the light. She was simply there — not hovering merely, but standing on the water: Nimue, the Lady of the Lake.

This was something that Mordred had not encountered. It did not puzzle him that the Fomor should think her ugly — he had come to understand that their standards were different from his. He thought she was only slightly less beautiful than his mother. She was clad in samite of an impossibly pale hue, and her copper hair hung almost to her hips. A cold beauty shone from her sharply delineated face, and it was good for Mordred that he was so young — for it was the doom of any man who beheld her in this, her more usual guise, to immediately fall hopelessly and fatally in love with her. Even as young as he was, Mordred was moved and greatly unsettled. *And anyway,* he insisted loyally to himself, *Mummy is a much nicer person. Still . . .*

Nimue's fierce eyes burned as she looked about her. Swiftly reaching out, she caught hold of a sprite who had failed to move back quickly enough or far enough. For a moment she just held the little creature at arm's length, an expression of distaste on her face as it ineffectually kicked and cursed and spat at her. Then she squeezed.

A scream split the air, followed by the wrenching, sickening sound of skin and blood vessels being ruptured and torn. Mordred could hear the thin, watery bubbling of escaping air as Nimue, without visible effort, tore the sprite's head from its shoulders. A look of frozen surprise was on the creature's face, and its tiny eyes had suddenly become so bulbous with astonishment that their sockets could no longer accommodate them. Nimue casually dropped the head into the pool, which boiled briefly and protestingly before finally engulfing it. The body she tossed into the clearing where, being rather stupid, it tried to crawl around for several seconds at the feet of the goat-man before it finally realized it was dead.

"Well?" she asked coldly. Shiny streaks of crimson smeared her pale gown as she wiped her hands. "What can I do for you?"

The Fomor were aghast. It had been a long time since anything like this had happened to one of their number. Even Morgause, as bad as she was, had never actually killed any of them. Never had they seen Nimue angry like this. Clearly they had gone too far this time. In confusion and dismay they retreated to a far corner of the clearing, where they huddled in fearful silence. Even huge Ruadan was attempting, with little success, to hide his terrified bulk behind the others.

Mordred said, "There was no need to do that. They didn't mean any harm."

The Lady of the Lake turned slowly, menacingly, but the fire had gone from her eyes. And when she saw who was speaking, she smiled gently. Mordred felt his insides swell and tremble as if something alive was awakening in there.

Oh . . . I don't know what love is, but I think I—

Then the smile faded and he was safe. Just.

"It's Morgause's little boy, isn't it?" She touched his

head in a brief gesture of polite indifference — soft, but enough to send fires rushing to his brain. Then she darted her swift, fierce gaze at the still-cowering Fomor. "It serves them right. How would you like it if someone threw a dead tree at you?"

Mordred had no answer to this.

"I hate them. They are vile. Vile!"

"Why?" He went closer. He longed to reach out. He would feel pain, he knew, if he touched her, but great delight also. But then she moved away and stood at the center of the pool. Mordred was not so foolish as to follow, but he went as close to the edge as he dared.

"Because they look like dung, and anything that does not resemble them they denounce as ugly."

"You are not ugly," Mordred whispered, wanting to placate her but not wanting to say it so loudly that the others would overhear.

"What's that?" She had heard him, but wanted to pretend for a moment that she had not. Mordred, embarrassed and uncertain, did not want to repeat himself. Then she looked at him and smiled again. "Oh, yes, but then you are a human, and we know what they're like." His warm blushes seemed to amuse her, though he did not think there was anything to smile about. "Still, it's very nice of you to say so — even if you are a bit young."

Perhaps shamed by Mordred's boldness, some of the Fomor had begun to move cautiously forward. "I'd like to give you something, my lady!" cackled one from the relative safety of the crowd.

Nimue's contemptuous gaze scanned their faces, then was accentuated by a savage grin when she beheld Finn, leering stupidly and, now that he had been spotted, rather uncertainly.

"So you want to have me, do you?" She addressed him in a gentle, sensuous voice. "You would like to give 'the monster' a poke?"

Entranced, the cyclops merely nodded, oblivious to

the thin, continuous stream of saliva running thickly from his toothless mouth down to his hairless and glistening chin. His gross lips quivered involuntarily. "Y-you are . . . not a . . . m-monster," he stammered in painfully slurred, pleading tones. His companions stared, uncertain whether to show scorn, pity, or simply to take to their heels. They could all feel it, even the females and androgynes — the heady atmosphere as Nimue shamelessly and irresistibly used her body.

She is not ugly, they thought, caught up in what she was projecting upon them. It is we who are ugly — ugly, repellent creatures. . . .

"No, I am not a monster." Her voice had dropped to a soft, provocative whisper. She was speaking only to Finn now, inviting only him. He lurched unsteadily forward. "Yes, why don't you come and try me?" And, stooping gently, she began to raise the hem of her garment.

Mordred did not understand why he felt it necessary to close his eyes, but he did just that. He heard the smooth whisper of silk over skin, then heard her whisper again, "Why don't you come and put it into me, you lovely, hideous fiend?" Suddenly, she screamed. "Then you can feel it wither and burn to nothing inside me!"

When Mordred opened his eyes again, the Fomor were back on the edge of the clearing and trembling like a single terrified organism. Nimue was rubbing her hands in a satisfied way. "All right," she said. "You've had your fun, and now I've had mine. What is it you really want?"

After a moment, egged on partly by the others, the Baobhan stepped forward. "It's the bastard. We want to know what to do about him."

Nimue nodded. "Ah, I see. You want a show?"

"Yes. Please, my lady."

Nimue did not let her expression relax, but she was pleased — both with the deference she was receiving and with the knowledge that her skills commanded so much respect. "Well, you didn't have to wake me up so rudely just for that. There are other ways, you know."

"We're . . . very sorry." The Baobhan turned to the others, who were attempting, as far as their mostly hideous faces allowed, to look convincingly contrite. "It won't happen again."

"Hmm." The Lady of the Lake looked skeptical, but on the whole she was satisfied. "You won't take my word for it — about the boy?" She did not want to appear too eager to display her skills, though in truth she rarely got the chance to show off. "She is dead, poor woman. . . . And he"— she glanced briefly at Mordred —"is destined for greatness, in a manner of speaking."

"We should love to see for ourselves," said the Baobhan, unaccustomed to being so importunate. "Please."

"Well . . ." Nimue shook her wrists free of the gown's irritatingly long sleeves and folded her arms thoughtfully. In fact, her mind was already made up; at her feet a grey mist rose silently as if from invisible pores in the pool's surface. "It's not really suitable for children, you know." There were whispers of anticipation among the Fomor as in thin streams the mist wavered and grew. Then the streams coalesced, forming a wispy, insubstantial curtain. Darker, more solid shapes began to move within.

"Did you want dumbshow or sound?"

The Baobhan was engrossed, staring into the mist. Already she thought she recognized some of what she saw. The others too were crowding forward, less hesitantly now, all eager for a good view but still anxious to stay out of arm's reach of The Lady. Because they still kept their distance, Mordred had the most comfortable place and the best view.

"Dumbshow will be fine," the Baobhan absently replied without a glance toward the questioner.

Nimue glided to the edge of the pool and let the show begin.

Mordred, as with so much of what had happened that afternoon, understood little of what he saw. Nor could he understand why some of the Fomor should keep casting looks at him, with expressions sometimes of puzzlement, sometimes of triumph. Was not the show, however confusing, far more interesting?

He loved the battle scenes; thousands of warriors, all dressed like his uncles and riding pell-mell at one another. He felt sorry for the horses, though, and was glad there was no sound. He saw his father — well, it looked like Father because he wore a crown — only this man seemed much older. Then he saw another, younger man also wearing a crown — the same crown! *But that can't be right*, he thought.

He saw an image of the pool — this was very confusing, for it was superimposed on the real thing, yet just as solid-looking, its black surface as still and uninviting as always. He saw a sword, dazzling in its purity, so brilliant as to be almost colorless. It sprang from the depths gripped by a white hand.

Mordred turned around but Nimue was still there, watching with satisfaction both her handiwork and her audience. He knew that if he were to peer round the thin screen of mist there would be no sword there. Oh, but it was so real. . . . The Fomor gasped when they saw it and some of them shielded their eyes and groaned, "Bad magic! No more!" But that passed and gave way to the final scene, which stirred them even more.

In the glowing, wavering mist a witch was being burned. Fiery bundles were being thrown at her feet until they reached almost to her knees. The smoke and flames obscured her face, but that did not seem to mar the enjoyment of the Fomor. There were muted cries of delight, and some of them were actually shaking with pleasure as they sat on their haunches watching the white-clad figure twitch and writhe at the stake. When at last she was mercifully suffocated by the fumes, the

Fomor too fell silent and strangely still for a moment, as if gathering breath. Then:

"Aaahhhh!"

Their collective moan of relief was so heartfelt and compelling that Mordred, though he did not like this last scene as much as the previous ones, could not help but join in.

All in all, it had been a wonderful day.

3

"SIR, IS IT REALLY TRUE THAT CAMELOT WAS built in a day?" Mordred asked.

Sir Palomides the Ethiope did not turn around. He had answered a great many questions this day, and his neck was beginning to ache fearfully. This had been a straightforward errand, little more than a day's ride in all, but how he longed for a hot tub and a bed strewn with pillows to caress his tired limbs!

Sometimes he worried that he was getting soft. At forty-six (or forty-seven, he could not be sure which) that sort of thing could easily happen.

"No lad, that was Rome." He frowned. "Wait a minute. That's not right either."

They were riding in the shadow of the walls, and Mordred, as he looked up, could not see where the battlements were or even where the sky began. Great blocks of granite, rank upon rank of them, stretched grimly out of sight. "I didn't think so," he said.

Though I suppose if you had lots and lots of men and they all worked very hard, you might build it in a week. Mummy built our house in a week. All by herself. Just me and a little magic, she said.

"How long—"

"No more questions, boy," Palomides growled wearily.

"Sorry, sir."

The knight's rough manner was understandable, for he was a bachelor. He had little experience with small boys. His heart was kind, though, and he had warmed to Mordred shortly after he had found the boy, seated in the doorway of his hut in an attitude of patient expectancy and gnawing quietly and systematically at a small bone that, once finished, he dropped onto the growing pile at his feet. Mordred had been waiting there for some days.

When Palomides entered the clearing with his sword drawn — out of habit rather than fear that any real danger might lurk so near the highway — the small, absurdly fat boy had not taken to his heels as many did when they saw him. Instead he studied Palomides with a simple frank curiosity and said, "Are you the one they call the Black Knight?"

Hah! Black Knight, thought Palomides at the time. That was a good one.

Mordred's face glistened, for he was a careless eater. He drew the back of his hand across his mouth and stood up. "Mummy said I was to wait here, and someone would come and look after me." He glanced behind him. "They try their best, but I do not like the food they bring me. They say it is chicken, but I do not think so."

"Did your mother say who would come for you?"

The boy did not reply. He was squinting as he looked up, and Palomides wondered if he was shortsighted or perhaps simply dazzled by his armor. He guessed the latter was so, for standing thus the boy looked the very picture of a simpleton. Taking his hand, he led him back to the road and the waiting horses.

"Can you ride?" Palomides asked.

"I have not ridden a horse before." When he saw the docile palfrey chewing contentedly at the grass by the roadside he added, "But it looks quite easy."

Palomides gave him a sidelong glance, but the boy had not meant it to sound like a boast. He had many times ridden whooping through the forest — and, twice now, through the air — on the backs of shrieking nightmares. The knight's horses, for all their size and quiet dignity, were gentle creatures by comparison.

"Are you taking me to your hut, sir?" Mordred asked as he was lifted into the saddle. The thought of leaving his home did not bother him, now that his mother was gone. He would not even miss his friends.

"I am taking you to Camelot," Palomides muttered as he mounted his destrier and then tugged at the palfrey's reins. Mordred, unprepared, was jolted backward and only grabbed the saddle just in time. The ground seemed a long way off, and he was beginning to wish he had not sounded quite so casual about this horse-riding business.

"You are going to live with your father," Palomides added.

Some father, the knight thought. He had stood in the crowded council chamber watching with growing dismay the king's anguished inactivity as the arguments gradually became more impassioned, more emotional, more hysterical. He was but a guest in the court, a foreign emissary, and had only been allowed to attend the debate because of his great prestige. Perhaps they had hoped to impress him with their colorful, democratic ways. But Palomides was not impressed. He had no right to speak, but had stepped forward nonetheless.

"In my country we order these things differently," he had begun. "We suffer witches and necromancers to live, and in return many do mend their ways and perform valuable services. They may bring rain to the desert or drive the locusts from the fields. Would it not be wiser and more humane to persuade this woman to relinquish her evil ways in the hope that she may prove useful to you?"

Some of the knights shuffled uneasily or stared guiltily at their boots. A few nudged each other and grinned. Palomides did not know about Morgause's many lovers.

Merlin, though he did not alter his counsel — he hated competition — had nodded shrewdly. He was impressed by the man's outspokenness, if not by his argument.

Arthur had looked at Palomides with a sort of desperate gratitude. He was doing everything but nod his head. Say something, why don't you? Palomides thought. You *are* the king. . . .

But it was old Sir Ector, Arthur's foster father and chairman of the council, who had spoken.

"We thank you for your observations, Sir Palomides. You may be sure they will be given due weight. But please understand that here in Albion, circumstances may be very different from those in your own country."

Not so different, he thought as he resumed his seat. Perhaps more civilized. Sir Ector's words had been spoken kindly enough. The old man had probably meant well. But he had also meant this: You are not one of us; you are a foreigner, and a dark-skinned foreigner at that. We have granted you a privilege in permitting you to observe our proceedings; do not abuse it.

He had taken no further part in the debate, though it continued for nearly an hour afterward. At times he was conscious of Arthur's gaze, silently imploring him to speak again to try and sway matters.

But he is the king, Palomides thought. It is his place, not mine.

He was not aware of the extent to which Arthur was constrained by laws that, though not enacted by him, he was bound by solemn oath to uphold. He could speak neither for Morgause nor against her, and when the vote was counted he was bound to give his assent, however bitterly.

It made Palomides bitter, too. If this was majority rule, then he was glad that his father would have none of it. But it was not bitterness that had driven him into the forest in search of the witch's boy, and he did not go in order to shame the Round Table. They have shamed themselves, he believed. This was quite clear from their down-at-heel looks and their strained conversations during the days that followed.

He went because he believed it was bad enough to have punished the mother; to abandon her innocent offspring would be worse than unforgivable.

And he went because Arthur had asked him.

* * *

There was no moat. Camelot's walls alone were sufficient to deter any would-be attacker. As they rode past the sentries and into the courtyard (Mordred had never been saluted before; that was exciting!), he wondered at the size and number of the great stones and what an effort it must have been to lift them, one upon the other, to such a height. "How—" he began but stopped quickly. The Black Knight seemed nice enough, but was probably not above cuffing a small boy if he became wearisome.

Arthur was waiting in the courtyard when they arrived, but the smile he gave them was more dutiful than welcoming. There was no one with him, and though it was a warm day he seemed shrunken and pinched, as if he was cold. *I expect it is because the courtyard is so big and I am so high up here,* Mordred thought, *that Father looks so small.*

"Hello, Daddy. Is Mummy here?"

Arthur mumbled something in a vaguely apologetic tone as he lifted the boy from the palfrey. But though he kept a firm grip on his son's hand, he would not look directly at him.

"Gramercy, Palomides," he said. He very nearly added, "Your skin may be dark, but your heart is great and fair." But somehow it did not seem quite appropriate.

Palomides, who still did not understand, said, "It was no trouble. The lad was easy to find. I think he was expecting me — or someone, anyway."

Arthur turned to Mordred, still avoiding his gaze, as he said, "Run along inside. There is someone waiting there for you. She will look after you." And Mordred, thinking it might be his mother, hurried into the keep, scraping his knees more than once on the edges of the high stone staircase.

"What will become of him?" Palomides asked.

"I will see to it that he is properly cared for. I will treat him like my own son."

"He *is* your own son."

Arthur said, "I really am in your debt. None of the others would volunteer to go, though they must have known it was my wish. I think they are a little ashamed of themselves." Perhaps sensing what the other was thinking, he added, "So am I, of course."

Palomides said, "I find this all rather hard to understand, sire."

"Yes, it must seem rather barbaric to you — this burning of witches." Arthur nodded slowly, and Palomides thought, How old is he now — late twenties? Yet his bearing is that of a venerable and bent old sage. . . . Burning witches, mutilating criminals, stoning the adultress while the unfaithful husband goes unpunished. Go to Albion, my father bade me. See the Jewel of the North and speak with the man who will do what the poor Carthaginians almost did — curb those swaggering Latins, send them scurrying back home, and make them sue for peace.

He had spent more than a year now sampling the various offerings of this cold, fertile country and had seen more that dismayed than encouraged him. About Arthur he was not yet sure. To his father Astlobar he had written, "I ween not what these people may do to the Latins, but me they do affright greatly."

Arthur was saying, "Morgause was not a good woman. Passing fair but evilly disposed. She was not as powerful nor as wise as she pretended, though; she was far less powerful than most people thought. In the forest she had things very much her own way — but outside, in the real world . . . . There are stronger things than magic there." The king sighed deeply, and Palomides again wondered at how much like an old man he had become already. A beardless, fresh-faced old man.

"I am not happy about it, you know," Arthur continued when Palomides did not offer anything. They were walking, rather slowly, across the outer bailey toward the Tintagel Tower. Arthur was wearing his careworn posture, bent slightly forward, his hands clasped pensively behind his back. His magnificent wolfskin cloak trailed in the mud, getting dirtier and dirtier, but he did not mind. I suppose that is part of what it means to be a king in Albion, thought Palomides, who came from a poor country.

"I thought I would enjoy being king," Arthur said, again hoping to elicit some kind of response.

"I am sure it is a heavy responsibility." Palomides tried to sound understanding, but not overly so. He dared not say what he was thinking, but all the same he was determined not to show this young-old man a great deal of sympathy.

Arthur took advantage of the opportunity, however small, that the knight's comment had presented him. "I am bound so tightly. By convention, by the past. My father Uther wanted to be remembered as a great lawgiver. He enacted many decrees — nine hundred fifty-seven, to be exact — most of them bad. That a witch must die, that was one of his."

"You can make laws too, sire."

"I can make laws, but I cannot break them. My father's system, The Pendragon Code, is, for all its faults, quite comprehensive. It leaves me little room for maneuver."

"You could still have saved her." It was a rash statement to make — he was not protected by diplomatic immunity or anything of the sort — but Palomides had become impatient.

Arthur was too depressed to be offended. "I am not above the law."

Palomides was weary of this sort of argument. "It has nothing to do with being above or beneath the law. You are the king. You *are* the law."

"I know what you say is true. I must be stronger, mustn't I?" And he fixed Palomides with such a look of loss and helplessness that the knight knew he was not expected to provide the answer.

"I am up against so much," Arthur continued. "The Druids with their absurd traditions. I have to keep on the right side of them. And all the people of the court who love nothing better than to give advice because they think they can do the job so much better than I. The only thing I've enjoyed about being king — really enjoyed, that is — was pulling the sword from the stone. That, at least, was something that no one else could do." He looked up at Palomides, who was a good head taller. "Did I ever tell you about that?"

"I have heard the story, sire."

"The trouble is, there aren't enough people who share my views. They are either sycophants or they are old-school. You know what I need?"

Palomides had been expecting something like this. Arthur continued after a heartbeat's pause, saving the Ethiope from having to answer the question himself.

"People with brains in their heads, instead of just more muscle. I noticed the way you spoke up for Morgause. Even though you had no right—"

"I'm sorry about that. It was—"

"It was commendable. You spoke your mind. To you, that was more important than convention. I need fellows like you."

Arthur turned, and they retraced their steps to the keep. Palomides knew he was expected to speak. He had just been given a great honor, but the only thing he could think of to say was . . .

"Alas, sire, I cannot tarry."

"Your father, in his letter, said you might be staying with us for some years."

"Aye, sire, but not with the court."

Arthur nodded thoughtfully, trying hard to hide his disappointment. He changed the subject. "You're not still trying to settle scores with Sir Tristram, are you?"

"He has my best armor and my best destrier. I mean to win them back if I may." Palomides found this topic an easier one; he felt more sure of himself and did not have to watch his words so carefully.

"You won't. You will lose your second-best armor and your second-best horse, and you will return home destitute and very likely maimed in the bargain. Your father will think we have strange notions of hospitality here in Albion. I love and respect Astlobar. I do not wish to incur his displeasure." This last was a form of words only — the two kings had never met. Still, it is nice of him to say so, Palomides thought.

"Tristram is very good," Arthur added.

"Which is why I mean to beat him."

"Most knights, even the best — especially the best — have other passions. Tristram is different. You've heard the old joke — how he was born in full armor, carrying a tiny sword. Sometimes I wonder if it is so great an exaggeration after all."

"He is not so bad," said Palomides. "We get on quite well, really."

"Yes, I know." Arthur smiled. "Rivals in arms, that sort of thing. It brings you much credit, much renown. But it's not very constructive, is it? It doesn't make this country a better place to live in."

They mounted the steps, in silence at first. Arthur's tone had been mildly petulant, and Palomides judged it best not to argue with him. Besides, in some measure he agreed with him. Then the king's voice softened as he added, "Well, I wish you well, though I would far rather you stayed here."

At the doorway they halted, the old man of twenty-eight and the young one nearly twenty years his senior, in a brief confusion of courtesy and protocol. Arthur said, "At any rate, I have enjoyed our conversation. You show much understanding for a—" He stopped himself suddenly, blushing hotly.

Palomides smiled gently and bade the king enter before him.

* * *

Mordred had not really expected to find his mother waiting at the top of the stairs. He had known for several days now that something was wrong, though he could not identify what. But he was still taken aback when, racing through the high, narrow doorway, he careered straight into a confusion of flesh and coarse linen that yielded only slightly, with a noisy exhalation of air, before bringing him up short.

For a moment he felt a curious mixture of fear and contentment. It felt pleasantly warm inside the folds of the garment, close to the body, and he sensed a faint milky smell that aroused dim memories. At the same time he thought he would suffocate if he did not quickly disentangle himself from this engulfing mass of palpitating cloth.

He felt himself pulled free and, blinking, saw daylight again. His upper arms were being gripped by two pink hands, and a round face was beaming down at him like a beacon.

"My, and don't you move fast for such a roly-poly little one?"

He was fairly certain it was a woman, though her voice had a deep ring and there were small dark hairs sprouting from a mole on her chin. She smelled like a woman.

"I am no roly-poly." There was some dignity as well as injury in his tone. *Who was she to speak? She was huge.*

"Come now, young sir. It's just my way. No need for you to take on so." Her fingers, playfully tweaking the roll of his stomach, were so plump that she could not move one without it brushing against its fellows. And where they met her hand, he noticed with vague horror, there were no knuckles — only tiny dimples, like black pinpricks.

Is this what I will be like when I am grown up?

His imagination, quick and obliging, began shaping a suitably repellent future self. He stopped the image from becoming fully formed by blurting quickly, "Where's my mummy?"

The woman's smile quickly faded, and as she drew Mordred aside from the doorway she shot a look of fierce reproach at Arthur, who was entering. He had overheard the question but chose to remain silent. "Why, bless you, child!" she exclaimed. "Has your father not told you yet?"

Arthur looked at her, at Mordred, then at the ground. "I thought it best that you break the news to him, Lile. You can do that sort of thing more gently than I."

She was not to be easily placated; she continued to stare at him, successfully trying to put him out of countenance. Then, abruptly and without a word, she turned and whisked the uncomprehending Mordred down the long hallway and up the winding staircase to the chamber she had already prepared for him.

* * *

She had some spirit, that Lile. She had the intelligence and looks of a carthorse, but she could stand up to my father like none of his courtiers could. I suppose she felt safe having been with the family for so long. Arthur, especially in his later years, was subject to moods of fearful melancholy, and at such times servants and knights alike went in fear of his unpredictable wrath. But she never acted that way. She had served Uther before, and "a more distempered king," she used to say, "you could hardly find." By comparison my father was easy meat.

She did not tell me the truth, of course. She sat me on my cold, hard pallet and knelt before me, contemplating me with big, gentle eyes while I fidgeted in embarrassment and tried not to stare too closely at the hairy mole on her chin and another I had just spotted on the side of her nose. I can remember it all so clearly. She said, "I'm afraid your mother was taken suddenly very ill. Some of us tried our best to save her, but she died."

I said, "Oh." And a little later, "May I get into bed now?" Mother's spell was acting like a strong sedative, losing its effect by degrees so that instead of becoming immediately inconsolable I vented my grief in manageable quantities.

Everybody was very good about it. They all assumed I was suffering from shock of some kind. I even remember Merlin coming to see me. He entered my room and sat down on a small stool beside my pallet. He did not say much; he told me that I could call him Uncle Merlin, but plain Merlin would do if I preferred it. He tried looking searchingly into my face but evidently found nothing of consequence there, for his eyes next wandered about the room, and he passed a few polite remarks about its size and the fair quantity of light it received. Then he muttered something else, possibly significant but quite incoherent, into his beard before quietly leaving. I think it may even have been an apology. He was a very busy man, and I supposed that to merit even that brief attention from so great a personage, I must have been considered of some importance.

And what of Guinevere? She made no protest at my presence. In fact, she was very kind to me. I think she saw it as some kind of test, and she was determined to come through with flying colors. But I fancy there was some genuine liking also. She did not try to overwhelm me with affection, and so our friendship developed slowly and naturally.

I should mention what became of Palomides.

He never returned to his poor Ethiopian kingdom. For years he and Tristram pursued their largely good-natured but perverse rivalry, Tristram just maintaining the upper hand. It turned sour eventually when both fell for Isolde, King Mark's agreeable but dangerous wife. She liked to flirt with Palomides, for of the two he was the more charming, and he entertained her with his erudition and his many anecdotes. But her love, strangely or perhaps predictably, went to the man of action.

Poor Palomides was heartbroken. I believe he had little experience with women, and so felt the rejection deeply. He became even more determined to beat Tristram, though when he finally did, after a wearing and bloody duel, it can have given him little satisfaction. They parted afterward with many bitter words, and neither spoke to the other in amity again.

Palomides, anxious for diversion and activity, threw himself into the search for the Questing Beast. This fabulous and apocryphal creature, loathsome spawn of an incestuous love triangle between a fay, her brother, and a demon, was said to possess the body of a leopard, the head of a snake, a lion's hindquarters, and the feet of a hare. Its belly housed thirty hounds, all baying and yelping as they drove the creature in a ceaseless quest for water to quench its insatiable thirst. Yes, I know this sounds improbable, but that is the story as told to me many times. I have also been told that the beast appeared on the night I was conceived, though neither Arthur nor my mother ever mentioned this part — I think understandably so, for the Questing Beast usually leaves disaster and tragedy in its ill-omened wake. I heard it once, or something very like it — the hungry baying of dogs on a clear and otherwise silent night. After that was when Lile first told me the stories of the beast and the knight who sought it.

Palomides made it his own quest and would suffer no others to follow it. Many times Arthur repeated his invitation but Palomides, being a singleminded fellow, had set his heart on this and would not be dissuaded. If he could not have Isolde, then he would have the beast and rid the land of a not inconsiderable nuisance. Then, he said, when he could be received with honor, he would join the Round Table.

He never did. He finally tracked down the Questing Beast and discovered that it was not the monster of fanciful legend but a man — quite mad, but wholly and pitiably human.

When the knight found him, naked, cold, and horribly bloated from so much needless gorging of stagnant water, he gave the fellow a cloak and some money and returned to his horse. He was probably not too disappointed. His quest was, in a way, complete, and though I hardly knew him I have always thought him to be a cut above the rest of those largely vainglorious swaggerers — the sort of man who would sooner offer charity than blows. I can picture him now, pacing thoughtfully back to his horse, a little self-satisfied perhaps and wondering what he should do next with his life, while behind him the Questing Beast, in uncanny silence and with huge stone upraised, was rushing forward. . . .

Tristram, when he heard the news, became utterly inconsolable and would speak to no one, not even Isolde, for days. After that he went steadily downhill, neglecting his lady and even the business of jousting. He began to lose — and worse, did not care that he lost. Eventually he gave up altogether. Isolde went back to her husband, who, deciding it was now safe to exact revenge for the injuries done him, had Tristram murdered. He sent four men to do the job, but the poor fellow put up so little fight that it could as easily have been done by two.

I cannot understand these knights and their curious conceits. Usually they are merely brutish, violent, and quite devoid of finer feelings. Then they proceed in this inexplicable and self-destructive fashion.

I thank the gods I was not made in that mold.

4

THE BOYS WERE ACTING UP AGAIN.

Dinas the Irish Druid was well aware of this, but he did not really want to catch someone pinching his fellows or playing Fire, Air, and Water, and so he finished drawing the diagram on the big parchment sheet before turning, with conspicuous lack of haste, to confront his pupils. If he did catch someone in a mischievous act, he would have to punish him, and discipline was not his strongest point.

But he did want their attention. This was a matter of considerable interest and significance. It concerned their heritage. That is why, instead of rolling his eyes heavenward in a gesture of pained indulgence, he fixed them with a sterner gaze. To the boys it did not seem quite like that. The Druid's small stature and beguilingly amiable face, pink and glowing in spite of his indifferent health, quite dispelled the effect. He looked like an old and benign dwarf who had suddenly been struck by some remembered hurt or disappointment. No matter; it worked well enough. When he turned, eleven expectant faces greeted his own, each one alert and poised.

Dinas's squinting gaze slowly scanned the tiny chamber that was all that could be spared for a schoolroom. It worried him, his eyesight. He was sure it was getting worse. So far it had not greatly affected his teaching but it made his real work, the task of his afternoons and evenings, much more difficult, and sometimes he wondered if he would ever complete it.

"Now, then," he began, grave and unsmiling. "In a few moments I'll be asking you to copy this representation onto your tablets. But first let us see who can recall what we discussed last week. . . . Sir Gareth: Whence came the stones?"

The boys liked the way he addressed them, though they had no right to any such titles. Still, it was not pleasant to be singled out this way and Gareth, coloring on his stool, thought, It's not fair. I didn't have my hand up or anything.

But at least he knew the answer. "Sir, ignorant folk believe them to be giants who were dancing in a ring when the dawn caught them unawares, and so they were turned to stone."

The Druid smiled. Lines, like secrets grudgingly revealed, appeared and turned his face into a network of deep creases. It always cheered him when his teaching penetrated what he regarded, without any malice, as these deficient sensibilities. Then he bent forward with a frown of pedagogic admonition. "But pray do not call them ignorant. They are the king's subjects still, like you or I." He stood upright again. "And can you tell me how we were able to refute this charming, though rather fanciful, account?"

The boy's face took on a pained expression, and he began gnawing frantically at his lip. No answer came forth. He knew that he should know it, for the boys had all laughed about it after the teacher told it to them last week. But then, they had been told so *many* things in the last several days. . . . Gareth dared to look up, but could see no pity in the Druid's face — only placidity and great patience, for Dinas could discern only a blur where the boy's face should be and had no idea of the torture the youngster was going through.

For a while nobody spoke. Many of the other boys

knew the answer, but it would have seemed to them disloyal to put their hands up. Gareth was a rather dull fellow, even by their undemanding standards, but he was well-liked and so no one wished to show him up. Also, the answer was . . . well, rather rude.

Eventually the tutor, sensing something was wrong, gently prompted. "Something to do with the construction of the stones?" He tapped the fingertips of his left hand with the palm of his right, forming a right angle. "Something to do with the positioning of the lintels upon the uprights, perhaps?"

A glimmer of comprehension appeared in the boy's eyes. Then he seemed to stiffen suddenly in his chair, as if he was bracing himself against a flood of recollection. "Nipples!" he cried with almost ecstatic relief.

Everyone else seemed to feel the relief, too; at any rate, no one smiled or even smirked, though they had laughed uproariously about it a week before. "There are holes in the lintels," continued Gareth, gathering confidence now. "And these fitted into the uprights — into the . . . nipples." Now a few grins did appear, but Dinas did not notice. Unfortunately for him the Druids had no knowledge of optics, so spectacles were out of the question; so the boys would continue to take advantage both knowingly and unknowingly, and in a few years he would be almost blind.

"Ah," he said. "Ah." He began pacing thoughtfully between the closely packed stools, weaving in and out along the front row. "So we do know the circle was built by men — hundreds, possibly thousands, of years ago. But what sort of men, and why should they expend so much effort?"

He came to a halt in front of the class and spread his hands as if in expectation of a bounteous harvest of speculation. "Come, gentlemen, hazard a guess."

After a few uncertain moments, some hands fluttered upward. Diomed, son of Sir Lamorak and at fourteen the eldest in the class, said, "People in those days were very primitive, Master Dinas. They made blood sacrifices to appease the gods. Perhaps the circle was an offering to their gods also."

Dinas knew that the young man had probably not thought of this himself, but he was too shrewd to ask him where he had picked it up. Instead he asked, "So you think we are advanced, then?"

Diomed, who had repeated almost word for word a conversation he had overheard in the library a few days earlier, could only nod uncertainly, suspecting some subtle trap.

"Blood sacrifices were quite common until the king put a stop to them," said Mordred. A ripple of quiet excitement spread through the room. First women's parts, now blood; their lessons were usually duller than this.

"And do we not still perform sacrifices in like manner?" returned the Druid. "Do we not burn witches to appease the demons of ignorance and malice that reside within us?"

"Oh, but they will always be there," said Mordred. "And anyway, witches are not burned anymore. My father has put a stop to that, too."

"Ah, yes." Dinas felt suddenly uncomfortable. This must be the best-kept secret in Camelot, he thought. And the ugliest. . . . Hastily he changed the subject. "It may be that the circle was conceived as a temple to a solar or lunar deity. We know that it can be used to predict phases of the moon and eclipses with astonishing accuracy. Our scientists with their modern astrolabes have proved this." Mordred's hand went up. Dinas pretended not to see it.

"Now," the Druid continued. He pointed to the diagram. A bird's-eye view, he had called it earlier. This seemed odd to the boys. When would they ever get a bird's-eye view? "Do we not have here the seeds of an enigma — a bit of a puzzle, in other words?" Sometimes he forgot his audience was a youthful one. "These people are so primitive and ignorant that they live in mortal fear of something as simple and explicable as a lunar eclipse. At the same time they are sufficiently advanced to construct a huge artifact which can accurately predict when such phenomena — happenings — will occur. Yes?"

Mordred, who did not like mysteries and who would be heard, said, "Could it not be that there existed in those times a group of clever people who knew about these matters, and who used their knowledge to make everyone else afraid of them and obey them?'

Dinas recognized this oblique criticism of the Druids and secretly admired the lad's acumen. To an extent he could even sympathize. He did not like these British Druids, so obsessively hierarchical and so coldly analytical. Learning, he believed, should be a joy — but the Druids of Albion considered that attitude to be trivial and unscholarly. Back home, things were very different. He could not say that in public, of course.

"There is no evidence to suggest that," he replied. And before Mordred could retort that there was no evidence to refute it either, he quickly added, "And now please, young sirs"— he tapped the parchment —"to your tablets. A good copy, mind. Take your time. We have plenty of it."

That was not strictly true. He did not want to keep the boys longer than necessary. But if they hurried, they would spoil their work. There followed a noisy interlude full of fidgeting and whispers as the boys took up their tablets and styli, but they became quickly silent as they bent to their work. After a few moments nothing could be heard in the room but the teacher's footsteps as he moved along the rows, briefly inspecting each hunched and concentrating form.

It would take them about an hour, he calculated roughly, for it was a meticulous diagram and showed the concentric circles and horseshoes of sarsens, bluestones, and trilithons. It had taken him a good deal longer than that to fashion the original, which was why he had still been putting the finishing touches to it at the start of that morning's lesson. He stood at the back of the room, beneath the tall, narrow window opening, and gazed with satisfaction at his handiwork and at the busy, silent figures.

Most of the boys wore fixed, intent expressions. Mordred's was clouded with gloom. He bent over his tablet, contemplating the empty wax-covered surface, idly testing its smoothness with his fingertips. It was not that he objected to his teacher; in fact, he thought quite highly of him — but he was simply not adept at drawing. Greek, mathematics, and arcana he could manage well enough — excel at, even, but copying was one task (there were others, too) for which being a king's son did not help very much. He had a stylus made from a unicorn's horn while the others had to make do with wood or bone, but still he made far too many mistakes. They were easy enough to correct — you simply rubbed the wax surface gently and everything would slowly disappear — but he seemed to spend most of his time rubbing out, and he was always the last to finish.

Glancing sideways but careful not to turn his head, he tried to catch Galahad's eye. But Galahad was totally immersed in his work; his thick eyebrows almost completely overshadowing his intense face, his tongue making swift, precise movements about his lips, just like the ones he was making with his stylus. Galahad was quite good at this sort of thing. He could bend his mind to such uncomplicated tasks for hours on end.

Mordred would have liked to look out the window. He had no idea what the weather was like. But you could never be sure with the old man; no one really knew just how shortsighted he was. Perhaps, they sometimes speculated among themselves, he was just pretending, and one day he would catch someone doing something really bad and they would all see his true colors.

Mordred did not think much of that theory. Still, it was not worth the risk.

* * *

"What these boys need is some education," Arthur had said after the cook, only partly mollified, had returned to the kitchen to repair the damage. "Some discipline, too, would not be amiss."

Kay's brows bent in suspicion. "What exactly did you have in mind, sire?"

"One of those Greek fellows," Arthur said after a moment's thought. "Or, failing that, an Irishman. Someone who will teach them their letters. And keep them in line."

Some of the other knights nodded in approval. Kay did not. Something had to be done, he did not dispute that. The boys were running wild, quite unchecked. That morning Diomed and Gwenbaus had charged through the kitchens flourishing their wooden drill swords, hitting each other and overturning sundry dishes and furniture in their mad, distracted play. The midday meal had been ruined and the servants had been upset. The Gallic cook had threatened to leave, and only a great deal of pleading by Arthur that stopped just on the regal side of dignity had persuaded him to stay.

The boys had been roundly punished; however, with little to occupy them, they would soon be doing mischief again somewhere. But was the solution to give them an education? To Kay the whole idea seemed dangerously effete. "Neither of us were taught our letters, sire," he reminded his foster brother. "Speaking for myself, it did me little harm."

Arthur thought it had done a lot of harm. Kay was not just illiterate, he was a bully and a braggart. A little learning might have softened him. "That chap Alexander, the Macedonian — he had one of those Greek fellows for a tutor. Isn't that right, Merlin?"

"Aristotle," replied Merlin from behind a bundle of manuscripts. He was just passing through the great hall on his way to the library and would not stop.

Arthur turned back to Kay. "You see — Alexander the Great, no less! Look what a little education did for him." Though illiterate, Arthur was not unlearned. He also had become a good deal more sure of himself since his conversation with Sir Palomides nine years earlier. He recalled that exchange often — and nowadays when he wanted a thing done, it generally was done.

So, Dinas was found and brought to Camelot.

"You're an Irishman," observed the king when introductions and obeisances had been made.

"I am from the west of Ireland, sire."

"What are you doing here so far from home, Master Dinas?"

Merlin coughed lightly and bent forward. "It is what we call a cultural exchange, sire. Master Dinas stays with us for ten years. In return, a British Druid goes to Ireland. We do the same sort of thing with our Gallic cousins also."

Arthur's brow became creased. "Whatever for?" he asked quizzically.

"Why, sire, to build bridges; to forge closer links within the wider Druid community."

"I do not think one Irishman is going to build many bridges," Arthur said. "No offense, of course," he quickly added in Dinas's direction. He leaned forward and in an almost conspiratorial tone asked, "Tell me, really, what do you think of life as a Druid over here?"

Dinas would have liked to have answered this frankly. If they had been alone, perhaps he would have done so. But instead, he began hesitantly. "Well, I—"

"Oh, don't you worry about him," said Arthur, indicating Merlin with a tilt of his head. "You can speak freely."

But Dinas caught the warning look in the chief Druid's eyes, and though strictly speaking Merlin had no hold over him, Dinas suspected that the man could nevertheless make his life even more uncomfortable than it already was.

"It is very different here, sire," Dinas ventured.

Arthur shrugged and sat back heavily. Then, seeming to change his mind, he gave a loud snort of derision. Dinas looked nervously at Merlin as if to say, I did not say anything, honestly I didn't.

"They're snobs, that's what they are," said Arthur. "Oh, brilliant, I grant you, but so class-conscious. You don't have that in Ireland, do you? Bards and Ovates and all that nonsense."

Dinas was agreeably surprised. Most Britons knew next to nothing of their fellow Celts, whether in Gaul or in Ireland. "It is true we do not have a hierarchical structure, sire. In my country a Druid is a man like any other; he may be a poet or a potter, a smith or a seer."

"But not a scientist," Merlin coldly interposed.

For a moment Dinas quite forgot about discretion. "It is true that we lack your skills in forging ever deadlier engines of war, Master Merlin, but we should not be considered backward on that account."

"Bravo!" Arthur laughed. "By Bran, I think this cultural exchange idea has much to commend it after all. I could send all my Druids to Ireland and bring all your folk here — what about that?"

"I am sure we would prove a poor substitute, sire," answered Dinas with an anxious eye on the king's formidable chief counselor.

But Merlin wore a smile of tired forbearance, and his face seemed to say, I have grown old in the service of my king. It is my duty to suffer thus. . . . Merlin was too shrewd to allow these sallies to upset him; he knew they were a measure of the king's impotence. Arthur would never dare touch the Druids, whatever he might say.

The king's tone changed, became more businesslike. "How much longer will you be staying with us, Master Dinas?"

"I have seven years left to serve, sire."

"And how would you like to spend them here in Camelot, as tutor to my boys — that is, the sons of The Round Table?"

The question did not take Dinas by surprise. He had long known the reason for this summons. But though he had given the matter plenty of thought he had not, even now, reached a decision.

Life in the Druid community to which he had been assigned was a far cry from the scholastic idyll he had been led to expect. Lately his British colleagues had discovered gunpowder, and the constant smell of sulphur was greatly detrimental to his studies. Worse, they seemed to have little idea of how to properly conduct scientific inquiry. Spontaneous explosions were becoming an all-too-familiar occurrence, and scarcely a day went by without someone emerging blackened and bloody but perversely cheerful from the underground chamber where they practiced their mad arts. To Dinas it seemed at times that he was surrounded by madmen who would quite willingly blow themselves into oblivion to advance, in even the smallest degree, their dubious cause.

Still, small boys could be dangerous, too. The sons of the Round Table were a wild lot, he had heard.

"You would not be expected to teach all day, you understand," Merlin said. "Only the mornings."

The Irishman's interest quickened at this point. "Then I should have the rest of the day for my own studies?"

"Indeed. And a chamber of your own in which to pursue them. And of course you would have unrestricted access to the library." How well he understands my needs, thought Dinas.

"What are you studying?" Arthur politely inquired.

"Master Dinas is devising an alphabet for our language," Merlin said. "Is that not so?"

Dinas nodded eagerly. For two years his endeavors had been virtually ignored. He himself had been been tolerated at best. Now here he was surrounded by kind people who wanted to know all about him. It made him feel useful again. "It has been my life's ambition. If we Celts can one day write in our own language, we should be free from the constraints of Greek and Latin. We should be able more fully to express our own ideas."

Arthur tried to look interested. "Jolly good."

"I have already given it a name: Gallo-Bretonic."

"Marvelous. Now, about these lads of mine. . . ."

"It would be an honor, sire," Dinas said, flushed with enthusiasm at the moment.

Arthur sighed. One weight at least had been removed from his mind. "They can be a bit of a handful at times, but I fancy they'll take to you."

And so they did. Not immediately, for at first they had greatly resented this sudden enforced and, to their minds, unwarranted confinement. But they eventually warmed to the gnomelike Druid who wore the reluctant smile. Perhaps they would have worked harder had he beaten them more, but they liked him because he did not, and so at length a tacit accord developed between teacher and students. They might act up, surreptitiously, when his back was turned; otherwise they would be diligent and attentive. He, in turn, would be sure to turn his back often.

* * *

I liked Master Dinas because he had the right ideas. He did not simply seek to implant knowledge into empty vessels, but drew it from us, like a gardener; nurturing rather than forcing growth, and intervening judiciously to ensure that things grew in the right way. He was constantly asking questions, inviting us to speculate — not just about stone circles but many things besides. Why is a triangle to be considered the perfect shape? Why was there so much hostility between the Celts and the Latins? What made a wise ruler?

There was a great deal of writing also, at which I did not excel. I simply could not get on with those wax-covered tablets. I longed to write on papyrus or parchment — to write something that would last — but those were expensive materials and not considered fit for the incoherent scrawls of young boys.

He was not a dull pedagogue. Sometimes, if there was an interval between the end of our lessons and our dismissal at noon, he would tell us stories, mostly from his own country. This was not wholly for our benefit, I believe. I fancy he was homesick and longed to see his homeland again. I enjoyed the stories very much, for they reminded me of my old friends in the forest — several of whom he mentioned by name. I was sorely tempted at such times to reveal my acquaintance with them, but I was afraid — partly that I might not be believed, partly for the sake of the Fomor themselves. They were having a difficult time just then, and would not have welcomed yet more attention being drawn to their precarious existence.

* * *

Today he did not tell them stories. When the noon bell rang some of the boys were still not done, and when he dismissed them his manner was unusually waspish. He was not pleased with those who had not finished their work — nor even, apparently, with those who had. "I ween I have been too soft with you," he said darkly as they filed silently past him. "It will not be so when next we meet."

But the threat was too distant to quell their spirits for long. They would not see Dinas for two days.

Normally in the afternoons they would go to the gymnasium, where they would run, throw the discus, and learn to box. This was another of Arthur's innovations. In those days he was a true eclectic, a cultural scavenger borrowing from other cultures the best they had to offer; education from the Greeks, a chivalric code from the Gauls, and military tactics from the Roman Republic. "For," wrote one of the chroniclers of those years, "when those of the king's party were sore opposed King Arthur turned to them and said, 'May we not overthrow our enemy more surely when we borrow of him his wisdom and leave him with his folly alone?'"

But today was the eve of Beltane — a happier time than the bloody feast of Samain, for it marked the onset of summer. There would be no school tomorrow, and their afternoon was free also. Most of the boys had already dispersed and were busy plotting some mischief or other. Mordred had intended to spend the afternoon in the library, but he had been caught among the arcana. Access to these shelves was strictly forbidden to children, and the librarian had thrown him out. Not before he had learned something useful, though.

"We need some agrimony, mare's dung, and the pelt of a tom that is not more than twelve weeks old," he told Galahad.

A look of patrician distaste appeared on his young companion's pale and delicate features. "What's it supposed to do?"

"Make us invisible."

They were sitting on the battlements of the Tower Perilous, enjoying the peace and the sunshine and occasionally tossing a pebble toward the people below. Arthur's serfs, a whole army of them, were building a moat down there. Galahad, vaguely recollecting what Dinas had once said about something called velocity, had brought a whole bagful of small stones with him in order to test the theory. "Make us stink, more like," he said as he stuck his hand into the bag. "Mare's dung — ugh! Why do these spells of yours always have such disgusting ingredients?"

"We don't have to eat it. Only immerse our bodies in the vapors. The effect is supposed to last for three or four hours." Mordred watched Galahad toss another pebble up and out. It fell in a gentle arc that became a straight line, vanishing finally into the shadow of the huge castle walls. "Think of everything we could do in three or four hours."

Galahad, glancing indifferently toward the ground, was not impressed. This was not the first time they had tried something like this. Mordred's spells never worked, and they always seemed to get into so much trouble trying them out. At least Galahad did. . . .

"Hello!" said Galahad. He leaned farther out over the wall, steadying himself with his free hand. One of the tiny figures far beneath them had collapsed and was lying with limbs comically outstretched, as if tied to a wheel. Other little people were converging about it, and the sounds of shouts found their way up to where the boys were perched. Galahad hoped he had not killed the fellow — that would mean more trouble for him, if he was caught — and both boys slid off the battlements before they could be spotted.

"What about the words?" Galahad asked as the two of them made their way hurriedly down the narrow, unlit stairway.

"There are no words." Mordred thought hard about this before answering; there had been time for only the briefest of glances before the librarian had spotted him. "Words are only for show," he echoed, less certainly.

"Don't be silly, Mordred. You know agrimony is a

common enough plant. It grows in the fields here. There *must* be words."

"We do not get it from the fields. We need the cultivated kind, from the herb garden."

"Oh."

"The flowers of common agrimony are yellow. Those in the Druids' garden are white, almost silver. The coloring is testament to their powers."

They reemerged, blinking, into the bright sunlight of the inner bailey. At the foot of the tower steps a number of cats were dozing or playing desultorily. Like most of the cats that hunted and scavenged around the castle grounds, these were sorry-looking specimens, and their reflexes on this warm, lazy day were unusually slow. Galahad sprang down the steps and scooped one into his arms. He came back to Mordred with a shabby grey kitten that might have been pretty were it not also half-starved. In its eyes was a look of dazed appeal, and though its mouth was open, revealing rows of little white thorns, it uttered no cry — it did not seem to know whether it should mew with delight or spit with fear. "Will this do?"

Mordred examined its hindquarters. "Yes."

Galahad grinned and deftly tucked the kitten inside his tunic. It scratched ineffectually for a few moments and uttered a feeble cry or two, but then, discovering its new home to be warm and quite comfortable, it curled up inside the capacious pocket and went to sleep. "You can get the mare's dung," Galahad said.

But it was the agrimony that proved to be the most difficult ingredient, for the herb garden was even more jealously guarded than the secret parts of the library. Here the Druid apothecaries nurtured the plants they needed for their work; mandragora for anesthetics, comfrey for broken bones, cinquefoil for the curing of ague and the flux.

The plants they cultivated were subtly different from

their cousins in the wild, and some were rare and delicate and served more sinister purposes. "One look from boys like you, and some of these would just wither away," the gardener had once said to Mordred and his classmates.

Then, perhaps because it was true, perhaps because he wanted to be doubly sure of deterring them, he added, "You know why the plants we grow here are so different? It is not just the way we tend them, you know. It is what we bury in the soil with them." When he had finished they had run away shrieking, leaving poor Dinas to admonish the gardener and chase after them with red face and soothing words.

Galahad remembered all this as they huddled like grotesque shadows in the moonlight, beneath the high wall of the garden. Even to be caught on the outside at such a time was serious enough. "Can we not try it without the agrimony?" he whispered

"Don't be silly. It won't work if we don't have all the ingredients."

Galahad preferred the sort of mischief that carried few risks — such as dropping pebbles on the heads of dull, anonymous peasants. Crouching there he could feel his courage draining away, down his legs and into the silvered ground. And all that replaced it was a dark chill, the unreasoning certainty of discovery. "It might. We might fade a little bit. That would give people a good scare."

Mordred replied with a forbearing smile. After all, he knew, it was Galahad who would be taking most of the risk. So his own resolve remained strong. "We don't want to just scare people. What's the good of going to all this trouble just to frighten the servants? We want to be really invisible."

Galahad knew he should want to be really invisible, too, so he nodded and placed his foot tentatively into Mordred's cupped hands. This was the only way they could do it. A watchman guarded the gate into the garden, and Galahad could never lift Mordred.

Only when he had pulled himself to the top of the wall and lay sprawled and panting along its length did Galahad stop to think how little thought Mordred must have given to the practical side of their venture. "How are you going to get up?" he asked in a loud whisper, feeling panic and a little irritation at the prospect of being deserted.

Mordred was the taller of the two, but still he could not reach the top of the wall by himself. There were no footholds in the smooth stone, and if Galahad could not lift his fat companion from below, then he certainly could not pull him up from above.

"You'll have to go by yourself." Mordred hoped that his bold tone might convince his wavering companion.

"How am I supposed to get down and then up again? You didn't think of that either, did you?"

Mordred could hear a frantic scrambling just above his head, but all he could see was part of Galahad's elongated shadow. Then a foot swung across his line of vision like a pendulum, coming within inches of his nose. He took hold of it and pushed it back up. "It's just the other side of the wall, Gally," he said, feeling impatient but trying to sound encouraging. "There are trees and bushes growing all along this part. You can easily climb back over."

He was almost sure about that. He had studied carefully the plan of the garden, but he had been caught and expelled from the library before he could properly plan an escape route. He wanted Galahad to get away. But he wanted the agrimony too.

At first there was no reply, and he thought Galahad might be sulking. Then he heard a dull thud on the other side of the wall, followed by a harsh whisper. "What do I do now?"

Mordred summoned forth the plan of the herb beds

that he had memorized — thoroughly, he hoped. "Close by on my right, just beside the wall. Look for tall plants with star-shaped flowers. It's the flowers we want."

"I know what they look like," came a petulant whisper. "But it's dark."

Mordred could tell from the sound that his companion had moved a few paces in the correct direction. "You're in the right place. Just grab a handful of whatever is near you and throw them over the wall." He heard a rustling and a tearing in the undergrowth, then something was flying through the air. A cloud of tiny white stars curved through the air on an oblique path over the wall, so that for a moment it seemed as if a portion of the sky was drifting slowly to earth.

The cloud hit Mordred in the face, preceded and accompanied by a shower of damp soil that pattered thinly on the ground around him. He quickly examined the plants. Some were clearly not agrimony, but there were enough of the necessary flowers for their purposes. He gathered them up with haste, clasped the bundle to his chest, and moved closer to the wall. "Come on, Gally."

Galahad did not follow. Mordred heard the shouts of men, followed by the sound of bodies making their way through the undergrowth from some distance away. "Oh, no!" said Galahad softly, then began to direct excuses and pleas for mercy toward the oncoming figures. The sky just above the top of the wall was faintly illuminated as the gardeners, with lighted tapers, rushed to the scene. Mordred knew it would not be long before someone decided to search the other side of the wall, so he took to his heels while behind him Galahad's entreaties turned suddenly to surprised, agonized yelps.

Red with shame and exertion, Mordred ran panting into his chamber. In a corner the mare's dung was slowly fermenting in its bucket, giving off an awful stench that was warm and sickly sweet. Mordred looked at it and felt his insides begin to swell horribly. He raced to the window while his stomach lurched to his throat. Flinging open the shutters, he thrust his head through the narrow opening as far as his shoulders would allow. Just in time.

He remained there for a while, his head protruding from the castle wall like that of a tiny, sickly tortoise from an enormous shell. At length his breathing slowed and his stomach returned to its rightful place. As he absently surveyed the scene before his eyes, he became aware of the surrounding darkness and the dim, distorted landscape it concealed, quite different from the daylight view. That line of trees with their thick, distended crowns, marking the very fringe of the forest, could well be an army of giants, silent and immobile as they waited for the dawn. A flash of white glimpsed briefly out of the corner of his eye might have been an owl, or some poor lost soul searching disconsolately among the trees for its owner.

None of these thoughts frightened him. The real terrors happened during the day. The night hid most of these. And the night air refreshed him; as he opened his mouth to breathe deeply, its smooth, chilly fragrance slid gently down his throat, helping to wash away the sourness within.

When he stepped down from the window the smell was bad but no longer unbearable. The kitten, which had been locked in the room for most of the afternoon, purred and rubbed insistently about his ankles. He sat down on the bed and the little animal followed, plunging unsteadily and rather aimlessly into the dense sea of Mordred's lap. *I could still do it*, he thought as the kitten's throat emitted a continuous hum of contentment. *I have all the ingredients now.*

He picked up the animal, its small back legs kicking in a lazy protest while the rest of its body vibrated with pleasure. *I just have to drop it into the cauldron and leave it for a few minutes. It would be a kindness, really, for it has no future out there. Then the agrimony — the flowers only — and finally the ordure.*

He stood up, cradling the kitten in his arms. Then he went to the door and stole downstairs to the kitchens. *Gally's sacrifice will not have been in vain. It should work. . . .*

He thought this again as he watched the starving animal devour the pieces of cold meat he had scraped from an unwashed cauldron. And again as he let it go, pushing it gently with his foot through the doorway because it was reluctant to leave him. Later, as he stole out to the cesspit with his stinking bucket in one hand and the incriminating and lifeless plants in the other, he thought, *If only I was invisible. This would all be so much easier then.*

* * *

Galahad did not betray me to the Druids. Nor did he hold anything against me afterward. Children are refreshingly pragmatic about the limits of loyalty, and he knew he would have done the same as I did. He spent several days in the infirmary — lying on his stomach all the while, for the Druids had been very angry. Still, the adventure won him considerable status in the eyes of his fellows, who queued up for glimpses of his backside.

Galahad's father showed remarkably little interest in the whole affair, though there were many who felt that the punishment — for a childish prank — was unduly severe. Nearly everyone in my father's court disliked the Druids, and most would have backed Lancelot had he chosen to protest about the treatment meted out to his son.

But he made no move. Lancelot was a firm believer in the school of hard knocks. He was disappointed in Galahad, whom he regarded as a milksop and rather gullible to boot. "It might teach him to look out for himself in the future," he said, catching hold of me one day, "instead of trusting in cunning fellows like you."

I looked up at him with wide, innocent eyes, as though I had no idea what he meant.

My conscience troubled me a bit, but more than anything I was glad that Galahad did not turn against me. He was virtually my only friend at the time. The others disliked me, for I was the king's son. You would think that they might have been a little more circumspect — I was, after all, their future lord. But it was an uncertain age, and anyway children do not think like that.

It did not help my popularity or my self-esteem that I was so terribly obese. I used to suffer from periodic bouts of self-disgust when I would sit, cross-legged and naked, before the mirror in my chamber, gazing with a dull reflective horror at the rolls of pale flesh, gross outpourings that in my more feverish imaginings would spread across the floor, engulfing everything they touched in a pink tide. Sometimes I would touch and embrace myself just to see if the images were real. There was nothing sexual about this, simply a child's fascination with its ugliness — in my case, horrified fascination.

It was many years before I was able to overcome this grave and embarrassing problem. In the meantime I was an easy target for my fellows, and they would taunt me mercilessly about it whenever the mood took them. Sometimes, after a particularly wounding day, I would lie awake in my room, nursing my pride and thinking back to those days when I had many friends. . . .

* * *

She moves so fast, he thought, gasping in the thin, cold air. *One moment we are on the ground, the next unbelievably high above it.* Even the beginnings of that thought had been left far below him as, clinging to the Baobhan's shoulders, he rushed through the air, the forest shrinking away below them. The roaring in his ears changed subtly each time he turned his head to view a different part of the world beneath. But it all looked the same; the great, green wood — The Forest Sauvage — stretched to every horizon like a carpet of green bubbles, millions of them, packed thickly to cover the land.

Except for one place where a toy castle stood on the forest's edge, in the only part of that vast realm where the forest had an edge. The fierce afternoon sun shone brightly there. He peered into its glare but he could not make out what lay beyond the forest, though he would dearly liked to have seen. Sunlight glinted from the tiny turrets so that, as they swooped and glided through the blue empty sky, the land rising and falling alarmingly each time, he had the strangest notion that the castle was signaling to him. Leaning forward, he shouted into the Baobhan's ear — or rather, into the hole where an ear should have been. "Is that my father's house?"

The creature nodded slowly. "And soon it will be yours too, I ween."

It was not a long flight. He had only enough time to marvel at the extent of the world and to briefly wonder at what might lie beyond those distant horizons before they were back in the clearing in front of his home.

He sensed something was wrong even before he slid off the Baobhan's back and began running toward the empty hut. It was not simply the silence, for that was normal enough in the forest; nor the sole testimony to some brief struggle — a cauldron lying on its side in the doorway. Nor even the fact that the Fomor herself had dared come so close to his mother's house. It was all of these, and something more. Something, he felt, had violated this clearing where for thousands of years the air had lain undisturbed but for the quiet presence of Morgause and himself. He could feel this restlessness even more strongly as he stepped through the doorway into the empty gloom.

"There is nobody there, you know." The voice came gently from behind him. But when he turned the Baobhan was already gone.

* * *

He never saw her again, though years later he almost did.

At first he thought it was the cold that had woken him, for no matter how energetically he tried he could never warm the whole of his huge pallet. He lay still in the darkness and tried to will himself back to sleep. Then he heard it: the faraway scratching. It sounded as if something with claws — they would have to be immensely strong — was struggling to gain a purchase on the sheer wall outside. *No,* he corrected, *not as if . . .*

Feeling quite calm, he tried to disentangle the noises outside from those within — his heartbeat, his breathing, the slow, sonorous rumblings inside his stomach. He was not afraid, partly because he was not fully awake and partly because he knew what was out there clutching at the smooth stones. He thought he heard a voice whispering through the closely shuttered window, but the wind frequently made a noise like that. He was not afraid, but he was tired, and eventually he turned his face away from the window and drifted back to sleep.

The next morning there was great excitement. Some of the guards said they had seen a hideous winged creature crouching on the battlements. For a moment it had glared at them balefully, showing huge yellow teeth, defying them to challenge it, but they were paralyzed with fear. Then it gave a shriek and sprang from the castle, its huge black shadow drifting lazily across the moon before it vanished. Not everyone believed the guards' story, but it provided meat for much discussion.

Mordred said nothing.

5

I WAS GENUINELY SORRY WHEN THE TIME CAME for Dinas to return home. Though I had long outgrown his lessons, we still held frequent and pleasant discourse together. Alas, his mind by this time was not what it had been. Shortly before his departure I finally told him about the Fomor. We were sitting, as we often did, in the familiar schoolroom, empty now, for it was late in the afternoon and already the light was fading.

His small, bony hands were folded reflectively in his lap and he listened with a meditative, almost somnolent expression. When I was finished he said, in the sort of voice that adults use when children's fantasies must be humored, "They were only stories, Mordred. I don't know if such creatures even existed. It was just something to entertain you boys."

"Oh, but they do exist, and I have seen them. It was a long time ago, but I can still remember." I recited some of the names, and he nodded politely and sometimes too in recognition, but it was clear that he had other things on his mind even if he did, finally, believe me.

He turned his head briefly in the direction of the narrow window and the grey light and shivered, though it had been a warm day. It was a little while before he spoke again. Now his voice was mournful and sonorous, filling that small chamber with an almost palpable image of its owner's despair.

"I am sorry to admit it, but it has been a waste. Such a pity to realize that when it is too late."

He was talking, I supposed, about his great failure, the writing of the Celtic.

"It could have been done, you know. In theory. Even in the little time I have left, I could have finished it. But for these . . ."

"Someone else could be your eyes." I fear I did not sound very convincing. It seemed to me such a barbarous tongue, hardly worth preserving in script.

"Ah, but not my heart — do you see? It is a task that requires a certain fixity of purpose. Yes, and a blind enthusiasm. Not many people possess such qualities." A thin, mirthless smile appeared and then quickly vanished. "Blind enthusiasm; that's good. Still, I must not be bitter, must I? It has been my privilege to act as tutor to the next king of Albion — an Aristotle to an Alexander, perhaps." He gave me a look of what I took to be significant enquiry, and so I laughed off the analogy as I thought was expected. At that, he seemed disappointed and hurt.

Then he said, "I am not prescient, you understand. I cannot tell you how you will fare, whether or not you will prove a wise ruler. But I think you will try." He nodded slowly to himself, as if even this small effort at speculation required great concentration. "Yes, I think so."

Leaning forward, I took the hands from his lap and briefly clasped them in my own. They felt small and tenacious, like a bird's extremities. But so cold! "I shall not forget thee, Master Dinas."

Then he stood up, and with a smile of acknowledgment but not a word, left the room. I am sure that in his heart he drew some comfort from the knowledge that he would shortly see his homeland again, but as I watched his small, frail body disappear down the corridor all that I could discern in that weary gait was sadness and a deep sense of waste.

As for me, by this time I was almost weeping.

But I was not left friendless for long. My next tutor, Crito the Macedonian, arrived at my father's court in the company of several amphorae of Italian wine, a pretty box of jewelry, and a ballista — all gifts from Lancelot, who was leading the forces in Gaul attempting to stem the Latin tide.

This Crito was an unprepossessing-looking fellow, diminutive and underfed, with lank straw hair plastered thinly across a narrow forehead. He carried his pitifully small bundle as if even that were too heavy for him. Arthur gave the ballista to the armorers to dismantle and examine; the jewelry he presented to Guinevere, who thanked him fulsomely and locked it away forever. The wine he gave to the Round Table, and the Macedonian he gave to me.

"He seems a learned fellow — that sack of his is full of books," Arthur observed. "It will be some company for you. I cannot put him with the other servants, for he only speaks Greek and Latin. Anyway, you know how I feel about slaves, Mordred. There is too much of that sort of thing in this country as it is."

"But I don't like slavery either, Father."

"Well . . ." He shrugged helplessly and contemplated the ground. He had the furtive look he usually wore on those rare occasions when we conversed; he was always affable enough, but beneath it all I could sense his embarrassment and his eagerness to be gone. I had lived in his home for fourteen years, and we had never had a proper conversation. "You can set him free, then; make the sort of gesture I am unable to make."

I nodded. I had long grown weary of hearing him bemoan his impotence.

"I do wish Lancelot was not so lavish," he sighed. "It's obvious what he wants. This is all so vulgar."

"Will you help him?"

"They are our brothers. Fellow Celts and all that." He

looked directly at me — something he hardly ever did. His dark eyes, fierce and penetrating yet reassuring, also seemed to me at that moment to be repositories of truth and utter integrity. "But I did not become king in order to lead my poor countrymen unwillingly to their deaths. We have a higher task, you and I."

These were unexpected confidences, and I was flattered and beguiled by being granted them. Only much later did I learn of his true intentions. Even so, I do not think he deceived me any more than he did himself. On this occasion, as subsequently on others, he was using me as a sounding board for the voice of his conscience.

But to return to Crito. Though he spoke no Celtic, I (thanks to Dinas) knew some Greek, so we were able to converse tolerably well.

His was an interesting story. He had been a student once, in Macedon, where he had learned about dialectic, physics, plane and solid geometry, and divers other subjects. But he was handicapped by Dame Poverty. Unable to afford the fees or to find suitable employment as a tutor, he had quickly incurred heavy and pressing debts. In desperation and on the advice of ill-favored friends, he turned to thieving, entering people's homes — usually at night — and making off with whatever valuables he could carry.

He was an incompetent thief and was soon caught, together with most of his partners. But while they were sent either to execution or the galleys, he, with his eloquence and flowing tongue, was able to charm a little mercy out of his judges and so was sent to the slave market instead. For several years he passed from master to master and province to province, traveling more widely than most freemen. He eventually fetched up in a small garrison town in Transalpine Gaul, where he held the comparatively comfortable position of chief house slave to the garrison commander — until Lancelot came.

"Oh, it was a shocking experience, noble master." He

wrung his hands and his eyes bulged horribly above hollow cheeks as if they were witnessing the whole scene again. "I was terrified — truly terrified. All the noise, the screaming, the killing! Really, I thought it was all up with me. I cannot imagine how I came to be spared."

Nor for the life of me could I. He told me he was thirty-five, but he could easily have passed for ten years younger or older. There was an abjectness in his manner that seemed a little too calculated, and the way he punctuated the account of his short-lived criminal career with so many contrite sighs and upturned glances irritated me. "I have learned my lesson well and truly," he would keep saying, or something like it. It was all intended, I suppose, to impress me with his trustworthiness. I had the feeling he had told the story more than once.

"They let me keep my books, too." They were lying in a bundle at his feet. "I have been so lucky."

That was another thing I could not understand. Most of the Gauls were illiterate. Galahad possessed a modicum of learning, but even if he had been involved in this particular battle I could not see him pleading for the life of such an unpromising specimen. It would be too much trouble.

"Of course it can hardly compare with your own collection, noble master." He glanced enviously, with genuine admiration, at the small but growing private library in my chamber. "But there may be one or two items here which you have not met with."

Indeed there were. For one thing, as I observed out loud, they were not made of the usual papyrus or parchment rolls. "Too expensive," he muttered as, crouching on the floor, he handed me several volumes. They appeared to be parchment, but the skins had been folded several times, cut, and sewn together between a pair of stiff covers. "It is vellum," he explained. "Calfskin."

I nodded as I turned the pages and felt the smoothness of the waxed surface. It was quite a pleasing sensation. *A woman's skin must feel something like this,* I thought. *Only warmer.*

"Some of these I had as a student," he said proudly. Indeed, many of them looked as if they had endured a battering. They gave off an unpleasant smell also, which may have been due to their age or to their being imperfectly cured.

"This one is in Latin," I remarked.

"You have taste, noble master. That is Quintus Ennius, a very fine poet. And this one"— he handed me another volume —"is Lucilius. He is what the Latins call a satirist. He is full of elegance and wit."

I took the book, turned it in my hand. "I have no Latin volumes."

He sprang to his feet, beaming and thrusting a handful of volumes at me. "Then please, master, take these with my compliments."

"We are not allowed to read Latin."

His face fell, and he gently pulled them back away from me. The poor fellow was trying so hard, and I was giving him hardly any encouragement. I reached out and took the books from his unresisting hands. "Perhaps you could teach me?"

He assented eagerly. Clearly such a task was vastly preferable to the normal duties of a house slave. I then explained to him my abhorrence of slavery. Somewhat to my chagrin, he was absolutely horrified.

"But what is to become of me? Surely, noble master, you cannot propose setting me free in this land of savages — I mean no offense."

I could not keep from being upset, despite his apology. "If you wish, you may stay here as my tutor. I will pay you for your trouble. In time you may save sufficient to be able to return to your home." I said this last as though I would welcome the event as much as he.

He brightened then, but I was still vexed and my manner remained cold for a time. My carefully rehearsed magnanimous gesture had met with a lackluster reception; I had cause to be annoyed.

But my doubts about Crito's other qualities proved to be unfounded. He was an excellent teacher, and I, being a diligent pupil, learned in the space of but a few months to speak, read, and write in Latin. In view of the political climate I could hardly boast about my new skills, but I was quietly proud of myself nonetheless.

It was not only my mind that improved during this time. Tired of the taunts of my fellows and burning with disgust at my truly awful appearance, I finally became determined to do something about it. First I approached my tutor.

"Crito, I have a healthy mind, but it resides in a body which sore displeases me. How may I right this?"

"You have a fine body—"

"That's enough. I want advice, not flattery."

He bent his chin. "Very well. You must eat little and exercise much."

"Is that all? I thought you Greeks were an inventive race. Can you not suggest an easier way?"

"You could learn to accept with equanimity what the gods have seen fit to give you. That is what our philosophers tell us. Most of them were quite hideous, you know. Personally, I find that rather comforting."

I did not, and for once I could not accept the quiet counsels of his philosophy. So I set about devising my own scheme, a rigorous regimen of green vegetables and unremitting exercise.

"Ugh, Mordred!" exclaimed Guinevere one day. "How can you eat such a mess? I would not give that to animals. It is peasants' food."

"Which is why our peasants are so healthy, Stepmother," I replied, tucking away my bowlful of boiled cabbage with a grim relish. Perversely, I welcomed her opposition and concern. It seemed to strengthen my resolve. How I would astound them all!

The attentions of my fellows were hardest to bear. No matter what time of the day I chose for my exercise in the gymnasium, they would always be there, commenting loudly about my portly frame as it lumbered gracelessly up and down the running track or rode clumsily at the quintain. Once their lessons were done, there was little for the children of Camelot to do with their time, so I provided a rare and much appreciated source of entertainment. All my life I had striven to hide my obscene body; now here I was exhibiting it for anyone to see.

But slowly, imperceptibly at first, a transformation took place. My convexities became concave; veins and arteries hidden for years began to bulge and twist as I flexed my new muscles. I began once more to go to the mirror and examine my body, only now a sense of pride rather than one of mortification drove me there. My face thinned out considerably, and my complexion acquired a sallow hue that I thought accorded well with my reflective nature — though Guinevere, wringing her hands, pronounced that I was bound for an early grave. Dark rings appeared beneath my eyes. These too, I thought, suggested the intense, scholarly image I was striving for.

"How do you find me?" I asked Crito after I had banished him from my sight for several weeks. "Tell me straight, mind."

"You look . . . interesting, lord," he replied. "You look like a man who should not be lightly regarded."

This pleased me greatly.

Of course, I could not extinguish all traces of my former self. My hands remained those of a fat little boy, white and soft and quite out of place on my new sinewy wrists. And I was disappointed with my beard — a thin, rather colorless affair. But, those few reservations apart, I was highly pleased with the new Mordred. After six months I could hold my own in the gymnasium against almost all my contemporaries. They still disliked me, but at least they left me alone.

Arthur, when he perceived the change in me, was full of praise. This pleased me most of all. "You look like the heir to the throne now," he whispered to me one evening across the table. Guinevere sighed, and her shoulders rose and fell in a demonstrative despair (*Why is it that women always wanted to fatten me up?*), but even in her I could detect a growing realization and acceptance of the change in me. She stopped treating me like a child.

I did not neglect my studies during this time, though it was difficult to obtain works by Latin authors. They were not exactly proscribed, but to have asked in the library would have meant enduring much raising of eyebrows and perhaps a few awkward questions. In any event it hardly seemed worth the trouble, despite the inevitable lure of the forbidden. I read all the Latin works in Crito's possession, but found nothing that fired my imagination. The poet Ennius, whom he rated so highly, I found dull and turgid. As for the satirist Lucilius, I could not fathom how someone could make fun of evil and injustice. He wrote of corruption and bad government as if it were all a rather fine and pointed joke. If that is what the Latins call satire, then they can keep it! Some of the playwrights I found mildly amusing, particularly Plautus. But, though entertaining, he lacked substance. My first love remained Greek philosophy.

* * *

"Your slave tells me you are reading Plato. The Republic. That's very interesting. We may have a scholar for a king yet." Merlin almost reverentially laid a white cloth across his work bench, carefully smoothing out the creases with crabbed but dexterous fingers.

"He is not a slave, but my tutor." Mordred wondered why the old man had called him down here among the jars and cobwebs and stale old smells of his cellar.

"Ah," said Merlin distantly. Bending down, he picked

up a chicken that writhed ineffectually in his hand as he laid it gently on the cloth. It had been trussed for nearly an hour and was still feebly flapping its wings, but it had long given up any real hope of escape. Leaning forward, Mordred thought he detected a look of resignation in its glazed eyes, though he knew full well that such a dull animal could not possibly have feelings.

Merlin took up a knife and a whetstone and began sharpening. His pallor was that of a man who has spent most of his life indoors; it seemed well suited to a world of shadows and candlelight. But though he was old — no one knew precisely how old — his face possessed a wonderful mutability. At one moment it would be saturnine and brooding; at another — now, for instance, in the knife's pale glow — his mild blue eyes would dance with a demented keenness.

He turned to Mordred with the genial smile of an ancient simpleton. "To tell the truth, I don't like doing this sort of thing. But it doesn't do to be squeamish, and it would be cowardly to give the task to someone else. Besides, I have to keep my hand in." He laid the knife down. "Your father suggested we have a little chat. You are, after all, heir to the throne, and I will be your chief counselor — if I am still around, that is."

Mordred watched in horrified fascination as Merlin stroked the hen with long, even caresses. The animal quickly became still and calm. Not lulled, but accepting. Mordred tried to imagine Camelot without Merlin, Albion without Merlin. . . . The old man had made Arthur what he was. Many disliked the fact, but there it was. "So you are reading Plato?" Merlin asked again.

"I think he has the answers to many of the problems that beset us, our world. Not all of them, perhaps, but many of them."

"So we have problems?" There was an irony in the old man's tone that caused Mordred to frown defensively. "Well, I suppose we do," he continued. "Terrible problems. Lack of discipline. No respect for authority. Rebellion." His eyes narrowed and his nostrils flared alarmingly. "Lewdness."

You know that is not what I mean, Mordred thought. "Plato states that there was once a golden age where all men were equal and virtuous. Do you think that such a thing is possible, Uncle Merlin?" There was an edge of nervousness in his voice. He thought, *This all sounds so ingenuous when I say it to him.*

But Merlin did not look scornful. He shook his head sadly. "I suspect that this, bad as it is, is as near as we shall get. It is certainly better than what came before and"— he lowered the volume of his voice —"immeasurably better than what will follow."

Mordred, concerned at the sudden, dark frown and the thin snarl that had appeared on Merlin's visage, bent forward. "Pardon, Uncle?"

"Just prattling, boy." And he murmured to himself, "Amid the glory there is rottenness even now."

"Still, there is always room for improvement, don't you think?"

"Oh, there's plenty of room. There is just so little time. Now, do you see this?" His attention was once more upon the poor chicken. "It lays eggs with two yolks. Not just once, but every time. What do you think of that? Could it have two souls, perhaps?"

Mordred thought, *Two souls, indeed. I thought you were beyond such silliness, old man.*

There was nothing delicate in Merlin's handiwork. He plunged the knife into the animal's breast and began hacking blindly. There was a dreadful shriek, followed by the slow beat of wings flapping reflexively against the bench. Mordred closed his eyes as the horrifying realization struck him. *My father's chiefest counselor, Merlin the Wise, is quite mad.*

When he opened his eyes again, all he could see for a moment was a drifting cloud of white feathers gently illuminated by the narrow window opening above their heads. Slowly the cloud dispersed, though a few feathers remained lodged in Merlin's hair and beard. He was gazing with great concentration at his bloody hand and the small, pulsing object that rested there. His eyes were ablaze with wonder, his voice strangely calm and dreamlike. "It still beats. Now, isn't that remarkable. . . ."

* * *

Later, when they had tidied up the mess, Merlin took Mordred's arm. After a long, searching gaze that left the young man feeling very uncomfortable, he asked, "Are you happy here? No regrets?"

"Regrets about what, Uncle?"

"You came to us from the great forest. You must have had some strange experiences there." Merlin's hand felt like the claw of a malevolent and repulsive bird. Mordred wanted to struggle free but dared not try.

"I remember so little of my life there. I was very young when I left."

"You remember the Fomor." His eyes came so close that Mordred could see the blood vessels, cracked and purplish; the madness dancing within.

"Well, yes, I remember them."

"Fascinating creatures. I should dearly love to study them more closely."

"Would . . . would you cut them open, too?"

Merlin released his grip with an angry gesture, almost flinging Mordred's arm away from him. "Do you think I am a barbarian? Is that it? It is your father's knights who do that sort of thing — and all their butchery is for sport. Mine at least has some value."

"Yes," said Mordred softly. Then, seeing some feathers still on the floor, he bent down to sweep them up.

"Oh, leave that," said Merlin. "I have servants to do that." But Mordred continued.

Merlin watched him for a minute, then shrugged to himself and returned to the subject he wanted to pursue. "You see, they know all about the old magic."

"I suppose they do," Mordred said, keeping his eyes averted and still sweeping grimly.

"We know about it too, of course, but they can still control it. We, with our modern ways, are fast losing touch with such things." Heaving a sigh, he gazed almost longingly at the narrow window in the ceiling, where dust motes slowly revolved in thin shafts of winter sunlight, just beyond reach. "I do envy your mother. It must have been a lonely life for both of you, but then she was so close to the heart of things."

"I really don't remember very much," Mordred said. He picked up the torn and mangled corpse by one leg. "What shall I do with this?"

"Put it in the sack with the rest. Didn't she try to pass anything on to you? About the Earth Spirit, for instance?"

"I was much too young. Earth Spirit. . . . I suppose there was such a thing in the forest. It is a strange place, certainly." The last was halfway between a question and a statement.

Merlin led the way to the staircase that rose out of the cellar, his long cloak dragging soundlessly behind him across the floor of packed earth, stirring up years worth of dust and detritus. Mordred followed, wrinkling his nose in disgust.

"I suppose it is a sign of the times," Merlin said when he was halfway up the stairs. "Our technology has blunted our senses, so that we are no longer even sure about such things. Your mother now, she could have told us so much. If only . . ." He pushed open the door, and they stepped into a long, empty corridor. The bare walls were stained with rivulets of dampness. This whole section of the castle, the Tower Bedegraine, was Merlin's alone.

"If only what, Uncle Merlin?"

"If only she hadn't fallen ill."

"Her magic wasn't good enough to save her from that," said Mordred without bitterness. "A good physician might have saved her." He longed to be outside in the open, no matter how cold it was. In the cellar there had been, despite the filth, a certain animal warmth. But everywhere else in the tower, in the corridors and in the dismal, sparsely furnished rooms, he felt a languid fear creep over him. Camelot was hardly a cheerful place; it had not been built for that. But in the Tower Bedegraine a special kind of gloom resided. It was wholly apart and wholly sinister, and Mordred wondered how Merlin and the other Druids who lived there could bear an existence so devoid of color and life. Unless, of course, they were all mad. . . .

Merlin reached the outside door, but to Mordred's dismay, though he laid his hand upon the latch he did not lift it. Instead he fixed his gaze once more upon Mordred. A strange new light was in his eyes now, something that Mordred had not seen before. It was not the light of madness exactly; it was far worse than that.

"What about the Lady of the Lake? You know about her, eh?"

"I did meet her once, though I was very young. She is called Nimue."

"You see? You have met the Earth Spirit — a part of it, anyway. You are fortunate. What would I not give for such an encounter!"

It embarrassed Mordred to see the old man's face contorted so by carnal eagerness. In the dim light his face glowed like that of an ancient satyr, and when he stretched a hand through the gloom and laid it on the young man's shoulder it was all Mordred could do not to recoil from the touch.

"I know that she is dangerous, Uncle."

Merlin smiled and pulled away his hand. "I am no ordinary mortal." He unlatched the great oak door and pushed it open. Outside the sky was a brooding grey. The brief sunlight had vanished, and rain was falling heavily. But Mordred felt his spirits lifted by the rush of daylight and cold air.

For a while Merlin stood in silence at the top of the steps. Without turning he said, "By the way, Mordred, I think it is time we dispensed with this 'Uncle' business, don't you? We are not related, after all, and you are no longer a child." Then, stepping briskly into the rain, he added, "Yes, I should greatly like to have a moment's discourse with her."

Mordred was about to try again to dissuade him from such a clearly dangerous course when something — perhaps the aura of corruption and stale lust he now sensed, or perhaps the fleeting and slightly puzzling references to his mother — made him suddenly decide that he should not concern himself too much with Merlin. As the old man stepped out into the rain, Mordred saw dark spots appear on his grey robe and watched the moisture spread like a rapid and virulent disease. *Very well. If the mad old goat is so bent on self-destruction, then I shall not stop him.* The sheer ferocity of that sentiment disturbed him. Mordred really liked to think of himself as a kindly soul.

* * *

Merlin too had been disturbed. He had made a careless slip and was anxious that he should not repeat it.

"Of course, he must be told the truth sometime, I realize," he said to Arthur a few hours later. "But not just yet, I think."

They were alone, the grey-bearded king and his ancient Druid, in a vast and vaulting chamber where their breath mingled in strange, outlandish shapes and where even their thoughts seemed to echo. This was the very center of Camelot. Here — when enough of them were present — the members of the Round Table would sit, swapping tales, arguing and getting drunk. Now Arthur sat alone on his high-backed throne, a lonely, regal figure staring pensively into an invisible distance. Merlin stood at his feet, dressed in simple grey garb, but his manner was not that of a supplicant.

"Hmm?" said Arthur, slowly coming out of his reverie.

The king had his troubles. From the remote and rarely visited north had come reports of tribal rebellions. The king of the Brigantes had repudiated his oath of fealty and was even now rallying others to his cause. Like all the other such incidents, it would come to nothing. Many more would rally to King Arthur than to some obscure and barbarous upstart. But it was a worry nonetheless, as were the constant importunings of Lancelot and the other Gauls, fearful of the gathering might of Rome.

Arthur turned his face to Merlin. Though careworn and prematurely aged, it was not unhandsome nor without dignity. "I don't give the boy enough of my time," he said softly. "Very well, Merlin, what's to be done?"

"Send him away, sire. It is done commonly enough at his age."

Arthur nodded. "To my uncle's castle, perhaps. Or were you thinking of somewhere farther away? What about Gaul? That should keep him out of mischief."

"The boy already has the makings of a fine warrior, sire. That part of his education could easily be completed here. No, I was thinking that as heir to the throne he should have a more fully rounded background." Arthur continued to regard him with interest. "I think you should send him to Glastonbury."

"To my academy?"

It was not Arthur's academy. The king had shown no interest and had played little part in the whole ambitious scheme. All the work, all the planning, had been Merlin's. But the old man inclined his head graciously nonetheless.

"I don't want him to become a Druid, Merlin. I have too many of those already."

"Glastonbury offers a wide variety of possibilities and opportunities, sire." This, at any rate, had always been Merlin's fond hope. The reality was disappointingly different. In spite of its grand title, the academy at Glastonbury was little more than a primitive seminary. Even the building work was only half completed.

"Well," said Arthur with no great enthusiasm, "I suppose it will do him no harm." To himself he added, If you cannot beat them, join them. "Very well, Merlin. I can leave the arrangements to you?" Slowly his attention returned to that invisible and intractable focus of all his cares.

Merlin, who in fact had already begun to make the arrangements, smiled and exited silently.

6

THE PLAIN OF GLASTONBURY WAS MARSHLAND that much of the year could only be traversed by the flat-bottomed boats used by the few inhabitants of its tiny islands. On one of these stood the Druid Academy. From another rose that loneliest of hills, Glastonbury Tor.

The buildings of the academy were in the Latin style, with whitewashed walls and red-tiled roofs, all grouped about a central courtyard much like the forum of a small Roman town. The Celts hated the Latins but borrowed freely when it suited them.

The principal entrance was a covered archway, rather gaudily decorated with pictures of Celtic deities — on the one side, the cultivated and almost omnipotent Gwydion, master of eloquence and poetry; on the other, the goddess Arianrod, an unremarkable deity who nevertheless had to be appeased, for the tiny island upon which the academy stood was held to be her sacred ground.

Around the courtyard were a lecture hall, a library, administrative offices, and the Druids' sleeping quarters, all linked by wide cloisters — but only on three sides. Due to a long-running dispute between the architect and the Druids concerning payment, the students' dormitory opposite the entrance remained, as it had been for many years, a partly built wooden skeleton. Inside, still in neat stacks, were the pantiles for the roof, the curved bricks for the columns and the stones for the walls. On some nights the plaintive howling of the wind through the timber framework would keep the students and their masters awake, putting them in mind of the fierce serpents that were said to haunt the lagoon.

Most people had grown accustomed to this part-finished state of affairs. The novices did not enjoy living in their crude round huts of clay and thatch close to the water's edge where the ground was damp and prone to flooding, but few saw any prospect of a change for the better — not in their time, anyway. Mordred did not care so much. He had his own quarters on higher ground and more important things on his mind.

"We are going to waste here, Agravaine. I cannot bear the thought of two more years of this. I simply cannot." Mordred bent closer to his friend, his voice sinking to a conspiratorial whisper. "Sometimes I have this terrible nightmare. I am living among people with whom I cannot converse, who cannot understand a word I say. Then I wake up, and the nightmare is real. Do you know what I mean?"

Agravaine said nothing. He did not believe that his friend really had such dreams; he was adding color to his argument. But he nodded and looked politely attentive, for he had found this to be the best response when Mordred was in these moods.

They were standing in the entrance. Behind them the muted conversations of their fellow students floated like ghostly whispers in the still, late afternoon air.

Mordred's attention was fixed in the other direction. Half a mile away across the black, still waters, Glastonbury Tor rose like a beacon, shadowy and mist-shrouded, inviting and threatening, so incongruous amid that flat, even landscape. He was thinking that if he were to continue staring, and with just a little imagination, he might see the mist about its summit assume some recognizable shape.

Though the tor was a sacred place to the Druids —

more sacred than the stone circles, because unlike them its purpose and origin were steeped in mystery — it was not forbidden to go there. Such strictures were unnecessary, and not only because boats were difficult to obtain. The tor had its own defenses against the merely curious. Even as Mordred watched, tenuous grey tendrils of mist twitched and shuddered gently, like an animal stirring in its sleep. He shook his head free of this disturbing vision, and he and Agravaine turned to join the other promenaders in the cloisters.

Though many people were talking, little could be distinguished. Life at Glastonbury tended toward the seemly and contemplative, and so people conversed in low voices and walked with pensive deliberation.

"I thought I would find so much here," Mordred said wistfully. "A community of scholars, a group of people like myself. . . ."

You mean malcontents, thought Agravaine as they turned and retraced their steps.

"But most people here, they are time-servers," Mordred continued, finishing the thought. He winced like someone who feels pain but cannot locate its source. "Can you not sense the futility of it all? The waste?"

They stopped for a moment, contemplating the bent and shrouded figures threading their way like grey shadows amid the columns and the winter sunlight. Only Agravaine and Mordred, as the sons of kings, were permitted to wear the more colorful tunics and trousers, called bracae, of the Celtic nobility.

Mordred was not finished. "Do you know what momentous subjects they are discussing so earnestly?" he asked sarcastically, then answered himself. "What will happen to the virtuous dead when the Isles of the Blessed become full? Or why is the heel stone so called? Or how long is the Spear of Lugh? What use is all that? Why, I learned about such things years ago. I cannot think why my father sent me here."

Agravaine nodded in sympathy. He did not always understand what Mordred was getting at, though sometimes he thought he very nearly did.

They were distant cousins. Agravaine's father, King Bleoberis of Northumberland, had consigned his son to the care of the Druids some six months earlier. Bleoberis was a bluff, likeable fellow, but he had little appreciation for culture. He had sent Agravaine south not to broaden his mind, but in order to save his life.

Back at home, a young servant had been discovered one morning in Agravaine's bed. Had it been a female, the matter would have aroused little comment. But in this case Bleoberis had been forced to take speedy and drastic action, for the moral climate of Northumberland was a harsh one, and the king had many enemies who would have eagerly exploited such an opportunity. So the relatively innocent victim, a kitchen serf, was hurriedly and discreetly dispatched, while the real culprit was placed under the watchful tutelage of the Druids of Glastonbury.

Agravaine had felt sorry for the boy, but he soon took to feeling more sorry for himself. He considered his punishment to be unmerited and unduly severe. After all, it was not as if he had any unspeakable tendencies. The incident had been a mildly pleasurable experience with some rather unpleasant consequences — for a time he had actually feared for his life — but he had discovered nothing new about himself. Mordred, he owned, was a handsome fellow — quite unlike the timorous and overweight nonentity he remembered from earlier visits to Camelot. But he was a comrade and a kinsman, and nothing more.

"Do you think there are others like us?"

Mordred's question caught him off guard. Agravaine's face wore an almost permanent expression of surliness, so deeply etched that many casual observers took it for a sign of some facial disfigurement. Suddenly it became suffused by deeper shadows of guilt and blushing confusion. "Like us?" he echoed.

"Seekers after truth. That's a good phrase of yours. The quest's the thing, eh?"

Agravaine had not told his cousin the real reason he had been sent to Glastonbury. He liked Mordred and admired his intellectual qualities, but he also considered him to be an innocent in some matters.

"But I should not complain so much, should I, Agravaine? Things are not so much better at home. And there are possibilities here."

"What sort of possibilities?"

"I mean that if we find things not to our liking, then we should forge opportunities to alter them so that they will be."

Agravaine recalled his father's parting words. . . . "Now then, son, if you can keep your nose clean for, say, a twelvemonth, then perhaps we can bring you back home again. I know your mother misses you already. So"— he delivered a painful slap to Agravaine's shoulder —"I shall be expecting good reports about you. List well what I say."

Agravaine had indeed listened and remembered. He hated the academy; the whole business of replicating and dissecting the sterile teachings of the pedants bore on him like a torturous weight, but he was determined to endure it in order that he might in time return home to his hounds, his hawks, and above all to his chariot. On such a tiny island as this, there were few opportunities for mischief, and because there were only two boats and he was a poor sailor, there was little chance of finding diversion elsewhere.

"I think," Mordred was saying, "that we should try to determine how many of these fellows secretly nurse similar grievances. We should make ourselves known to one another."

"Why?"

"Only so that we might converse and exchange views," his cousin silkily assured him.

* * *

"I was in error, I admit that." Agitated and flushed, Merlin was pacing angrily in circles about the council chamber. "It appears the academy was not the place for him. But then, I did not expect the future King of Albion to become involved in something so unseemly. There are things which even I could not be expected to anticipate." He stopped for a moment to gather breath and to fix an indignant gaze upon Arthur. "I am sorry to be so painfully frank, but these things have to be said."

"Oh, yes, Merlin. Quite." Arthur inclined his head slowly before turning to me with an expression of patriarchal gravity. He was annoyed and not a little embarrassed by the whole affair, but there was also, I fancied, a spark of merriment within those deep, unfathomable eyes. Merlin had actually confessed to being wrong!

"Is this true, Mordred?" Arthur was holding the letter from the academy authorities that had arrived at court a day or two before I had. "Did you actually strike one of my Druids?"

"Several!" Merlin's anger had manifested itself like a disease. His normally bloodless face was covered with purple spots, like weals. *He is choleric,* I thought with alarm. I had heard of men whose vitals had burst through too much display of ill humor, and I had no wish to see that happen, even to Merlin.

"Nay, sire." I continued to stare fixedly at the floor in what I hoped was a convincing attitude of reverence, innocence, and shame combined. "At least, such an act was not my intent."

"Uncias has written to me also." Merlin was addressing Arthur, but his baleful eyes were upon me. "He is still wearing the bandages."

His rancor did not frighten me; when in such a mood, he could be easily outmaneuvered. It was his icy calm that one had to watch. I really was concerned for his health, though.

So was Arthur. "Calm yourself, Merlin. I am sure this matter will prove to be less serious than it sounds. A case of high spirits compounded by a misunderstanding, perhaps?" He looked at me, and I nodded vigorously.

Merlin said, "A grave insult has been suffered by my people at the hands of the Pendragons. I look for an explanation." There was a short but significant pause. "Sire."

"Well," said Arthur. "Well, of course, Merlin, we do take this very seriously." He turned to me again. "Perhaps it is time we heard your version of events." His eyes narrowed shrewdly. "And the truth, mind you, Mordred. Merlin and I are not such a pair of old fools that we cannot distinguish truth from fiction."

As if I would underestimate those two so much! But the truth? That was a ticklish matter, for truth is a mutable and shifting substance that has different meanings from different mouths. But I am satisfied I told the truth as I saw it. For I really had nothing to be ashamed of.

* * *

"We shall call ourselves Young Albion," Mordred announced. This was the fourth meeting he had called, and he had decided it was time the group had a name, for its numbers were steadily growing. Tonight nearly twenty novices huddled around the crackling flames in the center of his hut. Many reasons brought them to Mordred — an escape from loneliness, the comfort of a warm hearth, the chance to mix with one of the great ones of the earth. But the most potent reasons of all were bitter disappointment and the sense of wasted youth.

These boys were the lowborn intellectuals of Arthur's

realm; farmers' and traders' sons mostly, ones who could never be content with menial outlets for their considerable energies. In later years, as part of his program to pacify the rebellious north, Arthur would inaugurate the great secular universities of York and Durham, and their lives, though tragically brief, would be glorious. But for the present there was only Glastonbury.

In some respects the Druids were far-seeing. They did not discriminate in the choice of applicants — members of all classes of society were admitted, and few individuals were turned away, for they believed that even those without apparent promise could, in time, acquire it. Poverty was no barrier.

But there was a price to pay. The Druid academicians demanded more than scholarly vigor and attentiveness in lessons. They required also unquestioning obedience to even the most trifling ordinances, for theirs was a closed, totalitarian society. It was also wholly celibate.

The two princes were of course among the few who were exempt from this particular stricture, but all of those who had gathered in the hut were not. Their pale and serious faces were pinched by more than simple poverty. These young men had realized that they had simply exchanged one bleak future for another. The only happy person among them was Mordred, for he was beginning to discover what a powerful driving force is the resentment of others.

There were some who, as they listened to Mordred's speech, kept one eye fixed on the doorway. Meetings of this sort were not expressly forbidden, but that was only because they had never been foreseen. There was a certain excitement to be had in running a small risk like this — providing it remained small.

Agravaine was trying hard to conceal his anxiety. He stood beside Mordred and the basket of scrolls that had arrived only that morning and prayed that the stewards should not take it into their heads to venture abroad this night. The weather was on his side. It was raining heavily, and outside the wind keened like a soul in torment, forcing itself through the cracks in the walls and quickening the flames as it chilled the backs of those in attendance. Agravaine told himself that the Druids would surely stay in their own chambers tonight.

Mordred did not feel the cold. For fully half an hour he declaimed to the crowded, upturned faces. He was warmed by their attentiveness, their enthusiasm — they liked the name Young Albion; there was an assertive ring about it — and by the satisfaction of knowing that here, at last, was something at which he excelled.

Despite his glum mood, Agravaine too thought it was a good speech. He did not fully understand it, though Mordred had practiced the presentation before him several times. He thought the bits about people determining their own future regardless of accidents of birth, and how youth should not bow to age when age was clearly in error, sounded very exciting — and very dangerous. Where on earth did his cousin get such ideas?

Afterward the two of them distributed the scrolls. The twenty-five copies of Plato's Republic were recorded on papyrus rolls each about ten inches wide and thirty feet long, made up of several sheets glued together. The papyrus came from Egypt, as did the cedar oil that both preserved it and lent it a soft, burnished glow.

Though Agravaine had thought about it often, he still quietly marveled at how the copying had been done — by fifty Druid scribes working in continuous shifts for six weeks. Not the Druids of Camelot, for they would do nothing of that sort on the authority of anyone but their leader. Instead, Mordred had approached the monks of Colchester. These were far from Merlin's influence, and were only too willing to provide such a service for their future king.

As are too many of those here, thought Agravaine, who could not believe that anyone would willingly choose to spend his precious leisure hours reading the thoughts of a dead Athenian. They all had enough of that sort of thing during the day.

Agravaine had no ulterior motives. They were different in so many ways, Mordred and he, yet their friendship seemed to thrive on this very contrast. He had never before had a companion like Mordred — someone who reflected on things and who weighed his words before speaking. His associations had so often led to trouble of one sort or another. He told himself that perhaps, despite his misgivings, things would be different this time.

"I should be happy for you to keep these," Mordred began, addressing the group again. "Unfortunately, Master Uncias would not, and so for safety's sake I must ask you to return them before you leave. Now then . . ." He quickly glanced around to make sure that everybody had a copy. "Tonight I should like us to consider some of the points raised in Book Four, Justice in the State." There followed a brief flurry of activity and much jogging of elbows as everyone tried to find the right place — no easy thing when there are no pages to be numbered or marked.

Agravaine did not have a copy himself and, after politely declining a neighbor's offer to share, found a space to sit and contemplate the fire and the studious faces — some less studious than others — that were grouped around it.

"I have chosen this section because it seems to me that no matter how often we examine it, there always seem to be fresh insights and new perspectives to be gained." Mordred's voice had lost its impassioned, combative edge. Now it was measured and discursive, and Agravaine felt warmed by its tones even though he was not really listening.

"It is in this part of the book also, of course, that we encounter some of the problems that lie at the heart of Plato's system — notably the apparent discrepancy between his broad definition of justice, which, taken at face value, would seem to prescribe a society not greatly different to that which we seek to replace, and some of his more detailed recommendations earlier in the book, in which he states, for instance, that property should be held in common and that extremes of wealth and poverty should be eliminated."

Do they really believe all this nonsense? Agravaine thought. Many of them were nodding in the right places, so perhaps they were indeed sincere. Perhaps they had even read Plato. He had made an effort. To impress Mordred, he had once asked to borrow the one copy in the academy's library, but the librarian had informed him that only ordained members were permitted to read that sort of thing. He could not see what the fuss was about. How could anything so dull be subversive?

"It is my belief, however, that these apparently warring elements can be reconciled, for the difficulty rests, in my opinion, upon a fundamental misunderstanding of certain crucial passages, including the one I wish to read now. From near the end of Book Four." He cleared his throat and paused a moment while those around him frantically scanned the narrow columns of text. Then he began to read.

"'Justice, therefore, we may say, is a principle of this kind; its real concern is not with external actions, not with the outward man, but with a man's inward self, his true concern and interest—'"

"What is going on here?"

This question was posed by a large man standing in the doorway. He had close-cropped, silver hair and a broad, muscular face that looked as if it had been assembled in a hurry — and a rather botched job at that, in the estimation of many observers. His heavy build was unusual in an order that, by dint of one privation or another, reduced its members by degrees to a kind of shrunken inconsequence. He looked as if he would be more at home on a battlefield than in the only institution of higher education in Celtic Europe. The narrow doorway and the diminutive stewards squeezing in beside him further accentuated his stature.

The Chief Bard was no soldier, but his mood at that moment was distinctly bellicose. He had been torn from his comfortable hearth by his frightened stewards, who had discovered a number of empty beds in the students' dormitories. For a while his fierce, searching eyes, presageful of some terrible doom, were the only things moving in the cramped and smoky room, and his angry breathing was the only human sound.

Agravaine, mindful of his father's warning, turned his face to the ground, pulling his cloak more tightly about his shoulders in a useless effort to render himself invisible.

"Master Uncias, I was not expecting you." Mordred was smiling, though at the cost of considerable effort. "You are indeed welcome. Please"— he indicated a seat and a chest that had been earlier pushed against the wall —"won't you sit down?"

This hardly placated the Druid, but it did calm the students. For a moment they drew back from panic and flight, their anxiety outweighed by a strong curiosity to see just what Mordred would do next.

Mordred himself had no idea. He was thinking on his feet — and dreadfully slowly, it seemed to him.

"What is going on?" the Chief Bard repeated. "Why are my students not in their beds?"

"Goodness, is it really so late? We have been so engrossed in our studies, Master Uncias, I think we have lost all track of time." Mordred was frightened too, but he was amused also when so many faces dropped in nearly simultaneous incredulity. *My, but you are a brazen fellow,* he told himself.

Before running to fetch their master, the stewards had eavesdropped outside just long enough to form their own conjectures about what was going on. Uncias had arrived expecting to find knives, metaphorical or real, being sharpened; an insurrection about to break out. He had posted guards outside, trustworthy fellows but unaccustomed to violence. However, the clubs that Uncias had pressed into their reluctant hands would, he hoped, inflict damage enough no matter how inexpertly they were wielded.

Seeing the novices holding nothing more lethal than papyrus rolls did not greatly lessen his irritation, but it did leave him momentarily confused. "I think I will sit down," he murmured as he threaded his way through the crowd of bodies. Some of the students tried to stand up, but he impatiently waved them down again. "Studies, eh? Perhaps you would care to explain."

And Mordred, daring to hope that he might actually pull it off, was only too glad to do so.

As he listened to Mordred's persuasive discourse, the Druid's mood gradually softened. It could not be countenanced, of course. This sort of thing had to remain the province of those who had been properly trained and equipped. But nonetheless Uncias felt a grudging admiration for the young man's enthusiasm. It would be no bad thing for the country to have an educated ruler for once, he told himself; it would do no harm to the academy's reputation, either.

Uncias knew he would have to express his disapproval. It might be necessary to make an example of one or two of these truants. But perhaps he would not be too harsh with them. . . .

* * *

"It was Agravaine who started it, really. Not that it was his fault. He was simply trying hard not to be noticed. He was so afraid of getting into trouble, you see. The more the poor fellow tried to conceal his identity, the more determined the steward in the doorway was to discover it. I suppose in the end his nerve snapped, because all of a sudden he was on his feet and shouting something quite unintelligible. Then before anyone could restrain him he leaped over the fire and made a rush for the doorway—"

"Agravaine?" Arthur interrupted. He and Merlin exchanged significant but to me quite mystifying glances. "You have been friends with Agravaine?"

"He is my cousin, Father. You told me he would be there."

"I meant you to give him my greetings, not your friendship." He sighed.

Now what have I done? I thought.

"What happened next?" Arthur asked.

"Oh, well, after that everyone panicked and made a run for it. It's a wonder the whole place didn't burn down. There were a few singed beards and burned soles." I paused and glanced at each of my inquisitors, but they obviously did not appreciate my attempt at lightness. Merlin's face remained especially grim.

"I think that Uncias had formed the impression that we were hatching some sort of plot. He had armed his stewards with wicked clubs, and in the darkness and confusion some people were hurt." I looked at Father, then at the floor. "I do sincerely regret the misunderstanding, sire."

He seemed rather disposed to accept this. I had the impression that there were other aspects of the matter that concerned him more.

But Merlin was not to be so easily placated. "Misunderstanding!" he huffed. "Is that what you have chosen to call it, then?" From somewhere amid the capacious folds and recesses of his gown he had at last extracted the letter from the Chief Bard. He held it up like a torch. "This tells the matter differently."

Arthur closed his eyes briefly. When he opened them

again, he seemed disappointed to see us still there. "No more, Merlin, pray. We have considered the matter long enough. Now here is my doom." He turned to me. His face, as usual when he was passing judgment, was quite impassive. "You will not return to the academy, Mordred. You will write to Uncias offering your sincerest apologies. And you will fully recompense him for any damages he may feel he has incurred."

"I will offer to pay for the building of the novices' dormitory." I had got off surprisingly lightly. Should I not be generous in return?

"That sounds fitting," said Arthur.

"Is that it, then?" Merlin asked coldly.

Arthur nodded heavily. It had been a wearing half-hour for all of us. "Look, Merlin, I do not wish to rub salt into the wound, but it was your idea to send the lad to Glastonbury." To me he said softly, "Some of these notions of yours, Mordred. They will not do, you know."

"They are wicked fancies," Merlin said in nearly a whisper. All his indignation had reduced his voice to a wheezing rattle, but he was not yet completely silenced. "This so-called philosopher you fancy so much talks like one of those wretched Hyperboreans who would dispense with all kings and lords. As for dialectics"— he sniffed scornfully —"if you knew your Plato half as well as you claim to, young man, you would know that no one under thirty years should assay dialectics. Young minds are simply not up to it."

"Some minds mature earlier than others," I said evenly, as though debating instead of arguing.

"And some not at all," Merlin huffed back.

"That will do," said Arthur. "Now, the question is, what are we to do with you?" And his face as he looked at me, despite its ingenuous smile, seemed to be saying, I have let you off lightly because it suits my purpose. Do not think you have fooled me completely with your sophistry and twisted truths. "I think you should run along now, so that Merlin and I may put our heads together about this."

I was only too glad to escape.

* * *

I wish I could properly represent the complex relationship between that curmudgeonly pair. On this occasion, I thought I had come away with the better of things — barely — but there were other times when I was quite at a loss in their presence; an ingenue caught between their cunning and wisdom — a little of both on each side. Then I sensed the poison in that union; like wary duelists, they sought to probe each other's weaknesses. Yet each needed the other. It was as if a grim symbiosis, a compound of rivalry and regard, bound them. Many times my father spoke with genuine affection of his Chief Druid — and this was reciprocated.

I do not know, even now, if either or both were truly wise or truly cunning, but I knew then that if I was to survive at that court I would have to become like them.

It was a depressing thought.

7

LANCELOT WAS ENTERTAINING GUINEVERE AND a few of the other wives with his latest adventure. He sat majestically in their midst while they reclined on cushions at his feet, gazing at him with beautiful, attentive expressions. Galahad and I looked on like dutiful attendants, and every so often Lancelot would turn to his son for spoken or unspoken confirmation, as if to say, Is that not right? Did I not do just that?

". . . I've no idea who the fellow was or whence he came, but he was a veritable giant of a man. There we were, Gally and I, riding peacefully along, minding our own business and enjoying the stillness of the forest, when there is a crashing in the undergrowth and out he comes, charging out of the trees pell-mell toward us. It was quite a shock, I can tell you. And if he was a big man, then his destrier was enormous — the largest I've ever seen. Isn't that right, Gally?"

"Yes, Father."

"Smoke flew from its nostrils like winter breath, and he careered down the bank toward the road with a thunder that made the ground tremble. He carried a lance the size of a battering ram." Lancelot took a pride in recounting his exploits and did not believe in false modesty. He did not embellish overmuch, but he did like to impress his audience with his colorful imagery.

"Poor Lancelot. What did you do?"

"I was quite helpless, completely unarmed. All my armor, my weapons, everything was in the wagon. All I had was this." He gestured toward his waist, indicating the empty scabbard that normally held his dagger — a fine, polite little instrument he used for cutting his food and paring his nails. "Not a lot of use against a giant on horseback, you might think." Some of the ladies shook their heads in agreement.

Lancelot was a gifted storyteller, there was no denying that. Already they could see the flying hooves amid the greenery, sense the panic and fear, the thrill of action and of narrow escapes. I am not ashamed to say that I also was not unaffected.

"I threw myself from the palfrey barely in time. Poor thing, she was knocked flying by the sheer fury of that brute's advance. But at least his very speed was to my advantage, for his momentum carried him onward, and so he could not turn immediately and dispatch me. As he rode by I could hear him roaring inside his helm; it sounded like a great storm. He was obviously incoherent with rage."

"A madman, perhaps?" Sir Lamorak's wife suggested.

"Or a jealous husband," said Guinevere. Her words — or perhaps the faint, knowing smile that accompanied them — seemed to confuse Lancelot for a moment.

"Possibly both. Or neither. Anyway, I reached for the dagger and threw it as hard as I could — more in desperation than anything else. I am not very handy when it comes to throwing things about. Gally here, he is a marksman with a spear — but if you know anything about me at all, ladies . . ." *Of course they did. He was the world champion. Undefeated, undisputed. Everyone knew about Lancelot.*

". . . you will know I am a man who relies on main force. Here lies my strength." As he leaned forward with his palms extended, his fingers almost caressed Guinevere's cheeks. He had pale, delicate hands, not unlike her own. "It was a lucky throw, and his back was unprotected. The knife sank in deep, just here." He indicated a spot between his shoulder blades.

"You killed him," said one of the women. For a moment there was a breathless silence.

"Me? No. That fellow was unstoppable. But I had given him something to think about. He turned his horse and made ready his spear, clearly intending to finish me this time. But he couldn't get the knife out. He kept on worrying at it, like someone with an uncommonly bad itch." A few of the ladies were stretching their hands behind their backs. "You see what I mean? It's difficult, isn't it?" They blushed and grinned. "Anyway, this went on for what seemed like an age. Gally and I looked on utterly helpless, not daring to move. It was as if an enchantment had been woven round us, wasn't it?"

"Yes, Father."

"Then, quite without warning, he turned round and rode off, giving me a parting look that seemed to say, There will be a next time."

"Goodness!" cried all the ladies at once, taking their cue neatly.

"Gally was all for arming ourselves and setting off in pursuit of the monster, but I do not think we would have caught him. Besides," he added in a tone of complete indifference, "we shall be meeting again anyway."

"Then I hope you will be better prepared next time," said Guinevere.

I glanced inquiringly at Galahad, for I was curious to learn how much truth there was in this entertaining mixture of modesty and magniloquence. He nodded, then shrugged, which left me none the wiser.

Then Arthur and Merlin entered, and the atmosphere changed perceptibly. Guinevere's smile became stiff and formal, and a sheepish hush descended over all the other ladies. Arthur looked around awkwardly, as if aware that he was spoiling their enjoyment. "Pray, don't get up, ladies," he began, but they did so anyway, curtseying becomingly and drifting off in search of other diversions.

Guinevere remained. "Sir Lancelot has been telling us of the ambushment he suffered on the way here," she said.

Arthur nodded gravely. "I have heard something of this. I hope it was not one of my followers."

"I think not, sire," Lancelot said. "Unless you count giants and ogres among your company. Anyway, it happened ere we took ship for Albion." He looked a little guilty and a little annoyed, like a man whose innocent flirtation has been misconstrued as well as interrupted.

"Whoever it was, he is a coward and a recreant," said Arthur. "I hope he is none of ours."

He sounded to me like a man of sense. Sometimes there is no other way to win save by guile and deception.

"I shall be ready for him next time," said Lancelot with aplomb. "And if he is one of yours, I shall send you his head."

There followed an awkward moment during which no one seemed to know quite what to do. Arthur and Merlin shuffled their feet rather self-consciously. The problem was one of protocol. They could hardly continue standing before this foreign emissary in their own court. Still less could they sit on cushions at his feet. Merlin coughed a few times, but to no avail. Lancelot remained entirely at his ease, leaning against the arm of his seat with good-natured indifference.

Guinevere ended the irksome silence. Softly but imperiously she clapped her hands, and within moments more chairs were brought into the room.

"I hope you shall be staying with us, Lancelot," Arthur said when he was finally seated.

"The Latins have retired to their pavilions for the moment. We have given them more than a few bloody noses this spring. I ween we shall have no trouble from them for a while."

Arthur and Merlin looked at each other. They did not seem entirely happy with this answer.

"But I hate this country," Lancelot continued. "Your climate. It is high summer, yet everywhere I go in this castle I am beset by draughts."

Although seemingly impervious to them outside, in court Lancelot was always complaining about physical discomforts of one sort or another. I suppose he was a sensitive creature. He was small in stature but finely built, like an intricate sculpture. His voice was small too, rather high and at times irritating in tone. His forehead was lined, but his face was fresh as a girl's, with cheeks the color of apples and small rosebud lips framed by a short, neat beard that he stroked constantly. Above his pale eyes were long lashes that fluttered sometimes as he smiled. Sometimes I wondered what women saw in him, but he was a doughty fighter, and those who allowed appearances to deceive them often paid dearly.

"We are a hardy people," Arthur said defensively.

"You are an unhealthy people. Look at me, King Arthur. I am your age, yet I look ten years younger. That is because I do not sit around in draughty castles and get plaguey joints."

I watched this exchange with interest. Lancelot was the only person in the world who could speak to my father this way. Even Merlin, for all his arrogance, was almost always scrupulously polite. Galahad looked embarrassed; clearly, he was wishing himself elsewhere.

Merlin looked angry, but he was also accustomed to the Gaul's casual impudence. His response was suitably crisp and dignified. "Sir Lancelot, you would do well to speak more judiciously. You are here to crave a boon, after all."

"And to perform a service for you, remember. Besides"— he leaned forward and, looking at Merlin, gently nudged Arthur's shoulder —"he knows I mean nothing by it. It is just my way."

Arthur smiled awkwardly and shifted in his seat.

"You should come back to southern Gaul with me, King Arthur. You would find the climate there much to your liking."

"No doubt you would like me to bring an army as well?" Arthur replied.

Lancelot laughed. "Of course, I should make you doubly welcome then."

The talk promised to get interesting now, and I was hoping I might remain unnoticed a while longer. But Merlin had been scrutinizing me archly from beneath his thick brows. He turned to the king and murmured something that I assume was intended to alert him to the situation.

"Mordred, perhaps you and Galahad would see your mother to her chamber," Arthur said. Then he winked at me. "Matters of state, you know."

Guinevere rose with a sigh, for she also did not wish to be excluded. But she smiled prettily, no doubt because she was aware that until she left the room all eyes would be upon her statuesque figure, and all ears would be attentive to her soft footsteps and the thickly sensuous whisper of her gown across the cool floor. Galahad, as he followed, gave me a look that suggested he was not insensible either.

* * *

When the three of them were left alone Arthur said, "Now then, Lancelot, tell us about the Grail."

"I know where it is," said Lancelot, and he smiled distantly at the huge ceiling.

That made Arthur momentarily furious, but he held his tongue. Knows where it is! he thought. He knows, too, that I am burning with curiosity, and that I may not demean myself by seeming impatient. Yet he insists on pausing for effect and to torment me.

"Pray tell us more, Sir Lancelot," entreated Merlin a bit gruffly.

But Lancelot could not bear to hurry a good story. "You have sent your men to scour the world for this treasure, King Arthur."

The king nodded wearily, still impatient but now resigned to letting Lancelot have his way. "Gaul, Wales, Ireland," he said. "And places much farther afield. Some so remote that we have not even names for them. Every now and then some rumor reaches us, and no matter how implausible there is always some poor fool of a knight who is willing to take it seriously. Sometimes he returns a year or two later, empty-handed and none the wiser. Sometimes he does not return. . . . Yes, Lancelot, we have scoured the world."

"What I bring you is no rumor," Lancelot said. "I am willing to stake my reputation on that. In fact"— and here he frowned thoughtfully, though the idea had occurred to him long before —"I will do more. I will hazard the adventure myself."

"You will bring the Grail to me?"

"By your leave, yes."

"Where is it?" Merlin repeated.

"Why, it is here, in this kingdom."

"Here?" Arthur's tone was a combination of relief and incredulity.

"More or less." Lancelot was enjoying himself hugely. "It is in the possession of some wild Caledonians. They keep it in a place called Carbonek. An impregnable fortress, or so I have heard."

"Not impregnable," Arthur muttered. "Formidable, though. Yes, I have heard of Carbonek. It is far to the north, in the highlands. It is in my kingdom, as you say, Lancelot, but no one ever goes there. You would need an army to get there." Arthur's eyes widened. He was finding it increasingly difficult to contain his mounting excitement. "I will give you an army to find the Grail."

Lancelot held up his hand. "That would not be a good idea. These people may be primitive savages, but they are not stupid. They would see an army coming and hide the Grail — drop it into one of their huge lakes, or simply into some hole. It would then be lost forever. No, this is a matter for guile and diplomacy."

Arthur was not convinced. He believed that the most effective form of diplomacy was the sort backed up by readily available force. But he saw Merlin nodding quietly and thoughtfully to himself, and so did not demur.

When he sensed he had won the last point, Lancelot went on. "Gally and I will fetch the Grail."

Merlin said, "Why should you want to do this service for us, Sir Lancelot, when you could have the Grail for yourself?"

"Oh, it's just an old pot, isn't it? I have no need of it." He waited for an explosion of wrath, but Merlin was not to be provoked so easily; he kept his indignation to himself. "I will do it for the love I bear King Arthur," Lancelot continued. "We will make it our quest, Gally and I. We have not been on a quest for years."

* * *

"He means to embroil me in his war with the Latins. That is why he won't let me send an army for the Grail. Self-aggrandizement and self-interest, that is what this is all about. He is trying to entrap me, Merlin."

The fingers of Arthur's left hand drummed in agitated rhythms against the arm of his throne while with the other hand he tugged fretfully at his beard. Years earlier, when the first grey hairs had appeared and he still had a little time for vain pursuits, he had been careful to pull only at the grey ones. Now these had become too many, and he was discouraged by that, though Guinevere said they made him look dignified.

He just felt old. People want me to be grave and sagacious, an even-handed dispenser of justice, he thought as he woke in the mornings. But that is not how I see myself. I do not want to be grey and creased like Merlin, for I still have the mind of an ardent warrior. . . . As the day wore on this despondency would lessen, but he dreaded the nights, for he knew he would wake with a sense of despair that he could neither properly fathom nor heal.

"I agree," said Merlin. "Lancelot is serving his own purpose here." Their two shadows, which had lengthened and then faded as afternoon gave way to dusk, suddenly sprang to life as servants with tapers hurried around the edges of the room, lighting the rushes. Merlin's shadow was thin and wavering, and it leaned across Arthur's like an attentive ghost.

"Why, then, do you urge me to accept such a bad bargain? Now that we know where the Grail is, could we not take it ourselves? We could reward Lancelot in some other smaller way, rather than sending men to battle the Latins with him."

"Now, sire, that would hardly do," Merlin said patiently. There was much about Lancelot that Merlin did not appreciate or respect, but he knew that Lancelot's strategy in this matter was the correct one. And he had grudgingly admitted to himself that Lancelot had a better chance of making it work than any other knight to whom Arthur might assign the task. He thought the king already realized these facts too, so he saw no point in discussing alternatives, and above all he did not want to be drawn into an argument on the subject.

Arthur sighed. "Oh, I suppose you are right. But you know how I feel about these foreign adventures, Merlin. They bring needless death in return for short-lived territorial gains. They do no good at all. And a war against the Latins would be a disaster for us. It would bleed us."

Merlin was nodding throughout. "That is what I have always counseled. But does not the matter of the Grail add a fresh dimension to all these considerations?"

"You would have us use it in battle, Merlin? A votive object?"

"What would you use it for, then?" snapped the Druid. And because Arthur could not immediately reply he went on. "We cannot afford to be too . . . principled, sire. Lancelot is an opportunist, I agree. He thinks to use us. But he is also right. The Latin threat concerns us as well as the Gauls. Look at the advances they have made, even in our own lifetime." On his fingers he began counting the Celtic nations. "First Cisalpine Gaul, then Transalpine Gaul. Soon all our brethren over the water will be overrun." He paused significantly, saving his ring finger till last. "Then it will be our turn. And we would have no allies."

"We would have the Grail."

"And if it has but a fraction of the power that men say, then it would be a mighty power in our hands." Merlin's hands vanished into the voluminous folds of his cloak. "But I would sooner have the Gauls on our side as well."

Arthur knew Merlin was probably right, but he was still unhappy about the whole thing. He desperately wanted the Grail. He had coveted it ever since childhood, when tantalizing rumors of its existence had first come to his ears. As a young man he had been sorely tempted to follow the quest himself, but Merlin and the responsibilities of kingship had forbidden it.

In those early days he had wanted it for the prestige and renown it would bestow upon his court. The Grail would make men virtuous, he thought then. Under its influence the Knights of the Round Table would become exemplars of virtue and prowess.

He still believed all that, but now he wanted it because it might somehow still the dread awakenings of age and the horrible ravages of time.

But he still had his doubts, and he needed Merlin to set them at rest. "I don't know. To use so sacred a vessel as a kind of secret weapon. . . . It does not seem right to me."

Merlin said nothing.

"And what about Lancelot? Can we trust him? How can we be sure he won't steal it for himself?"

"The man is insufferably arrogant," Merlin said. "And a blasphemer. It is precisely for these reasons that I do trust him. You see, he really does believe that it can do him no good. To him it is just a simple cauldron; he would much rather have a British army in Gaul. The fellow has no imagination."

Arthur thought about this.

"We could send Mordred along," Merlin prompted.

"Mordred?"

"We should not let foreigners reap all the glory, should we? There should be at least one knight of Albion among the company."

Ah, Mordred, Arthur thought. Whenever my conscience slumbers, there you are to prod it into wakefulness again. "He is not a knight, Merlin."

"That is a mere formality. He may not show any great enthusiasm for the martial life, but he has all the skills, I have noticed."

"The boy does seem remarkably fit these days."

"And it would do him a power of good. He has been moping about the court with nothing to do for too long now. We don't want him getting into any more mischief, do we?"

Arthur had no wish to revive that argument, so he agreed. "I suppose it is time the boy won his spurs."

"And the sooner he does so, the sooner we can give those Latins the hiding they so richly deserve."

"You seem uncommonly bellicose this evening, Merlin." Though smiling, he was genuinely concerned about the Druid's frequent changes of mood and the involuntary twitching that was sometimes so violent his whole face was a sea of taut, rippling flesh. Rumors had begun reaching his ears — of how Merlin might be found standing alone in dark corners at odd hours mumbling incoherently to himself, or walking about the castle wearing a fixed, purposeful stare, oblivious to anyone who passed him or greeted him. Mostly exaggerations, I am sure, he thought. Still, it will hardly do if my chief adviser is slowly sinking into senility. "Do not forget one thing," he cautioned, rising slowly, for indeed the draughts and the damp of Camelot did play havoc with his joints. "They have to find it first."

Merlin watched him go, his face a complex, changing pattern. He thought, He looked at me so strangely for a moment then. What was he thinking? Does he suspect? With jagged fingernails he harrowed his cheeks. Sometimes the pain stopped the spasms. Otherwise he was perfectly lucid. He had not suffered a serious fit for some days, though he knew that when the next one came no amount of violence could still it. The best he could hope for was that it might overtake him when he was alone or, failing that, that people would not scrutinize too closely the staring eyes and the frozen grimace; perhaps instead they would ascribe the trancelike stillness to some eccentricity and the whimpering groans of pain to a toothache.

It was inevitable, this madness of Merlin's, for his had always been a twisted as well as a supremely gifted mind. And there was the terrible, dark weight of the secret he had carried for years now. It nestled in the core of his mind like it nestled in the heart of Camelot; like a cancer. One day it would bring doom and ruination. He suspected that he could do nothing about that, but he knew also that he would not stop trying. Thus he had counseled the killing of Morgause, in the hope that her son might die of neglect in the forest. And for the same reason, he had just urged the king to send Mordred on an adventure fraught with peril.

He held no malice toward the boy. Mordred held

some strange notions, but such was the folly of youth. In many respects he showed great promise. And when Palomides had rescued him from the forest, Merlin had been almost glad.

But Merlin knew the secret of Mordred's birth. It ran deeper than even Arthur could conceive, and he knew that the fruit of such a passion, no matter how comely without, could only prove rotten and diseased.

For Morgause had been Arthur's sister.

8

"WE'RE OFF TO FIGHT THE WILD CALEDONIANS," Galahad declared. "And you're coming with us."

I did not respond immediately. It would be a welcome relief to escape the oppressive atmosphere of Camelot. So desperate had I become that I had even considered asking Master Uncias for one more chance. On the other hand, the prospect of spending a long time in the company of Lancelot and his son did not greatly appeal to me. Galahad may not have inherited quite all of his father's strange combination of savagery and effeminacy, but he had certainly changed a lot since we had been boys together. He was not as tall as I, but he had a certain stark presence. His slightly plump, boyish figure had become harsh and sinewy, and his once-genial face was now a region of bone and shadows within which a pair of sunken, calculating eyes glistened like dark gems beneath thick, lowering brows.

Lancelot had objected to the kind of upbringing that his son was receiving at Camelot — "Too many books and not enough beatings," as he had put it. So he had taken him back home to make a man of him. I suppose in this respect both father and son had been successful, for Galahad's reputation as a man of arms was second only to Lancelot's.

"We will take the Grail from Carbonek and restore it to its rightful owner." Galahad was punching his palm as he spoke, just as Lancelot sometimes did. "And we'll give those people a hiding in the process."

"Is my father, then, the rightful owner of the Grail?"

"He will be when we give it to him," Galahad said with a laugh.

"I am not yet made knight," I said.

"Your father is going to make you one. Haven't you heard?"

I shook my head. No one ever told me anything.

"It is just a formality. You passed all the tests long ago. Everyone thinks you will make a stalwart knight." He looked suddenly concerned. "I say, Mordred, you do want to come with us, don't you?"

There was something hearteningly familiar about his look of pained inquiry. For a moment I could see beneath the ruthless exterior. I thought, *Somewhere in there lies the Galahad I remember.* "If Merlin thinks I should go," I said, "then I suppose I should go."

"Merlin is wise. You should heed his counsel."

"I am not so sure. That he is wise, I mean. He has been behaving strangely lately." I fervently wanted to share my fears with somebody. But Galahad was in no mood to listen.

"That is just his way. Clever people often behave strangely. Now." He looked at me pointedly. "Do you want to go?"

"Oh, yes," I said. "Of course."

His smile was one of almost childish relief. "Oh, good." Then he looked at me and said, "You've changed a lot since we were boys together."

"We've both changed, Galahad. I have heard much about you. You have earned quite a reputation. Your father has taught you well."

"He is the best of knights and the best teacher. You will learn a lot from him."

"I suppose I will."

He clapped his hands gleefully. "It will be like old

times. Do you remember those, Mordred — the fun we had together?"

"I often think about them," I lied.

"So do I. Remember our raid on the herb garden?"

I smiled uncomfortably. I thought he would be as anxious to forget such episodes as I was. "It was a long time ago, Galahad. I don't really—"

"You had this idea for a spell. What was it now?"

"An invisibility potion," I said despondently.

"Oh, yes, marvelous. We had to get one of the ingredients from the garden. And I got caught and got such a whacking for it. I could not sit down for days after."

"I got away," I said.

"You always got away, Mordred." There was no ill will in his tone. "Father says that is because you are the cunning one. I had to learn the hard way. It's the best teacher, you know — painful experience." Again he punched his hand as a savage frown momentarily darkened his face. "Nowadays I do not get caught so easily."

"Your father says I am cunning?"

Galahad nodded eagerly. "He says you are verily the cunningest young man he knows. That is why he wants you on the quest. He and I, we are all right when it comes to bashing savages. But we need someone who can outwit them as well."

"I am glad you can find use for me." I said this with less sarcasm than I felt, so that Galahad did not catch my meaning. Then, as soon as it was out, I realized there was little point in taking offense at Galahad's remarks, so effusive and ingenuous was he.

"We shall have quite an adventure," he said.

"I cannot wait."

* * *

Merlin had arranged bottles and containers in a neat row on the bench before him. Though they were all inscribed with symbols, he examined each one carefully before adding some of its contents to the bronze bowl.

"Valerian, I think," he muttered, scrutinizing a blue earthenware bottle for a long time in the poor light. Then he removed the cork and spent several more seconds sniffing the contents. Only when he was finally satisfied did he pour out a few drops into his wooden measuring spoon. Mordred saw a thick liquid, the color of mortar, trickle out reluctantly.

Merlin repeated this ritual several times, sometimes with liquids, sometimes with powders from black leather pouches; all of them he would pour into the bronze cup, stirring occasionally.

And all the time he was muttering inaudibly to himself. Mordred could not tell whether he was reciting an arcane spell or simply the names of its ingredients.

"What does it do?" he asked when he could no longer restrain his curiosity.

"It is a cure for wind," Merlin replied. "Do not laugh. It is no laughing matter." He peered into the bowl to see if the color was right. It was not, so he added a little more hellebore. "It is whispered abroad," he went on in a distracted voice, "that the king's chiefest counselor no longer proffers advice, but only mighty farts. This will ease my disturbed vitals and quiet my trumpetings." He looked up sharply, but Mordred was managing to conceal his amusement. Then he prepared to add the final ingredient. "Oil of almonds. By itself a very sufficient remedy for freckles." He stroked the rust-colored bottle, smiling whimsically. "From this very jar I did anoint Guinevere's face."

"She had freckles?"

"As a young girl, yes. She was horribly sunburned too, for she loved to spend all her days in the open, like a peasant girl, much to the horror of King Leodegrance, her father. She was as brown as a berry."

"And yet my father married her?"

"When he first visited her father's castle at Cadras, King Arthur did not even notice her. But she set herself to have him, and so she came to me. The sunburned skin I banished by steeping a piece of copper in lemon juice, and her freckles — though to me they were comely enough — I treated with this bottle here." He banged it upon the table so that the noise echoed about the room. "Now, what am I about, telling you all my secrets?"

"It would make me giddy to remember them all, Merlin. And in the right order."

"Ah, yes." Unstopping the bottle, he poured some of its contents into the bowl. Then he took down a leather sack from its hook. "Some water," he explained, "for the taste will no doubt be foul." Gingerly he took a sip. "As I thought," he muttered. Nevertheless he raised it to his lips again and drank noisily. When he lowered the empty bowl, his beard was spotted with flecks of bright green like tiny emeralds. He wiped the back of his hand slowly across his mouth. "And don't you look at me like that, young man. You wait until you get to my age. You will have need of some of my little miracles then."

"Really, Merlin, I was not laughing. I just thought—"

"What? That I was busily concocting the elixir of youth or some such nonsense?" He began to replace the bottles and jars on their respective shelves. Every now and then he would stop and cough violently as if something hot and painful were lodged in his throat. He had brewed the potion too strong, and this did not improve his temper. "You think I would like to be young and foolish like you?" And before Mordred could demur he went on, "I suppose you think that all I have to do is mix a few ingredients together, mutter something unintelligible and meaningless, and I can do almost anything I want?"

Mordred shook his head and smiled sheepishly. "I used to think such things. We all did. We all thought you could do anything."

Merlin snorted, partly out of scorn, partly to clear his nostrils of the stinging vapors from his too-powerful concoction. "I can do a great deal, Mordred. Even now I am still learning. This is a new mixture, you know, quite untried. If it works, then no more will I suffer shame and embarrassment whilst counseling your father and his courtiers. And afterward I shall try to make it a bit more palatable." He drank more water, but that did not clear the aftertaste. "This had better work," he muttered.

"What about necromancy?" Mordred asked. He felt a sudden anxiety, a dread almost. All these years he had believed implicitly in Merlin's omnipotence. He had grown to fear it and to despise the arrogance of the man behind it. And yet it shook him to think that perhaps after all it had been mere illusion.

"Oh, that," Merlin said airily. "There is suprisingly little use for magic in the world of practical affairs. I suppose I could, if I wanted, render myself invisible or make others deaf to these explosions of mine. But I would rather have an effective cure than a spectacular treatment."

"If that is how you feel, why do you desire the Grail so much?"

"So you did not come down here just to be sociable." Merlin gave a sigh that might have signified disappointment, or simply that the medicine was doing its work. He paused awhile but did not seem offended when no denial came. "The Grail is earth magic, a very different matter from human sorcery. Do you know what I mean by earth magic?"

Mordred felt the pull of a distant recollection. Somewhere in time they had engaged in a discussion like this. "Yes, I think so."

"I cannot work that sort of magic. No mortal can. The Grail has power over life; that is why I desire it. Why your father desires it." Merlin's eyes suddenly gleamed wildly, and he gripped the sides of the bench as a spasm of pain like an icy shiver took hold of him. For a moment he feared the worst, but just as suddenly the cold embrace let him go. In his bowels he could feel a dull, leaden weight.

"Master Merlin, are you all right?"

He shook his head to clear it. "I do believe it works," he said brightly.

"Tell me more about the Grail," said Mordred, relieved. If Merlin had gone into one of his fits, he would have been at a loss. "What is this power over life?"

"It is strangely mutable. It works in different ways for different men, satisfying each one's greatest need, sometimes even fulfilling needs that one is unaware of. Thus, if a man is starving the Grail will provide him with nourishment. If he is a coward, then it will stiffen his resolve and fill him with a contempt for danger. It can cure the sick. It has even been known to raise the dead, though that has a price, and it must not be used lightly for that purpose."

"What price?" Mordred did not know whether he believed in the Grail and its powers or not, but he thought he should learn as much about it as possible.

"The Grail will raise a man from the dead if he be not dead for too long, and if the spirit of the Grail considers him to be worth the boon. But he will be without speech or hearing."

"It is a heavy price indeed," Mordred agreed. "But some would consider it worth paying."

"Not I. And the Grail is choosy. It doesn't work with just anyone." When he thought about it, Mordred was inclined to agree. Talking and listening were very important to him.

"But it does confer an immortality of sorts on everyone," Merlin added. "For anyone who drinks from the Grail is assured of eternal bliss in the otherworld — in Tir na Nog."

Mordred was not sure if he believed in the otherworld

either, though he was careful to observe religious form —just in case.

"But men will still die?"

Merlin shrugged. "Eventually. We must move on to make room for our descendants — that is obvious, surely. The Grail gives people something to look forward to."

"No matter how bad they are?"

All this questioning irritated Merlin, but he managed to summon a tolerant smile. In a few weeks the boy would be gone. "The purpose of the Grail — our immediate purpose, anyway — is to encourage prowess in battle. It is a sad fact of life that a strong right arm and a virtuous disposition do not always go together. That they should has been one of your father's fondest hopes. And one of his greatest disappointments. Do not be an idealist, Mordred. It will get you nowhere."

But Mordred desperately wanted to be an idealist, even though he had as yet no coherent philosophy of his own. "It does not seem right to me."

"Oh, it does not seem right to you?" As Merlin tossed his head scornfully, his white beard rose like an agitated animal. He began slowly stroking it. This calmed him, and these days he had to try, above all else, to remain calm. Conversing with Mordred did not help.

"What if a man is holy — makes sacrifices to the gods, succors the poor, performs good works?"

"Such a man has no need of the Grail, for he is assured of Paradise anyway." Merlin carefully stacked the last bottles on the shelves.

"Well, then, what about the ordinarily virtuous — people who do not perform great deeds but are good in simple ways? Showing kindness to others, that sort of thing?"

Merlin groaned inwardly. "Why concern yourself with them? They must take their chances."

Mordred sensed the misprizing of his opinions, and it made him resentful. "I still say it is wrong — that bad people should go to Tir na Nog just because they have drunk from a rusty cauldron that has been buried for centuries—"

"How dare you! This is sacrilege! Sacrilege and blasphemy! I will not tolerate such talk!" Merlin's startled beard rose once more, and his cloak billowed as if it too were part of his sudden outburst. But again he managed to control it and with great restraint added, "Do not quibble over trifles, lad. This is what your father wants. He expects great things of you. I know he does not always show you a proper degree of affection, but he really does think a lot of you."

Mordred was so taken aback by this that he was for the moment quite distracted from the old man's breathing and his quite violent facial tic.

"So, knowing what your father desires, and knowing how well he esteems you, should you not be eager to do his bidding?" Merlin was relaxing slowly. His breathing became quieter and more even. But he wanted Mordred to leave, and quickly.

He was already going. "Oh, yes." Mordred backed with respectful haste toward the stairs. "Yes, of course."

* * *

But it was several months before we were ready to go. This was not because the preparation involved was very great. It was simply that Lancelot was not to be hurried. The more he sensed the impatience of others — Arthur and Merlin in particular — the more stubbornly resolved he became to take his own time. Also, I believe he was not looking forward to making a long journey in a cold climate. But the longer he delayed matters, the more uncomfortable he made all our prospects. By the time we were ready to set off, winter was already far advanced.

On the eve of our departure, Guinevere called me to

her chamber. She sat on the edge of her bed and for a while contemplated me with an expression of wistful tenderness. I had the forceful and uncomfortable impression that she had already rehearsed this encounter in her mind.

"You must be sure to keep warm, Mordred. I hear the weather can be fearfully cold in those remote parts. I don't know what your father is thinking, sending you abroad at this time of year."

I was touched by her concern. If it was rehearsed, it was not entirely affected. "Lancelot says that at least it will be spring when we return. And if we wait any longer, we may never set out at all."

"Oh . . ." She stifled her protest with a pretty sigh, nodding compliantly in the face of this overwhelming male logic. Sometimes I wanted so much to chastise her for this emotional anemia. I am sure she was a much stronger person than she seemed. The empty-headed beauty was a convenient mask, no doubt, but to me it was not appealing.

"I have woven some garments for you. Be sure to wear them."

"Of course, Mother. Thank you." What she meant was that her ladies-in-waiting had woven clothes for me. Guinevere could never summon sufficient patience for such tasks. What little energy she could muster these days was spent on pampering herself — as she was doing now, pulling a fine-toothed comb through her luxuriant red hair with careful, languorous strokes. Her smile as she did this was innocent enough, but her movements and her eyes seemed to me to convey a different message. I scolded myself as I sat there reddening, enjoying her proximity yet feeling deeply uncomfortable at the same time.

"When you return with the Grail, you will be a great hero. Everyone will want to know you." Another sigh.

"If," I corrected. "If I return with the Grail."

She continued combing for a while in silence. *Let me do that for you,* I wanted to say. "Let us say when," she said at length. "I prefer to say when."

"I do not care for being a hero," I said. "I do not go for reputation's sake. I am not interested in such things."

"Then why?"

Just why was I going? "Because . . . I have seen so little of the world. My father's kingdom is vast, yet I have scarcely been out of this court."

"That can also be said about your father. He is not a great one for traveling these days." In a different tone she added, "But he manages to achieve a great deal nevertheless. He has never been where you are going."

"My principal reason, of course," I said hastily, "is because my father wishes it."

Guinevere nodded. "That alone is sufficient reason. We must all give your father what he wants."

I stared at her, for the irony in her voice was unmistakable, but she did not elaborate. Instead she put down her comb and placed her hands in her lap, patting her gown lightly so that in my increasingly wild imaginings I thought she was beckoning me to sit there. "So, Mordred, you do not desire fame or a reputation. What, then, do you want from the gods?"

"I can shift for myself. I do not need the gods." I was eager to impress Guinevere with my bold, independent spirit. She sat with a half-smile on her lips, her head a little to one side. "I wish to be a scholar so that I may become, when my time comes, what Plato calls a philosopher king." *How does she do it?* I asked myself. I had never spoken to Galahad of such things, nor even to Agravaine. Effortlessly, Guinevere had drawn from me all my secret hopes and ambitions.

"Plato." She furrowed her lovely brow. "Should I know him?"

I explained to her as best I could, and when I was done she said, "My, such things you know. Had I but a fraction of your knowledge, Mordred, I do believe my head would explode." But she laughed so prettily I instantly forgave this banality.

"And what else?" she asked, gently stroking the folds of her gown. "Do you not wish to take a wife? Is there no one at the court upon whom you look with favor?"

Ah, so that was what she was getting at! But I did not mind, for I was happy in her company, so warm and amicable was our discourse. "I wish to be ennobled by love," I declared.

A light of understanding seemed to flare suddenly in her eyes. "Ah, love . . ." Her eyelids dropped a fraction, and I thought, *Not only is she unconscionably beautiful, she is also not related to me by blood.* "That is a worthy quest. That is an even finer thing than the Grail." I followed her gaze to her jeweled fingers, plucking almost nervously now at the yellow silken folds. *Her body is all of a piece,* I thought. *It is possessed of a perfect, tapering symmetry.* The face, long and firmly pointed, the slender, white hands; the delicate feet; all were in a line. No doubt also perfect were those regions that only my imagination could penetrate, albeit with a disturbing vividness. Here I was, entertaining fantasies about my stepmother — and delighting in doing so! *This is madness,* I admonished myself feebly. Yet I could sense little shame.

My thoughts must have betrayed me in some way, for she looked up and gazed at me curiously for a moment before continuing. "I was greatly in love with your father; in much the sort of way you describe. He stole my youth, you know." There was no bitterness in her voice, and when next she sighed it was not from self-pity. "But I believe I have been compensated in an unsought way."

"How is that?" The atmosphere in her chamber seemed suddenly charged. It was like being in a warm meadow as a violent summer storm is about to break. *We are sharing confidences now,* I thought. *Like lovers!*

"It seems to me that I do not grow older, Mordred.

No, this is not just a vain woman's fancy, for there are many who have told me this, and for the most part they have no reason to flatter me. Rather, it frightens them." Her voice dropped. "There are some who whisper it about that I am a witch." She must have noticed how I caught my breath then. It was so audible to me that I almost choked. But she went on as if unaware. "I am not, of course. It is simply my just reward. I have been about thirty now for more years than I can remember. I believe I will never grow old." Her eyes were bright with a strange gleam, at once coquettish and percipient. "Now then, isn't that the strangest idea?"

I could not reply immediately, so clouded was my mind by images of corrupt delight. Then, with a little frown, she went on. "Though no stranger, I suppose, than your father's latest fancy. He is convinced, you know, that he has a sister living somewhere."

I thought, *What has this to do with me? With us?* The very idea seemed to me an intrusion on our intimacy. "Who told him this?"

"Oh, he dreamed about it. He has lots of dreams these days. According to this one, Igraine, your grandmother, had another child, a girl, years after Arthur was taken by Merlin to be brought up by old Sir Ector."

Most of that was well known. The atmosphere in King Uther's court at the time had been so poisoned by intrigue and jealousy that no one, least of all the baby prince, had been safe. With Igraine's agreement, Merlin had spirited Arthur away, for the kingdom's sake. He was not able to save poor Grandmother, who later fell afoul of one of Uther's mad rages and died of her injuries. I had never heard any story about another child, though. "What became of her? In this dream?"

"Ah. At that point he woke up."

"What does Merlin say about this?"

"He says that Igraine had the one child — Arthur — and that it is a dream and nothing more. But still Arthur persists in believing it." Her shoulders rose and fell slightly, and with them her breasts. "Ah, me. But I am not concerned, Mordred. This fancy will persist until he has another dream, and then he will forget about his lost sister."

"I am not concerned, either," I said firmly. "I set no store by dreams. You and Father are the only people I care about."

"Dear boy." I suppose she was pleased because an aunt would have had a prior claim upon my affection. I did not want that, either.

I rose to go, for I could feel myself blushing. I mumbled some infirm excuse, but she would not let me leave straight away. I felt her hand, warm and dry, encircle my own so that both, it seemed, pulsed in concert. Then she kissed me chastely upon the cheek — oh, how it burned! As I stumbled from her chamber and the cloying air within, I was suddenly glad of the winter and the purifying cold; glad that tomorrow we would be leaving.

Guinevere was right about her apparent agelessness. In the eyes of most men she never looked old. She was nearly sixty when she died, but only those who had known her for years would believe it.

I think my father was a perfect example of the blind fool. For is it not the blind fool who spends his life delving with his nose amid the filth of the world as he searches for perfect truth and perfect beauty — when all the time they are before him?

PART TWO

9

GALAHAD HAD DISCOVERED A SMALL POOL IN the hillside above our camp and, quite naked, was immersing himself fully. I stood shivering on the edge, staring down at the top of his head, only a little distorted in the perfectly clear water, when up he sprang, grinning like a demon, with curtains of water falling from his outstretched hands.

"It's so — exhilarating!" he cried, and, scooping some of the water into his hands, he hurled it in my direction. Though I stepped quickly backward, several drops stung my face. *How could the fellow be so insensible to someone else's discomfort?*

Far off the snow-capped mountains gleamed in the morning light. Soon there would be snow again in these valleys, too. It was bad enough having to drink the water straight from the pools and rivers, so cold that it would set my teeth singing. As for washing, well, I supposed I could go without until I could do it in a place of warmth and comfort. I certainly did not feel dirty yet.

"What are you trying to prove?" I called as he grasped the bank on either side and raised and lowered himself several times. His narrow frame was tense and trembling, his eyes closed in an ecstatic concentration, and so much splashing did he make with these athlete's exercises that he did not hear.

When he pulled himself from the water I discreetly

turned away, for there was something distasteful to me about the sight of his dripping, pale body capering about on that cold hillside.

"You should try this," he called to me. "Else you will stink ere long, and no one will ride near you."

I had not noticed any disagreeable odors, but I was made uneasy by the remark, for I took a certain fastidious pride in such matters. "I do not stink," I affirmed, not bothering to conceal my irritation.

He stood before me, crouched and shivering, and gave a loud sniff. "Not yet," he said with a laugh as he danced away again.

"Are we not going to stop somewhere?" I asked. "I mean, somewhere civilized?" I pictured in my mind a small castle, simple but homely, its cheerful custodian bidding us all welcome and leading us to soft beds and well-filled tubs.

Galahad laughed. "This is Wales. There is no civilization here."

"That is not true. Rience is a good king and well disposed toward my father." Then I said, "Farther on, then?"

Galahad was racing about the hillside, pulling up thick clumps of long grass and vigorously rubbing, almost scourging himself dry. I winced at the sight of that raw, angry flesh. *There is more to a healthy upbringing,* I thought, *than this daily inflicting of torture.* But at the same time I envied the way he could hold himself remote from pain and discomfort.

When he was dry he put on his tunic, his quilted vest, and his bracae. His mouth was open wide, and he was breathing heavily — a series of deep, contented sighs that wreathed his glowing face in a grey mist. "Why do you think we are taking such a winding way?" he asked in a condescending tone. "There are many castles to the east of us, King Rience's among them, but Father says we are to avoid them. No one must know of our purpose."

He pulled on his surcoat, still shivering. *One day he will overdo it and catch a fever.* "So, you'd better jump in. You might not get another chance. This thaw will not last. Soon the ponds will freeze over again."

This was becoming a disagreeable subject to me, so I changed it. "Where are we exactly?"

He turned toward the white-capped hills. "Those are the Cambrian Mountains."

They looked like the end of the world, for they encompassed the full span of my vision like a grey, frozen sea. "This is a desolate place," I whispered, for now that Galahad had finished cavorting and dressing I was aware only of a dread silence about me.

"There are dragons there, supposedly."

"No," I said, feigning disbelief, for I did not wish to dwell on such possibilities.

With a shrug Galahad turned and led us down the hillside. The reassuring sounds of human activity, of subdued voices and the clanging of pots and pans, drifted to my ears.

"Have you ever seen a dragon?" I asked.

Galahad did not turn around. "Father has."

The fire had been rekindled, and a cauldron of water was already boiling, so I was able to wash in relative comfort after all.

Later I asked Lancelot, "Why are we going to such trouble to avoid the inhabitants of this region?"

"Because they would want to know what we three knights, well provisioned and accoutred, are about, and it would be a poor return for a man's hospitality if we refused to answer such a reasonable request."

"But we have made the Grail our quest, and no one may interfere with another's quest without leave."

"Oh, you are naive, young Mordred," said Lancelot amiably. "There are few men who would cleave to vague and unwritten laws where a treasure like the Grail is concerned."

"You think they would try to reach Carbonek before we do?"

"I think they would let us do all the work, then lie in wait with strong forces to take it from us."

"You have a low view of human nature, Sir Lancelot."

"I have been abroad a good deal more than you, and I fancy I can read the hearts of most men well enough."

"Then you could tell them our purpose was somewhat different. That, for instance, you are seeking out the wild giant who ambushed you." All morning I had been torturing myself with tantalizing thoughts of warm bedchambers and hot dishes, and I did not want to give up on my dream so easily.

"Oh, I don't suppose we shall see him on this quest."

"Or that we are hunting dragons—"

"Ssshhh!" He cast an anxious glance behind him. "Be careful what you say, Mordred. The servants are nervous enough as it is. I already expect to lose some before our journey is done. If they hear you talking about dragons, then there will be a rout and we shall be left to shift for ourselves."

I did not see why we should not do so anyway. We had brought along five reluctant serfs to do the sort of tasks we could easily have done ourselves, except that Lancelot and Galahad would not bestir themselves to do menial work. It is generally accepted that on a quest everyone mucks in, regardless of rank, for when one is traveling among unknown dangers a sense of fellowship warms the soul and strengthens purpose. But those two did not see things that way, and were content to sit about idly or indulge in some desultory horseplay while others did the work. If they saw me helping — as I often did — they smiled to each other and made remarks like, "We have servants to do that sort of thing, Mordred."

"The pavilion must be folded correctly," I would reply. "It will spoil otherwise, and let in water."

And like small boys they would smile at one another

and, taking their swords, would go and demolish some inoffensive bush in order to test the keenness of their blades.

As that day wore on, my spirits slowly improved, for though our progress was slow we were at least moving, and I was happiest when there was some destination, however vague, in prospect.

When I was sure that we were out of earshot of the servants in their cart, I questioned Lancelot more about the dragons.

He did not reply immediately. His eyes were closed, and he was breathing deeply and noisily through his nostrils. His back was as straight as a rod. In such a contemplative pose he would ride sometimes for hours at a time and would suffer no interruption to his private meditations.

He had divers other quirks and fancies. He had an uncommon liking for salmon, especially the white-spotted variety, for these, he averred, have eaten hazelnuts that have fallen from the trees above their pool, and so the consuming of these fish would reveal hidden things and marvels.

However, it is not true that he would, after battle, feast upon the choicest parts of his slain enemies. I reveal this as I wish to be fair to the man, relating only his true faults.

He turned slowly, coming out of his reverie, and said, "My son tells me how you scoff at the idea. How dull it must be to be a skeptic and doubt everything because it is marvelous."

"Galahad tells me you have seen one."

"Have you not heard of the Lambton Worm that Sir Griflet slew by the wearing of spiked armor? When the worm coiled itself about him, meaning to crush him, the armor pierced its hide. Sir Griflet still lives, and he is a truthful man." He looked at me closely, and I nodded quickly, for I was eager to hear his tale. "Yes," he went on, "I have myself seen such creatures, though it was some years ago, when they were more plentiful." Raising a slender hand, he pointed to the distant mountains. "I chased one through there once; oh, five or six miles we must have gone before my horse collapsed beneath me."

"They are nimble creatures?" I asked. It seemed best to learn as much as possible about these prodigies, and so be prepared.

"No, they are very ungainly, and when stirred are slow to move. But they can outrun a destrier once they pick up speed."

"And how can such a monster be killed once it is caught?"

"Oh, I did not intend killing it. I chased the creature for the pleasure of it. They are huge creatures, but rather ludicrous in appearance and really quite harmless."

Such a sentiment was typical of the man. He seemed to care more for dumb creatures than for humans, who, he averred, brought more woe and corruption into this world than any other creature. Now he laughed softly to himself as he recalled the incident. "It had a smooth, grey body and tiny forelegs, and it galloped along on its giant hindquarters while squawking madly like a chicken. I have heard it said, Mordred, that they are the remnants of an ancient race of reptiles that ruled the earth in the days before there were men." He shook his head. "Imagine what preposterous creatures must have been about then!" So saying, he uttered several loud cries — in imitation, I suppose, of a dragon, though they sounded to me more like the wails of a distracted child.

Galahad came riding up. "What is the matter?"

"I was entertaining Mordred with one of my meaner exploits," Lancelot said.

"He was telling me about the dragon."

"I wish I could have been there to see it," said Galahad. "Father chased that beastie a good league or two before it flew off and left him panting."

"It did not fly away, Galahad. Oft I have told you; they do not have wings. Nor do they breathe fire. These are children's fancies."

I thought, *Nor do they need to, for they seem formidable creatures as it is.*

"Well, then," said Galahad, "I have more meat for this rare good humor of yours. The servants have been telling me jests — and very good some of them are."

Lancelot made a weary grimace, but I wanted to hear some of these jests, for it was a dreary and bleak landscape through which we were riding, though no doubt pretty enough in the spring. "Go on then, Gally," I urged.

"Here is one, then: A fishwife was at market, and a man was examining her wares, speaking of them cheaply — this fish is too old, this one is not well-gutted, and so forth. And she says to him slyly, 'Sir, if you will put some of my flesh (meaning her wares) in your belly, then you may put some of your flesh in mine.' To which the fellow replies, 'I will spare none of my flesh for one so ugly as you.' Whereupon she cries, 'What? Canst thou not put thy nose in my arse?' "

Now it was I who groaned, for I had expected something more elegant and trying to my wits. But Lancelot gave a huge, vulgar laugh. "I have not heard that one!" he said, adding another guffaw.

"Then here is another: A knight was riding hotfoot to greet his wife after a lengthy journey when his horse stumbled and threw him. A young woman, on seeing this, fell to laughing, which made the young man wroth, for he says to her, 'Take care, lady, for my horse always stumbles at the sight of a whore.' But she is quicker than he, for she replies, 'Take you care then, sir, for when you do meet with your wife you will surely break your neck!' "

When I could stand no more of this, I slowed my horse's gait and let them ride ahead until they were out of my hearing.

But I was glad of their company when we camped that night, for it was from those very mountains that we heard a loud, dolorous cry that was soon followed by others. In the end it sounded like a chorus of keening women crying in those far-off hills. There was no moon that night, and nothing could be seen but our poor fires and our pale, anxious faces. I watched Lancelot as he turned first to me, then to Galahad, and finally to the other fire, where the servants huddled and murmured nervously among themselves. Though I was uneasy, I was resolved not to speak up.

Presently Lancelot said, "Sometimes they set up such a wailing when one of their number dies, for they are gentle creatures and seem to feel one another's loss." He took a log and stirred it among the listless embers so that flames sprang up anew, cheering us a little.

In that yellow, crackling light I could see clearly the change that had come over him since we had left Camelot and its comforts. No longer was he the well-groomed, boyishly smiling courtier. His beard had grown thick and coarse, and his face had lost all the surplus flesh it had lately accumulated. It looked etched and shadowed, and he no longer seemed ten years younger than my father. This haggardness further increased my unease, for if we could not rely on Lancelot, then our prospects were bleak indeed. He glanced behind him again and gave a sigh. "I think this will bring us some trouble. I told the servants there were no dragons hereabouts."

Sometimes the mournful voices faded; at other times there were only one or two instead of several. I tried to picture the creatures, but it was hard to fashion in my mind the sort of monsters Lancelot had depicted. "It sounds almost human," I whispered, and I felt a lowness of spirits take hold of me.

"Truly it is so like," Lancelot said. The harshness of the climate had affected his voice also, making it deeper and investing his words with a melancholy insight.

The chorus of despair continued long after we retired to our pavilion, and we had little sleep that night. It no longer affrighted me, but it made my heart sore, for it seemed to me to speak of a grief older than time, and it set me thinking such dismal thoughts of the woe and misery that is woven into the very fabric of this world that in the end I almost cried myself to sleep.

The next morning we found two of the servants missing, together with a packhorse and a small quantity of stores. Lancelot tried to put a brave face on the matter. "I am not surprised," he said. "One cannot expect much from servants these days."

Galahad was all for galloping after them and giving them a good hiding, but Lancelot restrained him. "They have not been too greedy, and besides would be of little use to us in chains."

The matter was soon forgotten, for shortly after we set off a heavy snow began to fall. It drove into our faces, making our cheeks raw and our lips dry and cracked. There was no gentle banter or riddle-telling that day. But by dusk the snow had abated. We were able to collect enough dry wood to make fires, and our spirits soon rose again.

"Your father tells me you have lately taken some strange notions into your head," Lancelot said to me. "That you hold all men to be of equal worth. Is that why you insist on helping the servants with their tasks?"

"No," I replied. I did not greatly object to his questioning, but I was feeling tired from the continual buffeting of snow and wind and was thus in little mood to hold debate.

Galahad, picking some gristle from his teeth, said, "The king is worried that when you take charge of the kingdom you might give it away."

"How long have you been privy to my father's thoughts and counsels, Sir Galahad?"

I was perhaps a little haughty with him, for he suddenly looked confused and abashed. He was a tactless fellow sometimes, but he had probably meant no harm. "I do not think like that any more," I added. "They were but youthful conceits. I am a man now."

Lancelot gave me a sideways look but all he said was, "That is a pity, for now I shall have nothing to tease you about."

But he could not banish the matter entirely from his thoughts. The next day he said to me, "Do you know why your father wished for you to take this quest, Mordred?"

"So that I might prove myself worthy of the knighthood he has bestowed upon me."

"Ah." His sigh emerged as a perfectly white, opaque mist. "There are easier ways of doing that."

"Well, then, why?" It was snowing again, though this time it was falling in soft, gentle flakes so that Lancelot's beard became bejeweled by thick, melting drops.

"It is all these books you have been reading. Your father fears you will become a malcontent."

Since I was tired of contemplating the endless expanse of white that stretched before me and on every side, I was glad to try my wit against his. "For that I must thank you, Sir Lancelot."

"What?"

"Why, it was your gift of the slave Crito that set me on the path of enlightenment. Without his gentle guidance I should be a poor, benighted fool, groping blindly for wisdom in a veritable forest of learning."

"He was a present to your father."

"And my father made of him a present to me."

We rode on in silence for a while. Lancelot seemed pensive and, I thought, a little chastened. Presently I said, "It has always been a puzzle to me why you did not kill the fellow."

Lancelot shrugged. "He asked me not to."

Such a fellow was Lancelot. By turns mincing, charming, barbaric, and always utterly unpredictable.

"Come, Sir Lancelot. Surely there are others who beg for their lives as pitifully, if not as eloquently."

"Indeed there are. And because it is so little a thing they ask, I willingly grant it." He slapped his chest vigorously to dislodge the snow that had gathered there. He was wearing his hauberk — perhaps he expected his adversary, the giant knight, to rise magically from that dense white carpet. He said, a little petulantly, "You think me a heartless fellow, don't you, Mordred? Well, I suppose I am. You do not win battles unless you can give hard knocks. But I do not roast babies, and I have never defiled a woman. And I always show mercy when it is craved." Then he asked, "What became of the fellow, anyway?"

"When my father sent me to Glastonbury, I weened I would have no further use for him. He had saved some money while in my service, and so he took ship back to his own country. I have not heard from him since then, though he promised he would write." So it was with all my friends. All of them, in one sense or another, were far from me.

We heard no noises that night, for the mountains were far behind us now, but still Lancelot was not at ease. When Galahad and I retired for the night, he remained by the fire, and our candle was almost burned down when he finally entered, kicking the snow from his heels.

"There is someone following us."

Our heads almost collided in the darkness as Galahad and I sat up in alarm. "Perhaps it is the runaway servants," I suggested.

"No," he said with a weary certainty, "It is not that." He climbed beneath his blanket and blew out the candle. I heard the soft, chilling scrape of iron against leather as he took his sword from its scabbard and laid it beside him. Its dull, ghostly light shone through the gloom with a reassuring solidity. "I have given the servants the order of their watch. Let us hope that none of them runs away tonight."

My sleep was again disturbed and fitful, and attended also by many bad dreams in which divers creatures — howling dragons, a giant of a man on horseback, and a changeling creature who was sometimes Guinevere and sometimes Merlin — figured in ways that I could not afterward remember.

The next morning another servant had disappeared.

* * *

Let me tell you about the Grail.

It is one of the four magical treasures of the Celts — the others being the spear of Lugh, the sword of Nuada, and the stone of Fal from which Arthur drew the sword and which now stands in Camelot. But the Grail, the cauldron of the Dagda, is the most powerful and the most sacred. It is not large, no bigger than a drinking vessel, but it is finely and exquisitely wrought, being of bronze and finished in silver, its sides decorated in relief with the figures of the Dagda — the father of all — and many of the lesser deities.

Once all these treasures resided in the palace of the high king of Ireland, but in the days when the Fomor were waxing and were likely to have overthrown the race of men, the necromancer Bleise, later Merlin's master, took them privily into his keeping and brought them to Albion for safekeeping. When the high king learned about this, he was full wroth, for it was his intent to use them against his enemies. But though he roundly cursed Bleise and his interfering good intentions, there was little he could do about it.

For years afterward the treasures all vanished from sight and only lived on as magical rumor. Then, after the death of Uther Pendragon, the stone appeared outside the deserted gates of Camelot that Arthur might become king and the land thereby renewed. Yet the stone had little value elsewise, so next Arthur sought the Grail. In later years he would send knights to find those other treasures also, for with them, he believed, he would become a paragon among kings and his land a shining realm that would amaze the world.

But that is another story.

10

WE CONTINUED NORTH FOR A WEEK LONGER, until we came to the edge of the Forest of Bowland and the great hill known as Ward's Stone. There we turned northeast, toward Northumberland.

"We shall have to be careful from now on," said Lancelot, "for although King Arthur owns this land, he does not control all of it. We shall pass soon into the territory of the Brigantes." He gave me a look of warning. The Brigantes had recently joined the ever-simmering revolt against my father, and their king would no doubt be most interested to learn that the son of his greatest enemy was abroad in his land. But I was not about to betray my presence so carelessly. I was more concerned about the northeast wind that blew with a continuous, bitter keenness into our faces.

Only one servant remained with us now, a fellow of little account named Gruffyd. He drove the wagon, sitting atop it so that his fat belly protruded like a piece of baggage, and he wore on his face such an expression of melancholy it was as if tiny weights had been secreted within his cheeks. He drove the wagon but was good for little else, for he was such a laggard that it was frequently quicker for me to do the job myself. Oft I rebuked him with such words as, "Why do you not run off like those other churls? You are of little use to us — nothing but an extra mouth to feed."

He would endure my outbursts in silence and with a patient expression that seemed to say, Here I am once more being ill-used for my loyalty, yet I will suffer these undeserved rebukes and any more that my master sees fit to send me.

By the time we reached the Cheviots, I had conceived a hearty dislike for the fellow. Yet at least his idleness prompted Lancelot and Galahad to shift more for themselves, else I should have been left doing all the work.

The worst task was the night watch, for no matter how high we piled the fire it was always bitter and uncomfortable. And terribly lonely as well. But Lancelot was sure that we were still being followed, so there was no help for it. I saw nothing that struck me as amiss, though we passed many times through country so barren and exposed that nothing could have hidden from our gaze. But when I asked him how he knew, Lancelot would simply shake his head; in this respect knights errant are similar to Druids, for both guard the secrets of their lore jealously.

We crossed the land of the Brigantes without discovery and thence passed into the territory of the Votadinii where Bleoberis, father of my dear friend Agravaine, was king. These were still loyal to King Arthur, though from what I saw there they had little reason. One day we chanced upon a poor village in a valley of windswept, shrunken trees. Our stores were running low, and we could no longer live entirely off the land, so I was relieved when Lancelot compromised the principles he had espoused earlier and directed us toward the settlement.

The inhabitants of the place, when they saw us coming, took flight and vanished inside their hovels. They must have known they had nothing we considered worth stealing; could they have been afraid for their lives? At any rate, when they realized that we posed no immediate threat they emerged again, shamefaced and apathetic, watching in silence as we rode by.

I think it was the sight of all their children that unnerved me most. Thinly clad and shivering in the bitter cold, they regarded us with blank, hungry expressions so that I, in my princely clothes and mounted on my fine horse, was made greatly uneasy. I think the others were also not unaffected, for we dismounted in silence and tried fruitlessly to be inconspicuous as we walked our horses to the center of the village. There stood the largest house — imposing in size, but as ramshackle and weatherbeaten as all of its its fellows.

As we secured the horses, I became aware of a movement in one of the doorways and, turning, beheld a figure half-concealed in shadow, swaying on legs so thin and unsteady that it was gripping the doorpost simply in order to remain upright. I could discern no expression on that wraithlike face, nor determine whether it was man or woman. The only sign of life was in the eyes, which seemed to crouch in their sockets like tiny feral animals, alight with expectancy.

For a few seconds we regarded each other. Then, with what may have been a long, patient sigh or merely the shuffling of feet on the earth floor, it turned unhurriedly and vanished into the gloom behind the doorway. I do not think the others saw this, and even I afterward thought to dismiss it as fancy. Or a vision of famine; we had been on part rations for some time now.

From the large house the village headman emerged. He was not as wretched-looking as most of his fellows, and his manner not as distant but still wary. The man remained bowed and attentive as Lancelot put forth his request. Then he said, "The last harvest was a meager one, your worship, and illness and a long winter have further sapped our strength. But of course you are welcome to what little we have."

Because the man spoke respectfully — perhaps also because he was genuinely moved — Lancelot would accept no favors. "Gramercy, but I see that your straits are more parlous than ours, and so at this time will only take such provender as you can spare. And for that we will pay handsomely."

The headman bowed again. "I should invite you into my house, but it is a poor place—"

"We are in a hurry," interrupted Lancelot, "and may not stay."

So, bidding us wait, he gathered some of the other villagers and they went off in the direction of the granaries, though what they expected to find there I could not think. By now the novelty of our presence seemed to have worn off, for as I looked about me I saw people going about their business and paying us no more heed than if we had been churls like them — though the presence of three such knights as ourselves, bedecked in bright robes, must be a rare occurrence in such a place.

It was the children who fascinated me most of all. Their bodies were pinched and shriveled, and so unhealthy was their appearance that I could almost feel the multitude of creatures that must have been crawling about in their hair and on their bodies. I watched them at play — a listless, torpid affair, unattended by glee or abandon. They hobbled about in a strange, concentrated silence like little old men and women. Occasionally one would stop to scratch itself or to stand shivering for a few moments with a puzzled, vacant expression. Lancelot told me they were suffering from a disease that wasted and twisted their bones and that was caused by a deficiency of certain foods. "There are many who suffer thus in these parts, Mordred. There is no helping it."

I could not accept this. I thought I had seen want and the ugly face of Dame Poverty in the south, but the meanest beggar at Camelot was better served than this. These people were my father's subjects, yet many were clearly near to death.

I was of a mind to chide Lancelot for taking food from starving mouths — but it is as well that I did not, for his actions proved to be even more generous than his words. When the villagers had loaded their meager offerings — a sack of mealy flour, some stale oatcakes, and a quantity of salt pork that I judged to be only hours away from going to the bad — Lancelot gave the headman a silver pendragon, sufficient to feed the whole village for several months.

"Why so much?" I asked him when we had left the village behind us.

"I had nothing smaller," he replied with a grin. "Ah, Mordred, it is true that I am but a dull-witted knight and have no head for trade nor barter. Next time I shall leave those subtleties to you."

"Nay, Sir Lancelot. It was a generous and chivalrous act, and it is only for this that I marvel at it."

He gave me another of his sideways glances. Then, satisfied that I had intended no sarcasm, he said, "Did you see the look on that old fellow's face when I pressed the coin into his hand?"

What I remembered more vividly were the faces of all those others, and the terrible, blank despair etched so deeply upon them. For many nights afterward, they rose again to join the other demons that peopled my troubled dreams.

We passed other villages whose inhabitants were in a similarly sad state. Sometimes we entered and bartered for poor fare, and always at these times Lancelot was generous to a fault — so profligate, indeed, that I began to worry that we might ourselves become destitute. But usually we avoided such places, lest word of our presence spread around the countryside.

To that idle fellow Gruffyd I said, "Let this be a lesson to you. For all your self-pitying, you are as rich as Croesus next to the wretches inhabiting these lands." To my agreeable surprise he nodded submissively; his mind could be penetrated after all.

To Lancelot I said, "I wonder that they do not rise up

against the lord who permits such suffering, for he is surely neglectful."

This drew a sharp rebuke. "Do not talk so lightly of rebellion, Mordred. It is the evillest thing and puts all else at risk. It is as well for these people that they perceive that better then you."

"I think it is exhaustion and despair that keeps them in their place," I persisted, heedless of the risk. "But do you not agree, Sir Lancelot, that a lord has duties as well as rights?"

"It is the land and not the lord which is at fault," he replied, and then because he seemed to enjoy the alliteration he repeated it, adding, "It is not altogether the fault of Bleoberis that so many of his peasants starve. This has always been a poor land. The harvests are meager, and even in summer the wind blows across these dreary hills like a knife. I know Bleoberis, and he is, all in all, a decent enough fellow. A little neglectful, perhaps, but certainly not oppressive. He is not one of your robber chiefs, nor is he rich. His life is not so easy."

I thought, *It is an arbor of bliss compared to the life his subjects lead. Besides which, was not this King Arthur's land, and were not these — and King Bleoberis also — his subjects?*

It was becoming clear to me that there were two lands of Albion: the prosperous south, where even the poorest never wanted for the necessities of life, and this other, forgotten country, where people daily endured misery and privation with little complaint and less hope.

These questions troubled me greatly, and my ponderings seemed ever to lead me full circle, so that I felt I was digging in my mind a moat of dilemmas. I could not discuss these things with Lancelot. He had a kinder heart than I had credited him with, but he had very fixed views. As for Galahad, he took all his opinions unquestioningly from his father.

I should greatly have liked to stop at Bleoberis's castle and rekindle my friendship with Agravaine, for I thought he would be sure to provide a sympathetic ear. But Lancelot would not permit it.

"I am sorry, Mordred, but there is too much at hazard. Bleoberis may learn of our purpose, and, though he is an honorable man, such a temptation may prove too great."

I suppose he had a point there.

Thus far I had given little thought to the Grail — the cause of all our hardship and peril. Was I spending my days and nights shivering on these windswept moors simply so that my parents could be proud of me? Or had I too been seduced by Merlin's mad visions? In one of my dreams I saw my father at the head of an army not of the grim-faced and implacable but of men smiling to themselves, almost smugly, as if they knew that no harm would befall them. My father was carrying the Grail — in my dream it was a vague and shapeless object, like a tiny, dense black cloud — and every now and then he would turn and raise it in his arms, and there would break out a great clamor and baying as of hungry wolves. As they marched closer, I could see that this was an army of the dead — or as good as, for they were certainly careless of life.

"Do you think the Grail is good magic," I asked Galahad, "or bad?"

He looked at me suspiciously, for he did not know his father's opinion on this. "What do you mean?" he hesitantly replied. "Is it not the way these things are used, and the people who use them, that matters?"

"I don't know," I said, honestly perplexed. "I have a little knowledge of magic — as an observer, you understand, not a practitioner — and it has often seemed to me that the power that resides in such objects has a natural tendency to work either good or evil regardless of who wields it."

"Well, then, the Grail must be good — for why else

would your father desire it, and why else should three such virtuous knights as ourselves be sent off on this quest?"

"Sometimes evil things have a way of presenting a comely aspect so as to charm and cozen the virtuous." What on earth prompted me to utter such nonsense? I was a rational creature. To me the mind of a child contained more wonder and stuff for discourse than the meanderings of ancient necromancers. Those sorts of things had surely outlived their time.

But far from home, in a cold, hostile land, it was possible to believe in all sorts of things. In this environment the works of man seemed pitifully inadequate, of such poor avail.

Lancelot, who chased frightened dragons until his horses collapsed beneath him, had a suitably brisk and direct answer to his own question. "Why do we seek the Grail? Why, for the glory of the thing. Have you not grasped that yet?"

* * *

No borders marked our passage from the lands where most rulers acknowledged Arthur's sovereignty to those where none did, but Lancelot seemed to know when we had crossed over. I did not dispute it when he advised that from now on we should always wear full armor and carry our shields strapped to our mounts, readily available. As we rode farther on, the country became still wilder — and so did its inhabitants.

The first attack came five days after we had left Bleoberis's territory. Some twenty or so painted savages suddenly emerged from the rocks and scrub that bordered our straight path and began pelting us with stones and spears. When they had exhausted these, they descended upon us, screaming imprecations in their barbarous and incomprehensible tongue.

So great an uproar amid that pastoral quiet came as a rude shock, but Lancelot at least recovered quickly. With a murderous cry that chilled me as fully as did the whoops of the charging highlanders, he rode into their midst and began eagerly to lay into them.

Galahad and I stayed back to protect the wagon, for Gruffyd had thrown himself to the boards and could not be persuaded to drive the horses to a safer place. I do not blame the fellow, though it meant we were sorely assailed, for many of the savages who escaped Lancelot's sword threw themselves toward ours. Fortunately they were all on foot, and against our hauberks their crude weapons inflicted little harm, so that slaying them became so much sport — though I fancy my companions relished this more than I did.

In a few moments it was over. Of the twenty who attacked us, I saw only four who managed to flee to the safety of the thick undergrowth. Though he might have prevented them, Lancelot let these few go. He rode back to us, panting and flushed, but grinning also. While we briefly rested and searched ourselves for minor wounds, he and Galahad recounted in great detail the blows that each had struck and sustained.

But he also spared some praise for me which, coming from a man of such worship, pleased me greatly.

Our euphoria did not last long, for in the time that followed we were set upon almost daily. Sometimes our adversaries would reveal themselves and at other times they would not, choosing instead to strike from behind the rocks and impenetrable undergrowth that all too frequently bordered our path. On one such occasion a stone-tipped spear struck me in the side, driving the rings of my hauberk deep into the skin. But the immediate pain of this brush with mortality hurt me less than the realization that it was undeserved, for it seemed to me that while I took the greatest care in shielding and defending myself, I suffered far more scars and bruises than did my companions, who took no heed of their safety and yet emerged from each battle virtually unscathed.

We had to wear full armor even while we slept and this, besides being quite burdensome, caused our skins to chafe mightily — mine especially, for I was already suffering from a multitude of bruises, so that parts of me were the color of rotten fruit. Our progress became much slower, for the land about afforded many opportunities for ambushment, and all such places on our road had to be searched before we could pass.

One small thing among all this consoled me. The churl Gruffyd, perhaps realizing how fortunate he was to be with us rather than at the mercy of such fiends, discovered a sudden enthusiasm for his housekeeping tasks. So diligent did he become in laying fires, preparing food, and the like that he soon made himself almost indispensable.

Poor fellow.

For it chanced that during one particularly fierce assault, the press upon us was so great that we became separated from one another and from the wagon, and so were unable to protect it. Once again we suffered no great injuries, though my very bruises themselves became bruised, and soon enough the persistent savages were once again routed. But Gruffyd had worn no armor, and he was too timorous a fellow to wield any weapon to effect, and so he was slain where he cowered. Not only slain, but hacked and hewn most cruelly so that afterward, amid the confusion of strewn limbs and with dusk approaching, we had to content ourselves with burying those parts of him we could recover in a hurry.

"That fellow had a marvelous talent for making stew," Lancelot observed. "What a pity he found it so late. I shall miss him, though he was a melancholy soul."

"I hope we shall not have to endure much more of this," I gasped as I leaned on the pommel of my sword like an old man. "From now on one of us must ride the wagon, which leaves but the other two riders to fend off these Caledonians."

"Oh, they are not Caledonians," said Galahad. His dark eyes and sunken cheeks were alight with the excitement and waning fury of battle. I thought, *He does not tire of all this killing because he never reflects upon it. To him it is no more than hacking logs.* He went over to one of the bodies and turned it over with his foot. The head had been almost severed and, as it swung around, pivoted delicately upon a slender string of flesh before rolling heavily against one shoulder. I saw a bearded face that gaped sightlessly and with a stupid wonder at the darkening clouds and the faint, cold stars, its frozen snarl rendered almost comic by the purple, protruding tongue that it had nearly bitten off at the moment of death.

"These are Veniconians," Galahad was saying. "This is plain by the manner in which they paint themselves."

"It is truly awful," I muttered as I continued to gaze in horrified fascination at the intricate and indecipherable patterns etched upon the white, bloodless skin.

Lancelot stepped forward. "It is not meant to be pleasing to the eye." He was looking tired and drawn. Perhaps even he was satiated. "The Caledonians do not paint themselves. They believe that of all the highland tribes, they are the most fell, and as such have no need of cheap effects. It is almost a point of honor with them."

"And are they in truth so very fierce?" I was trying to sound confident, yet I dearly wished that I was indeed an old man and that my sword was a simple, harmless staff.

He regarded me speculatively for a second, then rested a hand briefly on my shoulder. "I believe we shall give a good account of ourselves."

11

BUT NO MORE ATTACKS CAME.

Perhaps our enemies had finally lost heart, for we had taken a great toll of them, and their numbers had not been great to begin with. Or perhaps it was simply that we had quit their territory. Whatever the reason, it afforded us little relief; how were we to know that we were indeed safe and that they were not simply licking their wounds and gathering their meager strength for a final, overwhelming onslaught? So we had to stay constantly on our guard.

For days we rode through a grey land beneath a grey sky, and the heaviness of these surroundings bore down upon us like a great weight. We encountered frequent mists out of which grey, spectral shapes would suddenly and hugely loom. Closer inspection would reveal these to be rocks or trees or sometimes, more disturbingly, nothing at all. It was early spring, yet even when the rain ceased to fall and the sun deigned to show herself we were scarcely sensible of it. Our destriers, instead of pacing proudly, languished with lowered heads whilst we became sunk in gloomy contemplation or else turned pettish and irritable, snapping fretfully at one another, usually over trifles. Even Lancelot, a veteran of lengthy quests, was affected.

He was still convinced that we were being followed. I think he sensed also our skepticism, which, though unvoiced, was plain enough. "I know what it is you are thinking," he snarled one day. "You think I am going soft and am running from shadows." And before Galahad or I could reply he was gone, cantering off once again in search of our shy, elusive companion.

He had a right to be vexed, for he was passing wise in such lore. But our doubt was understandable also. How could any creature pass unchallenged and unscathed through so hostile a wilderness unless it were a figment of the imagination?

One morning our senses became so confused by the fog that we could scarcely see one another, and so we determined to rise above it and find some landmark by which we might measure our progress. So it was that we found ourselves atop a circle of steep, terraced hills, unbroken save for a narrow gap far below through which two or three riders might pass abreast. Down in the valley the mist was slowly dispersing, as if in mockery of our efforts. It hugged the ground like a vast, receding lake, and on its still surface straw rooftops perched like conical hats.

"I did not expect to find this," Lancelot muttered. "We are a long way off the beaten track. There should not be people here."

Galahad, wearing a knowing look, decided to contribute. "Perhaps this site was chosen deliberately, Father. Perhaps these people do not like visitors."

Lancelot responded with a grunt and urged his horse forward.

"Are we going down there?" I asked.

"We are," he replied. "I am curious to know what sort of folk these are who hide themselves so effectively from casual eyes. They might also direct us to Carbonek."

How long have we been lost, then? I thought.

Galahad could not drive the wagon down so steep a hillside, and it was more than an hour before we found the path that took us through the hills to the village.

"Be ready to turn and run should I give the word," said Lancelot. "If there is trouble, I do not intend that we should fight our way out of it."

But we saw no blue-painted warriors in the fields as we passed, only farmers and their straining oxen absorbed in the spring ploughing. When they saw us, they stopped; a few ran toward the village. I raised a hand as we rode by, in hopes this would show that our intentions were peaceful, and I saw at least one man offer a hesitant wave in reply.

"There are no horses and no fortifications," Lancelot observed. "That is a good sign."

"Perhaps we shall at last meet with some highland hospitality," said Galahad.

It was a village of some considerable size; forty or fifty dwellings all told, well spaced and laid out in uniform rows, as if the place had been planned and built all of a piece and not over a time. A sizable crowd had gathered to watch our progress, and I suppose we must have appeared an impressive sight with the sun behind us and our armor gleaming. They stood on either side of the narrow path, neither frowning nor friendly but curious and silent.

They looked to me well fed, and their clothes, while shabby and faded, were adequate. At any rate, they were not starving or diseased or belligerent, and so my hopes were greatly raised that at last we might find a hospitable welcome.

One of their number stepped in front of us and raised his hand for us to stop. Lancelot, who was more accustomed to seeing peasants fling themselves out of his way than step officiously into it, muttered as he reined his horse. He was an old man, this peasant, but his gait was sprightly, so that at first I took him for a younger man. His face, though deeply lined, had a robust glow that Galahad later told me came from living in mountainous regions. He took hold of Lancelot's bridle — a bold and foolish act, for Lancelot was descended from twelve generations of Gallic kings; I wondered at his restraint in not knocking the fellow down. Perhaps it was the confident light in the old man's eyes that saved him, or else his smile, for with it he looked like a good-natured simpleton, and Lancelot was ever courteous to women and the feebleminded.

"Who are you and whence come you?" asked the old man.

Lancelot, swallowing his pride, responded with his own question. "Where are we?"

The old man's smile did not waver. "Friend, we are Hyperboreans, and how you have arrived here I know not, for we had thought ourselves safe from the prying eyes of strangers." I think he noticed my start of surprise, for he turned and contemplated me briefly before continuing. "However, if you mean us no harm, you are right welcome."

Lancelot looked like someone whose cheeks had been caressed by a leper, and for a moment I thought he was going to tear his bridle from the old man's grasp, but then he looked at the large crowd gathered watchfully about us and seemed to think better of it. Even unarmed, they looked a formidable array. "We are knights of King Arthur," he announced. "And it is the fortress of Carbonek that we seek. It is by chance alone that we happened upon you."

"Ah." The old man nodded gently to himself as if to say, That would explain your haughty manner. "We have heard of King Arthur, and Carbonek is but a few days' ride away from here. If your engagement there is not too pressing, perhaps you would care to stay a while and refresh yourselves."

Oh, yes, yes, I thought.

But Lancelot could stand no more of the churl's easy familiarity. Dismounting, he took back the reins and said curtly, "Now then, old man, we shall want a dwelling for the night if you can spare it. Also stabling for our horses. We shall require stores for our wagon — I will give you a list of these. If you can provide us with all this, then you shall have our thanks and be well paid for your trouble."

The old man's smile faded entirely. With a shrug and a small sigh he turned in the direction of the houses. "Follow me, then."

I hurried after Lancelot. "You cannot talk to these people like that," I said. "They are Hyperboreans."

The brief look he gave me said, I shall talk to them how I please. He turned and strode haughtily on.

They gave us a dwelling that was amply proportioned and comfortably furnished. There were already logs and kindling stacked in the hearth, so it was the work of a moment to get a good blaze going. It was all far more than we deserved.

"I have spoken to the headman," I said as I brought in some blankets from the wagon. "We shall be receiving some food presently."

My companions had reverted to their former ways, for they sat before the fire while I busied myself around them. Lancelot lowered his head — in contemplation or gloom, I was not sure which — and his son mimicked the movement. After a few moments of silence, I ventured a comment in a converstional tone. "We do seem to have fallen among friends for once."

Lancelot looked up. "Foolish boy. These are enemies, and we should not have stayed here." Then he dropped his gaze again.

Well, I thought, *if they want to sulk, so be it.*

The food the Hyperboreans brought was simple fare — porridge sweetened with honey, and a jug of ale with which to wash it down. Yet I welcomed it not only because it was hot and I was hungry. It seemed to me also to be touched by a certain beneficence. I cannot explain why I felt honored and privileged to be among such honest, self-effacing hosts. I only know that my companions shared none of my feelings.

"These are Hyperboreans, Mordred," Galahad tried patiently to explain to me as we lay abed and listened to Lancelot's thunderous snores. "They are your father's enemies. They are everybody's enemies, for they recognize no lords and hold King Arthur in contempt though they are no more than churls."

"Come now, Gally. They have shown us nothing but kindness, and you repay this with scorn and disdain. Where is the chivalry in that?"

"It is rather awkward, I admit," he said. "We should not have stayed here in the first place. This puts us in a very embarrassing position, accepting hospitality from our enemies."

In the pause that followed, I could almost sense his anguish as he struggled for a way out of this dilemma. "If Father pays them handsomely, then we can say that we have not accepted their hospitality gratis." After further thought he added, "Besides, Mordred, chivalry has two sides to it, don't you agree?"

"Hmm?"

"Well, chivalry means the strong protecting the weak, doesn't it? I suppose that is how your father would define it."

"Yes," I replied warily.

"If it is to have any meaning at all, then surely the weak must first accept their place in the scheme of things. But these people make no distinction between gentleman and churl. They recognize only a dull equality, each man as good as another." There was a shadowy stirring in the darkness, and Galahad's indistinct, pale face turned to mine. "Now tell me this — where is the knight's place in such a world?"

"Gally, that is not even sophistry. It is plain nonsense." And because Lancelot's snores would not let me sleep, I humored him for a while longer. "They are but a single tribe. What harm can they do, even if they are a trifle eccentric in their beliefs?"

"They set a bad example. If they were to be curbed, then perhaps your father would not have so much trouble with the other northern tribes."

I turned away then and, clapping my hands to my ears, tried to get some sleep.

The next morning I went off to arrange for the purchase of stores. Because the Hyperboreans considered that Lancelot had offended them, they would have no more to do with him or Galahad. But to me they were perfectly agreeable. I spoke again to the old man who had first approached us. "I have told my comrades that you are the headman of this village. Is that correct?"

He shook his head and looked mildly amused. "No, I am Anted." I think he was trying to be cryptic.

When we had loaded the wagon, he fetched a jar of mead from his house, and because it was a fine morning in early spring we sat down, leaning against one of the wheels, and drank to one another's health.

"I have heard of you," I said.

"I am flattered."

"Of your tribe," I corrected.

"Ah." Stretching out a tongue the color of dry mud, he licked absently at the stray golden drops trapped in his drooping moustache.

"Yes. Plato, the great philosopher, has written about you. And other writers."

"He never saw for himself, you know. He got all that from traders hundreds of years ago." He tugged gently at his woolen tunic. Once it had been richly colored; I could still barely discern a pattern of bold checks. "As you see, we are hardly living in a golden age. And the winters here are ferocious."

And yet he looked to me so comfortable, stretched out in the spring sun and licking his lips like an ancient and contented cat. "Then why do you stay?"

"Because we are left well alone. Our neighbors do not trust strangers, as you have probably learned, but they are rather in awe of us. We are simply good farmers who also like to dabble a little in such matters as herbal remedies and the like. But because even such modest skills are rare in this country, they think we are great magicians, and so in return for our occasional ministrations they give us respect."

"King Arthur believes that you should give him some of this respect also."

"Why? What has he done to deserve it?" And when I could make no answer to this he added, "Anyway, King Arthur is a long way from here, and no doubt has more pressing concerns than our obscure selves."

I shook my head. "You are storing up trouble for yourselves, Anted. Not yet. Perhaps not for years, but sometime. If you were to acknowledge King Arthur as your rightful lord, you would then enjoy Arthur's protection and might go where you please in his land."

"His land," Anted slowly repeated. "And how, pray, did it become his land?"

"Why, it belonged to his father, Uther Pendragon."

"And later, I suppose, it will be given to you?"

"In time," I said without thinking, and then I became flushed. *How did he know?*

Anted carefully propped the jar against the wheel, then slowly stood up. Yesterday he had not seemed like an old man at all. Now he stood before me looking rather decrepit, swaying slightly and gazing at me as if I was not quite in focus.

I believe it was a strong mead we had drunk.

Carefully he spat into his hands. "Then I will fight you for it, and if I win I shall give it to *my* sons." A mirthful smile spread across his face below his bleary eyes. He teetered — or at least seemed to — and I feared he might fall and do himself some hurt.

I could tell the drink had affected me also, for I was

in a merry humor. Considering my mood, and with my secret out, I found the right response easily. "Nay, Anted, for I will give it to you full willingly!"

He laughed at this, a sound like dry leaves, and sat down again.

I had to ask. "How did you know I was the king's son?"

"Some of us listened outside your hut last night."

"And did what you heard please you?"

His face became grave. "We do not counsel rebellion among the other tribes. They go their way, and we go ours. There has always been strife in this country. It has not been our doing."

"Perhaps not, but the king and his advisers must have some excuse, and you serve the purpose well."

"Ah, well." He seemed genuinely unconcerned. Heaving himself upright once more, he rested his hand on my shoulder. "I am glad to see that being a king's son and keeping such company as you do has nonetheless not entirely dimmed your perception." And, cradling his precious jug in his arms, he stumbled off in search of his house. "No doubt you will exercise what influence you can upon your companions."

But Lancelot's mind was made up fully and would not be changed.

"It is your youthful idealism, Mordred, that blinds you to the danger in all of this." With his arm he made a grand, sweeping gesture that encompassed the whole valley.

We were walking slowly up the hillside, for he had finally tired of skulking in his hut and felt a desire to see more of his surroundings before we left.

"Tell me, Mordred, what do you see as you look about you?" he continued.

I could see nothing unusual or amiss, and I told him so. "There are men and women working in the fields. Industriously, it seems to me."

He slapped me heavily on the back. "Quite. You know, the Celtic peasant is the salt of the earth. Diligent, conscientious, utterly reliable — as long as he is well led."

"But these Hyperboreans have leaders, Sir Lancelot. They elect them every year."

He sighed as he shook his head with good-natured forbearance. "That is not what I mean, Mordred. What if everybody were to do as they do — appoint their own leaders, hold the land in common, exalt the weak, and disparage the strong?" He paused significantly, but not long enough for me to gather a reply.

"I will tell you. First there would be no King Arthur, for men like him are chosen by destiny and not by the common and capricious multitude. Then there would be no Albion, for each tribe would shortly go its own way and the kingdom would fall apart. Lastly, there would be no Celts, for we should be overmastered and enslaved by the Latins. I suppose I should not be surprised that you should take their part, but you surely cannot desire all of that?"

I was stung by the suggestion. It was so unfair, and the logic of it was faulty. Yet so reasoned was his indignation, so genuine seemed his fatherly concern, that I had not the heart to take issue. This was not the man whom but a few weeks earlier I had regarded as an amiable buffoon. Ah, but he was full of surprises!

I said weakly, "But, Sir Lancelot, why can they not simply be left alone? They are a peaceful folk and offer no hurt."

"What makes you so sure of that, eh?" Turning, he began to retrace his steps, descending the hill with such long, purposeful strides that I, though a good head taller, had to almost run to keep pace. "Many times your father has sent emissaries northward, for he is a patient man and not easily moved to violence, and always these same ambassadors have returned scorned and sometimes bruised as well. The last expedition did not return at all."

"But how do you—"

"That is why I guarded my words yesterday as well as I did, for in their numbers and our weariness they would have overcome us else."

In the distance newborn lambs were bleating plaintively for their lost mothers. I thought, *There is either a grotesque misunderstanding here, or else someone is lying to me.*

"Do not judge by appearances, Mordred." Lancelot had slowed his pace a little, no doubt the better to press his advantage. "Your father is not a tyrant simply because he wants to pass on more than half a kingdom to his heir." He waved derisively at the houses below us. "And you should not think of these as gods in human form simply because of the words of dead philosophers."

"What is to be done, then?" His reasoning and his exhortations were affecting me, and I felt suddenly very confused and disheartened.

"Oh, I don't know." I think he was wearying of our discourse. He had, after all, only stepped out for some fresh air and a little gentle exercise. "It is for your father to decide such things. All I know is that Albion and Gaul must face the Latins together, or we shall be destroyed separately. And first we must destroy the enemies in our midst — especially those that try to beguile us with impossible dreams of felicity."

He must have seen the concern in my face at this point, for he added, "Yes, they are painful choices. The time will come soon enough when you have to make them yourself." He hurried on again, for it was his intention that we should resume our journey before the morning was far advanced.

When I came to take my leave of Anted, I found myself vacillating again, wondering how I could have been so credulous of Lancelot's argument. There were no fell warriors among these people, no houses brimming with weapons. They were not the homely, bucolic philosophers that I had read about in books, but that was not their fault. They were farmers, living a life of simple blessedness, and it saddened me to think that in time the growing power of Camelot would reach out and crush them.

Lancelot and Galahad, having already offered their own rather stiff, ungracious thanks, waited for me at the edge of the village while I settled accounts with Anted.

"I hope we have not been too great a disappointment to you," he said. "No doubt you expected all sorts of golden platitudes to fall from our lips. But really, the truest wisdom is also the simplest; plant in the spring, harvest in the autumn, lay by sufficient for lean years. That sort of thing."

I asked him the way to Carbonek.

"It stands like a citadel on a hill," he said, pointing into the distance, "and there is a great lake behind it. You cannot miss it, for it is a notable landmark. You follow the quest of the Sangrail, I suppose?"

It did not surprise me that he had guessed so much. "It is there, then?"

"Oh, yes." He contemplated me with narrowed, appraising eyes. "You are not the first to have assayed the quest, but you may be the first to succeed. In which case I wonder if I have done the right thing in directing you."

"Is it really so powerful, then?"

"The faith of men makes it powerful, yes. Possession of the Grail would increase your father's strength a hundredfold. That can hardly bode well for such as us."

"All the more reason why you should bend a little," I said. "What difference can it make? It is a form of words, no more."

He shook his head. "You surely take us more seriously than that."

"Well, then." I mounted my horse. "I admire your

principles. I hope you can keep both them and your lives." He smiled at that, and we shook hands warmly. "If you can keep yourselves out of harm's way until I am made king, then I shall grant you unconditional title to this land. You and all your tribe."

Gently he slapped my horse. "It is not yours to give." As I rode away he added, "No offense."

Some people just will not be helped.

12

SOMEONE WAS CALLING TO ME FROM FAR AWAY. No, there were two voices; one stern and authoritative, the other a thin, pitiful whine. I struggled toward wakefulness, for the voices were growing nearer and demanded an answer. But I had gone to my bed greatly fatigued, and though I was strangely aware of my body stirring listlessly beneath a burden of weariness, I could not fully awaken.

"Be careful!" Galahad cried good-naturedly as he peeled away the sheepskins from my bed. "I woke you because you were suffocating, and you repay me by trying to black my eye."

I sat up with a start and looked about me. "Where is your father?"

"Mordred!" This time I heard but the one voice.

"He has been calling for some time." I saw that Galahad was almost dressed. Still drowsy and confused, I tugged on my shoes. "I think he was right after all about our being followed." He shook his head as he waited for me to put on my tunic. "Who would have thought it, eh?"

Pushing aside the flap of the pavilion, we stepped outside. As usual, a cold mist enveloped the world outside and a cruel dew was underfoot. I took a tentative deep breath but there was nothing invigorating about the air; it tasted damp and unsavory.

We rubbed our shoulders vigorously and huddled

close for illusory warmth as we peered into the dismal grey curtain.

"I cannot see anything moving out there," I muttered.

"To me everything is moving," Galahad said.

Lancelot called again, but still it was impossible to say whence his voice came. At least it no longer sounded urgent. Rather, it was relaxed, triumphant. See what I have found, it seemed to say. "We shall be eating humble pie for days after this," said Galahad gloomily.

At last we saw him, a gaunt figure astride his mount, slowly emerging from the mist as if from the depths of a thickly translucent pool. And something else had come into view in front of him, keeping pace with the horse's measured gait. It shuffled along with the utmost reluctance, prompted largely by the point of Lancelot's sword and softly moaning to itself all the while. This figure might have been man-high, save that it was bent almost double by some infirmity and the weight of its monstrous head. And in that head—

"Mordred!" called Lancelot.

"Mordred!" echoed the other figure in a pitiful, wheezing, ancient voice.

"This fellow claims acquaintance with you." Lancelot, his face aglow with exertion and triumph, sheathed his sword and dismounted. "I must say, Mordred, you keep some strange company."

I went toward the whimpering form, bent and shivering in front of the destrier. "Careful," Lancelot said. "I have bound his arms, but he has a batch of prodigiously sharp teeth."

"It is all right," I said and, crouching, gazed into the single red-rimmed eye that stared with terrified uncertainty into mine.

"For a moment I feared you would not remember me. You do remember me, don't you, Mordred?" Now that its owner had ceased his dreadful whining, the voice was surprisingly soft and delicate. It sounded sad and venerable too, and should have seemed out of place emitting from so hideous a mouth, yet curiously it did not — though I had to turn away my head for fear of choking on his foul breath.

"Of course I remember you." Even after twenty years I had recognized him instantly, once I had got a good look. "But you are in a bad way, aren't you?" His few clothes were unrecognizable rags, and the exposed parts of his hunched, misshapen body were covered in sores.

He nodded abjectly.

"He is indeed a friend," I said to the others. "Though one I never thought to see again, and certainly not in such a condition."

"Well, I am not to blame for that," said Lancelot irritably. "He was in this state when I found him. And I thought he meant to make a meal of me — that is why I bound him." He stood stiffly, watching us with folded arms and chewing his upper lip in thoughtful displeasure. He was clearly disappointed with the reception he had received. "If he is your friend, then tell us his name, for he would not give it to me."

"Assuredly. His name is Finn, and he is one of the sons of Balor."

I heard Galahad gasp. Then he vanished back inside the pavilion.

"Actually, I'm the only son now," Finn corrected.

"Oh. I'm sorry." I watched a thick tear course down his cheek and disappear into the folds of cracked, yellow skin. A few more followed, and then he rubbed his eye with a fist, just like a baby. I wondered if the other eye, huge and bulbous behind its permanently closed lid, was crying also.

"All dead," he blubbered.

"I am sorry," I repeated. "But tell me, why were—"

I heard the tent flap being thrown aside and turned as Galahad emerged. Most of him was concealed behind his shield, and he moved forward with a heavy, anxious deliberation. But the sword he was weaving slowly above his head carried menace enough.

"Turn away quickly, Father! Look not into the creature's eye, else it will petrify you!" His voice sounded thin and tremulous and rather endearingly boyish. To do him justice, he showed enormous courage. The prospect of being turned into stone — sentient, perhaps, but forever helpless and unmoving — must have been a terrifying one, even if quite unfounded.

"It is all right, Gally," I assured him while Finn shuffled behind me and buried his head in his arms. He was whimpering again. He could have made a run for it. His hands were bound in front, so that should not have greatly slowed him. But he was too far gone for resistance or flight.

"Stand back, Mordred. I mean to consign this foul, unwholesome beast to the pit whence he came."

I stood up slowly and raised my hands. His blood was up, and there was a savage contrast between his white, determined face and his black brows. I chose my words carefully. "Gentle Sir Galahad, put down your sword and shield, for it is difficult to remonstrate with a wall of wood."

He glared at me with such ferocity that for a moment I thought he might attack me first, but I summoned my courage and stood my ground and eventually he lowered the shield. With his sword he pointed to the quivering mound of flesh I was risking my life to protect. "This is the son of Balor? The cyclops?"

"He is harmless, Gally. You can see that, surely. The evil eye is closed quite and can never be opened. Even if he wills it." I gave the bundle behind me a light, good-natured kick with my heel. "Look up, Finn, and wither your enemies with a single glance."

Up went Galahad's shield again. From behind me came a gentle sob. "Nay, Mordred, do not tease me when I am in my direst peril."

I touched him again with my foot. "Be not afeared. You are among friends, though they do not know it yet."

Lancelot, who had watched these proceedings half with amusement and half with concern, finally intervened. "Put down the sword, Gally. I did not keep the thing alive this long in order that you might carve it up." He turned to me. "Find out what it wants. It told me that it followed us for love of you. No offense, but I do not believe that for a moment." He led Galahad away. "Why was there no fire to greet me on my return?" I heard him complain as they vanished into the fog.

I turned to our captive. "Well, Finn, what have you been up to these many weeks?"

As he smiled, some of the pustules about his dry, cracked mouth burst open. The smile turned to an apologetic grimace as I recoiled in disgust. "Gentle master, for that you have saved my life I give thee thanks."

"Never mind that. Answer my question." I wondered how I had once been able to regard such a monster as my friend. I had been a perceptive child, so there must have been a good reason.

He groaned, wiped his lips, then gave another cry as he inadvertently touched the sores. "Oh, but these bonds do hurt so. I fear my hands will drop from my wrists."

I cursorily examined the ropes that bound him. "You will be all right for a while yet. Now, tell me, do you know about our errand? Is that it?"

He cast down his face like a guilty child; a smelly, ill-favored child. Also a dangerous one. Regardless of my assurances to Galahad, Finn was not to be trusted. His cunning was as childlike as his intellect; he would loudly protest his good intentions in the teeth of all the evidence until he wore down his accusers by his sheer persistence. Then, once he had convinced them that he was, if not innocent, at least harmless, he would creep up on them unawares and in the night would snap their necks like dry twigs.

That is how he had lived in the old days, feeding off the unwary, and I had no reason to suppose that he had changed his ways since then.

But for the moment I told myself that it suited my purpose to keep him alive. And in spite of all, I could not help but feel a residue of pity and affection.

"If I was younger and had my wits about me, I could break these cords. You know I could. But I am sad and old and terribly confused." The words came out in thick, choking sobs.

"You have never had your wits about you, Finn, and you should be thankful for it. It was your stupidity that saved your life today. It is your only endearing quality."

He looked up, beaming. "Do you mean that?"

Lancelot had been out most of the night and was chilled to the bone, so we did not set off straight away but lit a fire instead. It was a smoky, fitful affair, for all the wood we could find was damp, and so it did little to improve our spirits. Lancelot allowed Finn to be untied while we ate. The cyclops sat beside the fire gratefully, his feet virtually resting on the smoldering branches, quite oblivious to the choking smoke. I found some garments to replace the rags that were dropping from his body — as much for our sakes as for his — but I could do nothing about the frightful sores. We had brought some salves and ointments with us, but he was beyond such meager help. With Lancelot's grudging permission, I offered him some fruit, which he accepted and devoured greedily.

"I thought the Fomor ate only live meat," Galahad petulantly observed. He had been cheated of his kill, and his frustrated aggression was turning into bitterness.

Finn seemed not to notice the attitude with which the comment was delivered. "Ah, but these days it is eat or starve. For my people there is no other choice." Turning to me, he added, "Dear friend, if you might see what misery we suffer, your heart would surely weep."

Embarrassed, I looked at Galahad. He was scowling silently across the fire, his shadowed eyes enlivened occasionally by a cruel gleam whenever they alighted on the son of Balor.

"Your father's knights have pressed us hard, Sir Mordred. They deem it great sport to carry away our heads to adorn their chambers and horrify their ladies. Even in the deepest parts of the forest we are no longer safe." He shook his head with a puzzled gravity. "Ah, such times these are. . . ."

I knew all about this, of course. It had been going on for years. And I fancied I knew the cause, for it came of my father keeping so many knights idle about the court. Starved of chivalrous pursuits, they turned to barbarous pleasures instead. These were at any rate far more enjoyable than the succoring of widows and orphans. I disapproved of the whole business; what civilized person would not? But there was little I could do. If I had championed the cause of these ill-favored creatures, I should have been laughed out of court.

Though his feet were thrust so far into the fire that they themselves were seemingly beginning to smolder, he was still shivering. "There are so few of us left now. The Baobhan—"

"She is dead?"

"Sir Lamorak had that honor. She was so old that she could neither fight nor fly. But he got little for his troubles, for afterward her head became so shriveled as to be unrecognizable." His own head fell slowly to his shoulder as he stared mournfully into the smoking fire and beyond. "The Oakapple Elf, that handsome fellow Ruadan, most of the others, they all hang in the halls of your father's knights." He closed his eye and gave a loud sniff. "And their souls stumble blindly in darkness."

I had not heard such eloquence from him before. "Cannot Nimue help you?"

"I daresay she could. But she won't. She has always

regarded us as interlopers. I think she wants the humans to come into the forest."

"Since you may not save your people by doing this, why do you follow our quest?"

He smiled ingenuously. "Who knows the power of the Grail?"

Lancelot, who at first had taken little interest in our conversation, was now gazing speculatively at this creature hugging its arms and mumbling to itself in the comfortless firelight. Perhaps he was wondering why he had troubled to spare it; such behavior was not in his nature. I think that Lancelot possessed a crude sort of compassion, but surely it did not extend that far. He rose and stretched his arms. "We have delayed long enough, I think." He touched Galahad's shoulder. "Help me make the horses ready." As he walked away he said to me, "Bind him, and talk to him." A moment later his disembodied voice added through the mist, "But be careful of those teeth."

Had he looked closer, he would have seen that they were quite rotten and mostly broken, but I appreciated his concern.

When we were alone, Finn turned to me with a look of desperation, his hands outstretched and imploring. I took up the rope and deftly wrapped it around his wrists. His mouth fell open, and he looked for a moment like one betrayed. I half expected to hear a howl of anguish that would bring Lancelot and Galahad running with swords drawn. But he contented himself with a grunt of dismay and a resigned, accepting shrug.

"It was the Baobhan who sent me to you," he explained as I tightened and tested the knots. "Just before she was slain. She told me the words I should say to you, but I have forgot most of them because I am a fool. Must it be so tight?"

"She taught you in vain." I let his hands drop. "I am sorry to tell you this, for it is plain that you have endured much hardship of late. But the Grail can be of no use to you. It does not work like that."

His head bobbed grotesquely in stupid agreement. "Of course not, of course not. But it could do you no harm if we were to borrow it for a while." He leaned closer so that his warm, stinking breath flowed all over me. "We looked after you."

"Stand farther off!" I snapped, more out of fear than loathing. As I recoiled from the close gaze of his unblinking eye, huge and white and hideous, I thought, *What must the other one be like? What if he were to open it and show me?*

Clearly hurt, he moved away. "You only looked after me because it suited your purpose," I said defensively. But I knew he was right. Had it not been for the Fomor, I should have starved in the days between Mother's mysterious disappearance and the equally inexplicable arrival of Palomides. In the years that followed, I had pondered often these puzzling inconsistencies. "Yes, you did save me," I assented. "But you were also very unkind about my mother. I remember that, young as I was."

Finn shook his head vehemently, scattering some of the thick drops of saliva that had gathered about his fat, wet lips. "You do not understand. She hated us. And she wanted to use us in her plots against King Arthur. But we wanted no part of her schemes. She was a meddler and would have got us into trouble."

"My mother would never scheme against my father. What nonsense are you talking?"

He clamped his bound fists to his mouth and shook his head wildly.

"Come, Finn. If you know something about my mother that I do not, then I charge thee to tell it to me."

His eye grew wider, but he remained silent. Perhaps I could have threatened him or bribed him, but something told me that I should not pursue this particular question. So I simply asked, "Why did you hate her so?"

"She used to try out her new spells on us." He shuddered at the memory. "Imagine that. She would summon one or two of us to her house — how we dreaded those summons. But we had to go."

"That could not have been pleasant for you," I agreed.

"At first we befriended you because we knew she would blame us if any harm befell you. We thought we should keep a close watch on you for our own sakes. But later we came to like you as well. Some of us did, anyway. I did. I would never have let you be harmed." As he struck his chest it boomed hollowly. "Never."

"But mainly it suited your purpose."

"You owe it to us," Finn said, returning to our earlier topic. There was a note of petulance as well as pleading in his voice. "We should not keep it for long. A day at the most. Perhaps two. . . . Oh, please, gentle Mordred, I have braved so many dangers to follow your quest." And because I would not suffer him to touch me, he prayed to me instead, his gnarled, laced fingers reaching out to me like the intertwining roots of a long-dead tree.

Then he winked at me — a horrible sight, for he had no eyebrows or lashes, and so for a moment the top of his face was quite featureless save for those black, wrinkled slits. I thought, *He has endured a great deal in pursuit of this forlorn hope. Surely it would be churlish to forsake him entirely. . . .* "How did you evade capture for so long?" I asked.

"I have my tricks," he answered. "I can still do them. I could help you."

That was a point to be considered. Very soon now — Lancelot thought the next morning by the latest — we would be in sight of Carbonek, yet what we would do next Lancelot had not told us. Nor do I think he knew himself. As a child, I had been greatly impressed by Finn's tricks. They were often clumsy, but sometimes they were effective also. *Yes, he could be of use to us.*

I suggested as much to Lancelot as we rode together.

Finn was in the wagon. He was still securely bound, but Galahad protested nevertheless at having to carry so unwholesome a passenger. He drove slowly, openly sulking.

"He is a shapeshifter," I explained to Lancelot. "That is why we never saw him."

"You mean he just changed into a tree every time we looked around?" He sounded skeptical.

"It is not so simple as that. Shapeshifting is a skillful art, requiring great dexterity and suppleness of body." I knew that I was showing off my knowledge, but there were very few areas in which I could demonstrate any superiority to the peer of knights. "Merlin used to be quite good at it, but he is getting too old now."

"Indeed."

"The son of Balor is not a skilled practitioner. His body is hardly supple. But he was always careful to keep himself at a great distance and thus avoid scrutiny. Tell me, Sir Lancelot, how did you capture him?"

He thought about this for a moment. "I was passing what I took to be a large stone in the mist. It seemed to me that the stone moved." He shook his head. "But that was a trick of the light, or of my mind. When I caught him, he was as you see him now."

"You caught him because he panicked and resumed his normal shape in order to run away."

Lancelot twisted around in his saddle. The wagon and its petulant driver were lagging farther and farther behind. He gestured angrily at Galahad to hurry up. Galahad's expression did not change markedly, but the horses did move a little faster. Turning to me, Lancelot said, "Why does he not shift himself out of this fix he is in, then?"

"Because whatever shape he assumes, he will still be bound hand and foot."

He snorted derisively. "You have an answer for everything, Mordred."

"He could be useful to us."

Lancelot looked at me. "I hope you have not promised him anything. You know that the Grail must be delivered straight to your father. I have pledged my word on that."

I shrugged uncomfortably. "We will see" was all that I had said to Finn, but I knew how desperate he was and how much faith he would place in even the vaguest of promises. "I think he is near death. Do you not think so too, Sir Lancelot?" I glanced around. Behind Galahad I could see the outline of Finn's hunched and shrouded form, huddled as if deep in contemplation, jolted frequently by the stony ground but uncomplaining all the while. "You only have to look at the state of him."

"I hope you are right, Mordred. Else we shall have to guard him all the way back to Camelot, and I think we shall have worries enough by then." His gaze moved to the distant line of hills that lay across our path. "I will tell you what I think. I think that Carbonek lies just on the other side. What is your opinion?"

13

ONE DAY AND SEVERAL HILLS LATER, LANCELOT lay on his belly in the long, damp grass at the crest of a rise. Twisting uncomfortably, he thought, Well, I was almost right.

Below him a narrow plain stretched for about half a mile to the banks of Loch Morar. He could see the sun sparkling on the water's surface while a sharp, stinging breeze carried the smell of the sea and stirred the water so that there was a scattering of white amid the steely blue brilliance. The sun shone too on the high fortress of Carbonek beside the loch, picking out details of the dozen or so tiny buildings inside its walls. It was warm on Lancelot's back, for he was in a place sheltered from the wind, but he felt more keenly the penetrating damp from the ground. As he shifted again in his discomfort, he thought, I am getting too old for this business.

Carbonek was no Camelot. It had no vaulting walls of granite, no grim towers crammed with helmeted soldiers or the devilish engines of King Arthur's Druids. But it was formidable enough; two rings of wooden palisades, each protected by a deep ditch. The main gate was the nearest thing he could see to a weak point — but from the entrance the ramparts turned outward to form a narrow corridor along which an attacking force would have to thread its perilous way before it could storm the gate itself. Not only were the ramparts securely built, they had been so erected as to follow the contours of the hill and so give a clear view in all directions.

To Lancelot it was a disheartening sight. He had half expected to find the place in a state of neglect and disrepair. The Caledonians were the dominant tribe in the region and, had they followed the usual pattern, should have become lax and complacent as a result. It is having the Grail that keeps them prepared and alert, he supposed. How are we to take it from them?

"We must go closer." He spoke the words, but to himself. The others were in the camp at the bottom of the hill, far out of earshot.

Rising to his feet, he felt a painful twinge along the whole length of his back, which added to his other discomforts. As he walked slowly and pensively down to the makeshift camp, he felt a sudden longing to be back home, where the damp and strained muscles would not trouble him. He thought about the castle at Benwick, the ancient home of his fathers. He saw the whitewashed solar, that most pleasant of rooms, where he slept and took his private ease, steeped in the warmth and golden light of the Provençal sun streaming through its high, narrow windows.

This is the last time I undertake such a journey, he quietly but firmly resolved. Once the Grail is taken (the question of how this was to be achieved he laid aside for the present), I shall give up quests. I will immerse myself instead in a life of tranquil pleasure and the undemanding responsibilities of a country gentleman. And I shall find a wife, that most of all. Someone like Guinevere, perhaps.

Yes, and who shall drive away the Latins in the meantime? asked a small, objectionable voice. For if you do nothing about that, then soon you will have no lands to tend at your leisure and no castle to which to retire.

But Galahad will do that, he answered the voice. It is his turn. He is young, and it is the duty of the young to renew the folly of life and the taking of it. This love of slaughter is fast deserting me. I take no pleasure from it any more. Look at me; I have even spared Mordred's shambling pet.

It made perfect sense to him that the older he grew, the more he should want to cling to life, and not just to his own. More and more it seemed to him that the whole of suffering humanity was somehow vaguely bound, perhaps by a vast, invisible web. And the breaking of one strand would send tiny vibrations along the whole — not enough to cause any great damage, but just sufficient to act as a reminder of the fragility of the system. Lancelot disliked philosophizing. He would always dismiss such talk as prattle, or at worst walk away embarrassed. But these unfamiliar and strangely sophisticated concepts had troubled him a lot lately.

And one of the consequences was the realization that he could not allow himself to sink into the placid idyll he had so enjoyed painting for himself.

He savagely kicked at a stone that rolled down the slope and into the camp. Three small, white faces turned toward his.

I cannot simply relinquish so many responsibilities, he told himself. I cannot give Galahad a free hand. The boy has a murderous look in his eye sometimes. He looks at Mordred's monster as if he were wondering where best to hit him, yet I cannot think where he gets it from. His mother was the gentlest creature living, and while I have been a cruel fellow in my time, my violence has ever been of the hot-blooded kind, a wild demon energy. There is something chilling and methodical about Galahad that horrifies me at times, and until he learns to control his murderous urges then must I be around to curb them.

By the time he reached the bottom of the hill, his mood was thoroughly sour and irritable. "Get up, you idlers. It is time we parleyed with these folk across the valley." So fierce was the look he gave them that the others complied swiftly, without complaint; even the normally sluggish Finn sprang lightly into the wagon and, settling himself into a position of relative comfort, lapsed into a contemplative silence.

What does he think about? Lancelot wondered. Lately it had occurred to him that the creature could in fact think. He had noticed this when last he had discussed Finn with the others. The monster all the while was clearly conscious of his loathsomeness; in his pale eye was written apology and shame. Yet he had a residual pride also, and on at least one occasion Lancelot had caught a gleam of resentment, a brief look that seemed to say, Take care that you do not lightly regard me, for I may do much that will astonish you.

Finn had stopped complaining about his bonds and his other discomforts, and spoke only when addressed. Instead he would sit quietly, regarding the others with a polite unconcern that they found vaguely unsettling. In that white, impassive stare of his there was an immutable calm, so that hideous as he was, there appeared to be a wisdom about him that at times almost commanded respect. I do not regret sparing him, thought Lancelot, but it may prove necessary to dispose of him later, and that I ween I shall regret.

As they rode across the narrow plain, he could hear urgent whispers passing between Mordred and his son, though he affected not to notice and did not turn around when Mordred called from the wagon. "What plans have you laid, Sir Lancelot, for dealing with these wild men?"

They were close enough to see tiny red faces crowding the ramparts. He waved at Mordred to be quiet.

The hill was steep but unguarded, and their approach to the outer ramparts went unchallenged. Lancelot could sense the excitement among the waiting Caledonians as keenly as he could feel the wind from the sea on his face and in his hair. Dozens of men with fierce beards and set expressions peered down at them; sunlight glistened on their helmets and spear tips. Though they had passed in safety thus far, Lancelot could detect the menace in the silent gaze of each observer.

They passed along the narrow, fortified corridor, the wagon wheels creaking loudly. If they were set upon now, they would not be able to turn the wagon around. But, despite all those inhospitable stares, they were not attacked, and this Lancelot took for an encouraging sign.

At the gate he stopped and looked up. "I would speak with your chief. Pray make our presence known to him, for we are knights of King Arthur who would parley."

A chorus of low murmurs greeted this request. Lancelot could discern no words, but the tone was perfectly clear, and he wondered if he should have left the wagon at the entrance to the corridor. The laws of chivalry, he well knew, did not obtain here, only the rough and ready customs of capricious barbarians. At any moment they could take it into their heads to hurl those spears at our heads, and we have no escape. He spoke again. "Gentle sirs, I pray you answer, so that I may state our purpose."

There was another pause, silent this time. Then a face leaned over the wall. It was not far from Lancelot's; if the two men had extended their swords, the weapons might have touched. The owner of the face spat onto the ground and said cheerfully, "Ooh, laddie, forgive us our manners, but we are unaccustomed to receiving guests."

Lancelot could see nothing funny in this jibe or in the manner of its delivery, but the ripple of laughter it evoked from the surrounding onlookers was another encouraging sign. If they are in such a good humor, he thought, then we may come out of this alive.

He supposed the man who spoke was the Caledonian chief, though there was little in his voice or bearing to confirm this. His thin face was red from so much exposure to the biting, salt-laden wind, and his red moustache stretched to his chin. In his narrow eyes lay a shrewdness that suggested he owed his position as much to cunning as to prowess. This Lancelot did not take for a good sign. He did not like to deal with cunning foes. They are not straightforward, and they do not play fair. I shall have to go carefully here, he told himself.

"Aye, well now," the thin-faced man continued, "we weened ye were indeed of King Arthur's court, else we'd have cut you down long ere now. You'd be Sir Lancelot, I suppose?"

And Lancelot, marveling at their intelligence, could only nod in reply, which seemed to give their chief great pleasure. "This is Galahad, my son," Lancelot added. "And this is Sir Mordred, the son of the King of Albion."

The chief was unimpressed. "I had heard that Lancelot was a giant of a man who picked his teeth with the tops of trees. You're but a wee fellow." Shrewdly stroking the side of his hawklike nose, he added, "I suppose King Arthur would not risk sending three such prizes unattended." He stretched his gaze into the distance. "But where are the rest of ye? We have heard that a puissant army was on its way, one that has slain many good Highlanders."

Then Lancelot was relieved, for even if their intelligence was remarkable, it was also patchy. "We are but the van," he lied.

The other nodded thoughtfully and replied, "Well, we have received you, and though we have sent you back empty-handed, yet we have tended you no hard knocks nor harsh words." Then to Mordred he said, "I hope you will tell that to your sire when next you— What is that?" In turning to Mordred he had noticed something moving diffidently in the back of the wagon.

"This is Finn, the son of Balor," Mordred promptly replied. "Say hello, Finn."

Finn turned to face him, but the Caledonian chief did not appear shocked by the horrid grimace or the brown and broken teeth within it. "So this is your secret weapon, is it? I know about this fellow." He glanced behind him as if to briefly reassure his followers, some of whom did look shocked. "You will never get that eye open, you know," he added helpfully.

"We did not choose to bring him with us," said Lancelot, who was anxious to talk about the business at hand. "I suppose if you know our names, you know also our purpose."

The chief smiled graciously. "I wit also that you are wasting your time."

Lancelot saw a line of approving grins spread on the faces of the men before him. "But the Grail is here?" he asked.

To this the chief did not reply, but Lancelot, sensing a slight movement behind him, turned in time to see Finn nod briefly to Mordred. The look in the creature's eye gave him the answer he needed. Leaning forward in the saddle, he called up, "This realm is King Arthur's, and you, though you like it not, are his subjects. Therefore I may rightly claim what is his."

The chieftain raised his eyebrows and waited for Lancelot to continue.

"I will tell you what I will do. I will fight your champion man to man. And the victor shall take the Grail on behalf of his lord. What say you to that?"

The men on the ramparts laughed. Their chief shook his head.

"Two of your champions, then. Two against one."

This time the laughter had an uncertain edge, for their manhood was being called into question. But the chief said, "We will not put so great a treasure at so light a hazard, for that will anger the gods." And this seemed to the rest a satisfactory answer.

Lancelot reached into a pouch that hung from his saddle. "In that case, I shall set your treasure against mine." He held aloft a purse that he then emptied to the ground. A thin shower of coins fell and lay glittering.

"There is a purse of these for you and for every member of your tribe."

He was lying; there were not so many gold pendragons in the whole kingdom, and anyway Lancelot had only the one purse.

But the Caledonians, even if they believed him, remained unimpressed. "What do you take us for?" asked their chief scornfully, and with his arm he swept the starkly beautiful but empty landscape around them. "What would we do with your baubles?" With both hands he prized open the torc that clung to his neck and dangled it from the parapet so that Lancelot could almost touch the twisted strands of gold. "We have treasures, too," he said as he gently pulled the terminals apart before replacing the torc about his long neck. Lancelot felt suddenly at a loss.

The Caledonians watched in silence as Galahad, at his father's behest, dismounted and picked up each fallen coin. They wore patient, expectant smiles as if they were waiting to hear what further inducements Lancelot might offer. But Galahad, who felt keenly the indignity of his position, believed himself to be the object of their wry, amused stares. By the time he had bent down to retrieve the last coin, his face was crimson with mortification and as he stood up again he gave the wooden gate a savage, ineffectual kick and called out, "Send out but a dozen of your savages, and I will show you who is fit to be master of the Grail!"

That has wiped the grins from some of their faces, thought Lancelot a moment later. But his satisfaction turned to concern when the Caledonian chief, clearly displeased, turned and gestured angrily to some of his men, who retreated from the ramparts. He thought, Now, did Gally mean twelve against one or twelve against the three of us? He did not think these warriors would prove such easy meat as their ill-armed brethren of the hills.

Galahad was standing too close to the gate to see

what was happening above him, and Lancelot wondered what his son was thinking as he stood there, feet firmly apart, hands defiantly on hips. He was proud of his son, though worried too.

Then the men who had been sent away returned, carrying a black cauldron above their heads. It was not the Grail. They tipped it over the ramparts, and a pale, yellow stream fell upon Galahad's upturned face.

"It is the Grail that is the master," their leader called out. "Were you to slay all my warriors, you would not change that."

Galahad, soaked and sorry-looking, black hair plastered across his face, arms hanging limply, turned to his companions with an expression of pathetic bewilderment. "They have showered me with water!"

"That's not water, laddie," called down one of the Caledonians, and the others gave vent to such coarse and raucous laughter that Lancelot could bear to stay no longer. "Come on, son," he said gently as he handed Galahad his horse. "Let us go and clean you up." And so he led them all away, steadfastly ignoring the jeers and taunts that followed them.

14

"OF COURSE," SAID LANCELOT AIRILY WHEN WE had rekindled the fire and Galahad had changed, "I did not think for a moment that they would accept our proposals. It is plain that they value the Grail too highly for that. But I needed to get close enough to examine their defenses." Galahad gave him a sour look. His own proposal had not been lightly made. Lancelot continued. "It does not look very hopeful, I'm afraid. A great deal of woodland has gone into the building of those walls, and the ditches around are steep. Some of the work looks as if it was but lately done."

"They were expecting us," I said.

He shook his head. "They were expecting an army, not three men and a—" He looked across the fire and stopped. But Finn, as he did so often lately, was staring abstractedly at something in the flames and paid us no heed.

"We must gain entrance somehow," said Galahad. "For I mean to be avenged." His initial pain and humiliation had gone. Now his voice sounded dangerously low and determined. We had thrown away most of his clothing, and boiled water for him to wash with, but still an odor lingered about him. It was sharp and pungent, and my nostrils stung whenever I went near him. Lancelot looked up but said nothing.

"If the only way in is through the front gate"— I waited until their full attention was on me —"then we must induce them somehow to open it."

Galahad heaved a disappointed sigh. "Bravo, Mordred," he growled. But Lancelot eyed me shrewdly and nodded thoughtfully to himself.

I went around the fire to Finn and touched him gently, almost gingerly, upon the shoulder. He did not respond straight away; such had been his manner since our arrival at Carbonek. When I nudged him again, he seemed to waken slowly. "Come with me," I said.

As we walked away from the camp I heard Galahad mutter, "There goes the prince with his tame monster." Quite unjustly, I felt more annoyed with the inoffensive Finn than with Galahad, and snapped at him to move faster.

When we were out of sight and hearing of the others, he drew level with me and said in a voice both mournful and confiding, "It is here."

"We already know that."

"It is calling."

"What?" I stopped and looked at him. "What do you mean? Calling to whom?"

"To anyone who cares to listen." He placed a twisted finger over his mouth. I could hear the wind blowing across the wide, white-capped waters of the loch. "What does it say?" I whispered.

He gave a contemptuous wave of his hand. "You are not listening." Then he sank onto his haunches and became once again distant and contemplative.

"We must open the gates," I said.

He nodded absently.

"That is difficult for us."

He nodded again, and it was plain that mine was not the only voice that was vying for his attention.

"Perhaps it is not so difficult for you," I continued.

"Perhaps not," his voice dreamily echoed. Then suddenly he was alert again, scratching energetically at the sores on his soft, hairless head. "Do you want me to tell you where it is?"

"Please."

His pale eye became bright and intense. "First they placed it in a shrine, in one of their houses, on a high altar with many candles about. But though the room was fast shut, a great wind came in and blew out all the candles, and when they were relit so also were they extinguished again. So they placed it instead in a deep pit, for, being men and creatures of the light, they feared this thing that so hated the light."

"And this pit — is it such a deep one that it may not be reached?"

His head rolled slowly on its thick stalk as he seemed to scan an unseen horizon. "It is not deep," he finally pronounced. "And the object may be fetched up by anyone brave enough to do so. It lies in silence and in darkness, useless, doing neither harm nor good."

I wondered at him, at the strength and wisdom in his voice and in his words. "It is not right," he intoned, "that something so ancient and powerful should lie idle."

"Then must we two fetch it up," I replied.

He became thoughtful for a moment. Then a look of childish cunning crept into his face. "Perhaps we could help each other."

I said, "I will do what I can."

This went a little further than my earlier promise but still, I felt, did not bind me too closely. Did I intend doing anything at all for the poor fellow? In the light of subsequent events, I like to think that I had some notion of helping him and his fellows, and if my promises were vague it was only because I was uncertain of how best to fulfill them. But I did feel a stab of guilt as his credulous and trusting face creased with pleasure.

We went a little farther off, as I did not wish to be disturbed. "I cannot do this if I am bound," he said, extending his hands.

"Yes, you can." I do not think he would have tried to run away, for he needed us as much as we needed him. But I thought of Lancelot's wrath and would take no chances. "You are only practicing, after all."

He gave a mildly petulant shrug, and for a moment I thought he might prove difficult, but all he said was, "I am out of practice. I have only done stones and trees lately. They are easy."

"Could you mimic one of those warriors we saw?" I was not very hopeful.

"Alas, I think I am too like a human for that."

This sounded to me like heinous blasphemy, but I wanted to encourage him, so I said, "What about an animal, then?"

"I might be able to do that. Something they would open the gates for, but not eat straight away." He snorted with laughter, then abruptly stopped as a look of concentrated seriousness appeared on his face. He took a noisy, deep breath through his nose and held it for several seconds.

The seconds turned to minutes, but still I did not see him breathe out. Nothing else seemed to be happening, so I became convinced that this was not going to work after all. Then his mouth disappeared, and I realized that I was indeed witnessing a transformation, but one so slow as to be imperceptible till now.

The process quickened; first his face, then his whole body began to flow and contract in spasms that started tiny but grew bigger and moved faster. I felt suspended between incredulity and terror as one by one the rest of his features disappeared beneath engulfing folds of new white, rippling flesh. Each time I blinked and looked at him again something else had gone — his eyes, then his mouth, even his clothing — until all that remained was a large, slightly quivering mass, featureless except for the rope biting into the soft flesh where the wrists had lately been. Somewhat egg-shaped, the body (if it could be called that) rested heavily on its foundation of wrinkled skin and trembled with a quiet, obscene expectancy.

This was the most horrible of the visions that I beheld that afternoon; still I could not forbear touching it, despite my repugnance. But as I bent forward the trembling increased as if in warning, and when I looked down upon the thing I saw that its body was partly translucent, and that buried deep within was something black and coiled, like a worm. It pulsed and expanded even as I watched, so that I sprang back with all haste lest it come bursting out upon me.

Your mother may have been a sorceress, I chided myself, *but still you are out of your depth here.*

Slowly, accompanied by a hideous tearing as tortured flesh and twisted bone strove to accommodate itself to its owner's commands, the egg-thing began to change. Veins and arteries burst to its surface; an intricate network of black and purple canals that coursed their way about that writhing and now shapeless mass as it stretched itself in all directions. From within there came a constant bubbling and boiling and occasional claps like a great breaking of wind. Also I could hear a deep, painful groaning.

But something else was happening too: Oh, wonder! The thing was covering itself in a brown, leathery hide, and even before this was finished I saw a scattering of coarse hairs that spread and thickened rapidly. There was another deep groan as something pushed its way bloodily out of that painfully gestating mass. It was a hoof — soft and newly formed, but distinctly recognizable! — and I bit my knuckles to contain my mounting excitement.

Another hoof appeared, and I almost cheered, except that I did not want to bring the others running just yet. Then, in the next heartbeat, Finn had appeared again, sprawling in a mess of blood and bile, his legs kicking spasmodically in the air.

"Oh, but it hurts!" he sobbed. "I cannot do it after all. Ohh!"

I dragged him from his noisome pool and helped him to his feet. His face was an even ghastlier color than usual, and tears were coursing down both cheeks. *It does cry, then,* I thought.

He rocked slowly on his trunklike legs and hugged his stomach. "It is too much."

"Come on." I punched him on the shoulder for encouragement. "You nearly became something I recognized."

"Can I not do a tree? I am good at trees."

"No," I said firmly. "A tree is no good to us. Have a rest, and then we will try again." He gazed at me imploringly. "There is no other way," I said.

I believe the poor creature really was in terrible pain at times — imagine trying to turn your body inside out. But though I felt for him and the unimaginable torments he must have suffered as he writhed and contorted his way from one grotesque mutation to another, I could not let up.

I wanted the Grail, you see. Every bit as much as Lancelot, and probably as much as Arthur and Merlin. I am not sure why; perhaps I had finally succumbed to the lure of the Quest, no matter its purpose.

Whatever the reason, I was now determined that we should succeed, and so intent and singleminded did I become that it never occurred to me to laugh at Finn's ludicrous failures — the two-legged cow that rested pathetically on its haunches with its udders dangling from its throat; a man-sized cony with yellow teeth that spat savagely at me so that I dared not approach. Perhaps strangest of all was a creature with the face of a dog and great back legs, upon which it sprang ceaselessly up and down. "I do not know what it was," gasped Finn when, exhausted and tearful, he resumed his normal shape. "I cannot see what I am, so how should I say what I am called?"

"There was a pocket of skin in your belly," I said with a grimace. "Is that where it feeds?"

He nodded to himself as if recollecting. "That is where it keeps its young." He held up his wrists again. "It does not help, my being bound like this."

I pictured him hopping into the distance and vanishing from our sight ere we could even saddle our mounts. "Later, when you have made something of yourself," I promised.

"A mirror, then. That I may at least see what I am doing."

There was no such thing in the wagon, for Lancelot had left his vanity at Camelot. So I fetched my helm and polished it with my sleeve, and this did to some extent suffice.

* * *

It was almost dusk when I returned to camp. Lancelot looked up from a crouch and watched me approach from a distance. I thought he might come running when he saw me returning without Finn, but he kept his place. Then, when I got close enough to see his face plainly, he stared at me irritably. "Where have you been, Mordred?" In his hand was a sharpened stick, and the ground at his feet was stirred up, bearing traces of the many abortive plans he had sketched and erased. "And where is the son of Balor?"

"He is no more," I declared, and waited just long enough for their mouths to drop open before adding, "But see what I have brought you instead." I motioned back toward what was hiding behind a large nearby tree and stood to one side to watch the fun.

I do not know which sight occasioned me the most amusement — Finn as a ludicrous, mottled heifer that hobbled along on three legs because the fourth was too short to reach the ground, or the faces of my companions as they rose unsteadily to their feet in staring disbelief. Galahad almost fell backward into the fire as in his panic he reached for his sword.

"Calm yourself, Gally," said Lancelot shakily, taking the boy's arm. "I am sure Mordred has an explanation." And he looked at me and shook his head, though whether in wonder or in disapproval I could not tell. "What have you been up to?"

"Come and see." I stepped forth and gently patted the cow's broad back. Its great nostrils twitched; it wheezed heavily as if the simple matter of existence required great effort. But its eye — yes, there was only the one — was blank and unregarding as we gathered around and examined it.

"Their chieftain joked that this was our secret weapon," I said with justifiable pride. "Well, so it is."

"And how do you propose to use it?" said Lancelot, drawing back in distaste from the grey-and-green mottled skin that in places was like a furry mold.

"The cattle are kept in an enclosure outside the walls. If they are expecting an army, then they will shortly bring them inside."

Lancelot nodded. Galahad laughed softly to himself as he examined the useless hind leg, dangling halfway between its hindquarters and the ground. "It is quite the ugliest beast that ever I have seen." Gingerly he poked its back. There were places where the moldering hide had not quite covered, and these still had the texture of human skin, though the colors varied — white, pink and purple. "Ugh!" he exclaimed, stepping back as the animal gave a snort of pain.

"Be careful, Gally!" I said sharply, for Finn had started to tremble violently, and I recalled that thing of evil that lay coiled deeply within. "He still has his sores. And he is sensitive in other ways, too." To my relief the trembling subsided. "If you must carp, then do so out of earshot." To Lancelot I said, "We can smuggle him into the enclosure tonight. It is not guarded, being so near the fortress."

Lancelot's eyes were narrow and skeptical. "That . . . that thing; it smells of death. It smells of the grave, Mordred. Did you not notice?"

For goodness' sake, I thought. *This is no time to be having such scruples.* Then he said, "Still, it is a bold plan, and I ween we must try it, for we have no other."

"There are at least forty cattle in that enclosure. Among so many he should escape scrutiny."

"At night, perhaps, but not in daylight. If they are to move the cattle, then it must be at night."

Galahad came up behind me and said in a low voice, "Let us fire the enclosure tonight. Then they must bring in the cattle."

I turned toward Lancelot with alarm on my face, but he seemed to think this was a good idea. "Will he run from the fire?" he asked me. "Or will he stay?"

I looked across at Finn, bovine and placid and tugging at the grass with his broken teeth. But evidently he had not learned what to do with it next, and so he spat it out again. "Whatever we do," I said, "we must act soon, else he will starve to death."

Lancelot eyed me sternly, still waiting for an answer to his question. "I do not know," I said. "It was not easy to get him to do this, you know," I said. "We have been practicing for hours. And he took some persuading."

Lancelot folded his arms impatiently. "Will he stay or will he run?"

"If he thinks he will have the Grail, then he will stay," I said quietly.

"We cannot tell him that."

"I must tell him something. This is our only chance of getting inside."

"It would not count," Galahad said helpfully. "Any promise you make, you cannot be held to. You are a prince." He patted my shoulder soothingly. "Princes do not make promises to churls, and that thing is far lower than a churl."

Lancelot sighed gravely. "Do what you think is best. But I do not want to know about any promises made or broken." He cast another look at the sorry creature. "I have promises of my own to keep," he muttered as he stalked away with Galahad beside him.

I think he was feeling rather uncomfortable at that moment.

But then, what about me?

15

IN THE SLOWLY DYING DARK, THREE RIDERS SAT waiting for the dawn. Occasionally one of their mounts would nod its head or a bridle would gently ring, but for the most part they were motionless and soundless, like grim, forbidding statues.

The eyes of the middle rider were trained toward the east as he watched for a sign. When he saw it — a dark rift of water lightly streaked with grey — he nudged his horse gently forward, down the slope to the valley floor. His companions followed, the darkness clinging to them like a fog, blurring their shadowy outlines. They did not speak much, for they were concentrating on the pace of their mounts. It was their intention that they should reach the other side of the valley at the very crack of dawn — not too long before, and certainly not a moment after. When they did converse it was briefly, and in low, urgent voices that seemed to travel through the thin tunnels of cloud formed by their mingled breath.

"Are you sure he understood you?"

"Yes, yes. Do not worry."

They passed close by the enclosure where the cattle were kept — until last night, that is. They could not see it, but they could detect a few embers glowing faintly, and the wind brought the smell of smoke and ashes to their nostrils. That part of the plan had come off quite perfectly.

"Can they see us yet, Father?"

The hill across the valley was a dark and shapeless blur, and Carbonek was still hidden in its encompassing shadow. Lancelot thought, I know what daylight is and I know what the night is, but I have never seen this long moment, when the two are delicately poised. Never really seen it, that is. Without turning he said, "Can you see them?"

"But they will see us," Galahad muttered behind him. "At any moment."

"And when they do it will be too late," Mordred assured him.

"If he opens the gate," whispered Lancelot as the black sky turned to overcast grey. "If he has not taken the Grail for himself and privily made away with it." When they had talked at all during their long, uncomfortable vigil, it had been about this.

"He will not do that," said Mordred. "I have made him a promise."

"Ah, yes," said Lancelot, not happily.

"I mean to honor it if I may," Mordred added in impulsive defiance.

To this Lancelot made no reply.

By the time they reached the valley's farther side they could see each other quite clearly; pale faces encased in black armor, anxious because they had endured a long wait and could not be sure that the waiting had not been in vain. At the foot of the slope they halted briefly. There was a sigh of iron on leather as they drew their swords, and Lancelot whispered, "When the gate is opened I will ride in first and take up the son of Balor, for my destrier is strongest and may more easily bear us both. You, Mordred, will fetch the Grail, for it behooves you as your father's son—"

"And I will slay their proud and orgulous king," Galahad declared.

"You will not. You will hold the gate until we two

have safely made our escape. Then you will straightaway follow."

Though he did not raise it above a whisper, the anger and frustration in Galahad's voice was plain enough. "He has shamed me, Father. Aye, and all of us."

"I know, Gally." Lancelot was genuinely sympathetic. "But you must put that aside for the moment." To them both he added, "Our purpose is much higher than the settling of old scores, and it must be achieved first. Now then." He looked up, seeing the walls of Carbonek slowly detaching from their surrounding shadows. "Watch and listen."

They rode at a measured pace up the hill, praying that the horses would make no noise (thanks to the soft ground and their riders' skill at keeping them calm, they did not) and with Lancelot leading the way, for along the narrow corridor no more than two could ride abreast.

Lancelot saw the ramparts, a black row of evenly pointed teeth, and along their top a figure that was slowly pacing. He could even hear the muffled slaps the guard sent out as he pounded his arms to keep warm. Let us reach the gate before he sees us, he prayed.

He saw the guard halt in his tracks and peer through the half-light, and he pictured to himself the disbelief on the man's face as he bent over.

Then he realized that he could not see the guard's face — the man was looking away from him. Whatever it was that claimed his attention was happening within the walls. There was a moment of silence as Lancelot watched, puzzled; then the guard gave a choked cry of surprise that was partly drowned by the creaking of iron hinges.

A thin bar of grey light seemed to split the ramparts. Then, as the beam of light slowly widened, the guard shouted again, finding his voice this time, for he gave a harsh, animal-like cry that, though wordless, was loud enough to waken all those who slept within. Galahad, who was a peerless shot, hurled one of his short spears, and the man disappeared from view.

* * *

My two stalwart companions raised their swords and rode through the gateway shouting, "For Arthur and the Grail!" I know that sort of thing is good for morale and steels a man's resolve, but I felt too self-conscious to join their hearty chorus though I made all haste to follow their advance.

Finn, now that he had pulled the gate back on its hinges, was cowering behind it, resisting Lancelot's efforts to pull him out, while the Caledonians, heavy-eyed and partly clothed, stumbled from their huts, fumbling for their weapons and peering confusedly in the half-light. Cries of alarm were echoing about the courtyard, but though they made a dreadful din, I judged we had a little while before our adversaries organized themselves into some semblance of order; perhaps even enough time to complete our task and make good our escape.

Except that Lancelot was pulling at Finn's arm and shouting, "Where is it, man? Where?"

And Finn, almost human again, was jumping up and down with an expression of agonized dismay while he pointed wildly in several directions. "I tell you, I do not know! It was there! It was there! Now it is gone!"

Lancelot cursed him roundly while Galahad looked on, grimly bemused. I was keeping my eye on the Caledonians. They did not try to attack immediately; though caught unawares, they were no fools and meant to gather their strength first, for they were forming themselves into an orderly mass about the edge of the courtyard. I turned to the gateway and to the sight of the slowly advancing morning light across those valleys and hills. There was safety there. Above the din of the Caledonian war trumpets I called to Lancelot, "It would be no shame to flee now. Rather would it be folly to abide when we are so overmatched."

Even as I spoke it, I did not really expect to dissuade Lancelot with such a remark. But I supposed I might get some support from Galahad, and perhaps his father would relent if he saw that both of us were of a mind. Galahad said nothing, however, and as I glanced in his direction I thought I detected scorn in his shadowed face. *How can he not agree?* I thought, feeling the irritation rise in me. For his response, Lancelot merely shook his head reluctantly while Finn stamped his feet like a child having a tantrum and cried out, "It is still here. It wants to be found!"

"For that reason only do we abide," Lancelot said, using words that addressed Finn and myself at the same time. Then, directly to the Fomor, he added, "Else we should leave you to fend for your miserable self!" He closed his eyes briefly, resignedly, then turned his destrier and dressed his shield to where our enemies were hastily assembling. The sweat inside my hauberk felt like a warm extra skin, and to still my trembling I had to grip my sword so tightly that the contours of the hilt pressed painfully against my palm. But I was as much angry as afraid. Rage rose rapidly inside me.

"Keep together!" shouted Lancelot above the clamor, but I was already gone, for I was determined to show Galahad — as Lancelot had seemed to realize — that my last comment had not been made out of cowardice.

A knight's warhorse, laden with its rider's armor as well as its own, can go no faster than a canter, but that is quite fast enough. Before my eyes the mane of my steed dipped and rose like a ship's prow while the line of our enemy seemed, by comparison, fragile and tiny. Already I fancied I could see the fearful expectancy on their faces as they warily dressed their shields and braced themselves. Reason got the better of me again; instead of plunging forward by myself, I pulled lightly on the reins and slowed my horse's charge. Then Lancelot and Galahad were beside me, their swords upraised, the noise of their mounts' hooves a remorseless drumbeat that for a moment drowned out even the awful cacophony of the war trumpets.

For one deluded moment as we neared the line of men, I thought we might fly right over their heads. But then came the horrible moment of impact when we plunged into a solid wall of human flesh and felt the gigantic pressure of bodies all about us. It was like riding into an enormous pillow, though not a very soft one. The screams of the enemy seemed suddenly as close to me as my own. My destrier slowed, and for a moment I thought he might grind to a halt, but I dug in my heels and he slowly raised his head and continued his progress. Those who would not give way or, because of the press of bodies, could not, were mauled by his hooves, while many others I slew with a blind, savage recklessness. Together we cleaved and trampled such a bloody passage through the Caledonians that his legs unto the fetlocks and my sword unto its hilt glistened darkly.

But their discipline was such that they quickly regrouped, hurling themselves at us with such eagerness as if they counted it an honor to have their limbs hewn. Amid so heavy a press I took little notice of individuals. Once I marked a huge, bearded fellow who advanced on Lancelot blowing a shining horn with a bronze mouth cast in the shape of a boar's head. So hideous a tumult did he make as if he thought to cast the knight from his saddle by the mere force of it. Lancelot spared him hardly a glance but swung his long sword in a slow, graceful arc that split the man's face and his fine instrument too, driving it into his teeth. For a second or two he remained unsteadily upright. His huge eyes, bulging with glazed concentration on either side of his shattered mouth, made him look as if he were desperately striving to extract one last note before he fell.

But in the main I meted death in a blind, anonymous fashion so that the faces of the men I slew blurred into a single ghastly image of snarling pain, and I marked only a messy series of hacked limbs and split skulls. Though afterward I did give some somber thought to the many widows and orphans we made that day.

As mounted knights we could withstand a great number of men on foot for a short while. Of course they tried to bring down the destriers, but their flanks and breasts were well protected, and those who dared approach from the rear were dealt such blows from their swift hooves that they soon changed their minds.

But we could not keep this up forever. For every man I killed, another stepped forward. I was reminded of a great wind that brushes over with ease the trees at the edge of a forest, yet loses its strength as it goes deeper in and the wood closes thickly about it. Thus far I had not been touched, for I kept my wits and my shield close about me and wielded my sword with a savage dexterity. But I could feel myself rapidly tiring; I was sweating profusely in my iron cocoon, a great, numbing weight that now tried to pull me down. My sword was so pitted and gouged that I weened it would be useless after this fight, whatever the outcome. And with weariness came doubt. *This is madness. What are we doing here? Has all my philosophy brought me only to this?*

Yet when the constant buffeting finally ceased, I was so taken aback that I nearly fell from the saddle, so great was my surprise and exhaustion.

Looking to where all the other heads were turned, I saw a great ball of noise and dust race into the courtyard. Within it, insubstantial and almost like a character in a dream, stood the chief of the Caledonians in his war chariot, his arms upraised — holding in his hands the precious Grail!

I say it was the Grail, yet all I could see when the driver with his fluttering whip finally halted that wild, spinning onslaught and the noise and dust subsided was a blurred, shapeless thing, vague and shadowy, yet blacker than night. The chariot was a beautiful thing and reminded me of Agravaine's as he had described it to me. Its wicker sides were decorated with golden rivets, and the heads of the ponies were clamped in bronze so that fire as well as steam seemed to dance from their angry nostrils.

Despite this finery, my attention was drawn inexorably back to the tiny storm cloud that swirled and danced in the chief's hand, swallowing all the light around it while I, straining to discover what lay within, felt awe and trembling much like that of a savage witnessing his first eclipse. All about me doughty warriors cowered like frightened children, and though I knew I should tear my eyes away as they were doing, I could not, for fear of tearing my soul also. At last I knew what Finn had meant. The Grail was calling me now; wordlessly, soundlessly, with ageless wisdom and infinite patience. I felt steeped in a restful calm, as if I were sinking into warm water that would drown me, though I cared not.

It was a cry from Lancelot that woke me from this insidious drowsiness, just as I was about to fall from the saddle. I stirred myself and raised my head in time to see him unbuckle his lance from its vertical mounting. At first he moved slowly, as if with a curious reluctance; then twelve feet of sharpened ash were set in rest, and he slammed down his visor with a crash that resounded through the courtyard.

Lancelot began to move forward, his powerful mount gathering speed with each step, its hooves hammering thickly on the packed and blood-soaked earth. The destrier reached a heavy canter, and Lancelot became a silver blur, leaning across its neck so that his eyes would not alight upon the Grail but on the ground racing beneath him. It was said that Lancelot could joust with his eyes closed.

The look of confidence on the chieftain's face turned to alarm when he realized what was happening, and he reached for his shield as his driver strove desperately to turn the ponies out of the path of danger.

Lancelot struck.

I should not feel sorry for the chieftain, for he was discourteous and unknightly, but against this onslaught he stood not a chance. His shield was made of thick planks overlaid with bronze, but Lancelot's spear tip burst through it as if it were parchment, split the man's chest, and hurled him into the dust. He lay there, kicking and bubbling horribly, while next to him the Grail rocked gently on its side. Whatever power it had held was gone for the present, for now I could mark clearly its shape and nature: a bronze cauldron, no bigger than and quite similar to many of those that served as cooking pots in my father's kitchens, save that it was exquisitely wrought and chased in gold and silver. It looked harmless enough.

Lancelot, who feared no man, did not think so. He was edging forward with caution, ploughing with his spear tip a shallow groove along the ground as he endeavored to lift up the Grail without touching it. Galahad and I watched in silence these deft maneuverings; the Caledonians too, for they were still shocked and uncertain yet how to act. So none of us noticed the approach of the thief.

Lancelot raised his spear, the Grail poised delicately at its tip. He turned to us and raised his helm so that we could see his face glistening with exertion. . . . And then it paled with fear.

The next moment he was cowering in the saddle, dropping both his lance and the Grail as he shrank from the huge shadow that encompassed him and the ground around him. I looked up to see a massive blur of feathers and beating wings sweep past my head, and then it landed heavily on the ground. The biggest raven that ever I have seen — for I swear it was half the size of a man — plucked up the cauldron in its great yellow talons and flew off again with such a shriek as if a hundred demented souls nestled in its belly.

Finn's practicing had paid off.

He perched briefly atop the ramparts and turned to regard us with a single eye that was not quite raven and not quite human. In that parting look I believe he was conveying more than one feeling: defiance, because he knew we could not follow; triumph, because he, a poor, misshapen thing, had outwitted the proud and overweening humans.

And I thought I detected a look of prophecy, too, in that pale, red-rimmed eye; he held in his claws not just the last desperate hope of his people, but their rebirth also. You will see great things, I pictured him wordlessly saying, when the people of the forest emerge to claim what is theirs.

Then the great wings rose and fell, and with a final, chilling shriek he vanished from the ramparts.

But I did not see him rise above them.

Galahad was the first to mark the significance of this. While the rest of us had been reeling with astonishment, he was noting carefully how slow and ungainly were the great bird's movements, how weighty the Grail seemed in its thick, horned talons. Even as the raven sprang shrieking from the walls, he was riding for the gate and groping behind him for his second spear.

Lancelot and I speedily followed, though to what immediate purpose I was not sure. Unheeding, we plunged through the still-cowering ranks of the enemy and reached the gateway as Galahad careered down the hill and across the valley, his spear upraised and his arm already drawn back, straight and taut.

Finn was only a little way ahead of Galahad, his wings beating with a slow, rhythmic heaviness as if the air about him was somehow thicker than for us on the ground. He was aware of his peril; he was weaving desperately from side to side. Even from such a distance, I could see that he was more human than bird, and I could sense his fear as he turned to view his implacable pursuer. I could sense too the agony in those tiring wings as they struggled to bear him farther aloft. The Grail was such a tiny thing, almost lost in the grip of those great talons.

He was not falling, but he was not getting any higher either, and I knew that Galahad would not miss. I knew also that I should not aid him, for his true intentions were clearly more mischievous than he had led me to believe. As I spurred my destrier ever harder, outpacing Lancelot and slowly gaining on Galahad, who had drawn even with his prey and was slowing to take aim, I shouted, "Let go! For your life, let go!"

I know that he heard me. Just as I am certain that it was human terror that I saw in his eye as he twisted and saw Galahad rise in the saddle to hurl his spear. But he would not let go.

The spear did not kill him. It flew straight through one of the black wings, leaving his body strangely twisted and momentarily frozen in mid-air before it plummeted soundlessly earthward. He managed to straighten his wings sufficiently to glide the final few feet and thus land gracelessly and with several bumps, but otherwise safely, on the soft ground.

I saw him change even as he bounced for the last time — a transformation so swift I might have missed it had I so much as blinked. I saw him make a futile grab at the Grail when his feet could no longer grip it, but though his fingers may have brushed it, the cauldron willfully rolled in another direction, and he was too sore and confused to immediately follow. I did not concern myself with the Grail; it could clearly take care of itself. Finn was rocking slowly back and forth on his haunches, lamenting with dismal human cries his loss and his bruises while he rubbed furiously at his eyes. There was quite a large hole near his shoulder but no blood as yet.

I dismounted and went toward him; I think I had some vague notion of comforting the wretch. He hardly deserved it. But neither did he deserve what happened next.

Galahad was both nearer and faster, and his sword was already out. Had I been closer, I could perhaps have stopped him. But I was moving with a dreamlike slowness while Galahad was fully awake.

As his head was roughly drawn back, the son of Balor gazed up at his murderer with a look of sadness and contempt. Unmoved by this, Galahad, wearing a grisly and implacable smile, brought down his sword and drew a glistening red scar across Finn's white throat. Then he sprang back in sudden alarm as the blood that issued in thick rivulets burst upon the ground to rise again as an incandescent wreath of steam that wove itself about the dying creature. I could see Finn's body, obscured within this swirling pillar, writhing in a sort of exquisite agony while on his face, as he strained upward, there was an expression of rapt concentration. His eyes rolled toward the sky as if they were following an invisible passage and I thought, *Can a man see his spirit as it leaves his body, as some Druids claim? And can something so contrary to nature have a spirit?*

The pink cloud slowly dispersed, and all that was left was a stiff huddle of grey flesh and tattered clothing. Yet there was something curiously restful about him now, too, as if death were really his preferred and most natural state.

With an expression of part satisfaction, part foreboding, Galahad sheathed his sword. "There was no need for that," I said rather limply. "The wretch was harmless."

"He was trying to open the evil eye. Another second and he might have succeeded. You should be grateful. I have saved us all." Galahad would not look at me.

"He was crying." A faint breeze from the sea was stirring the rags on that lifeless body. Beneath the overcast sky I shivered.

"Nonsense." He had the look of a man who is beginning to suspect his error, but is determined to put a brave face on things nonetheless.

Galahad turned to his father for support, but Lancelot was contemplating the Grail and had no interest in our quarrel. He had dismounted and picked up the cauldron. Now he turned it gently in his hands, stroking the intricately worked surface as if it were the skin of an animal or a lovely woman, and he was muttering softly to himself as he recognized the various scenes carved on the bowl. Then he turned to stare in puzzlement at the dead eyes and the huddled, shrunken form, already cold. "It feels so light," he said. "Almost as if . . ."

* * *

Arthur said, "I had the strangest dream last night."

Guinevere was cutting an apple for her breakfast. First she cut it into wafer-thin slices, then she cut the slices into tiny squares and rectangles. She took an age over this, for she knew how it irritated her husband; the faint, measured thud each time the blade bit into the table, the tiny lines of concentration that disfigured her brow — both of these things he hated.

Arthur, wincing but determined to be heard, went on. "I was alone in a dark tower without doors or windows, and as I wandered blindly in search of an exit the air about me seemed to press ever thicker and warmer, so that I was almost choking and could scarcely breathe, so thick and hot did it become.

"Then came a great blast of wind that blew cold and refreshingly clean against my face, and when I next looked about me I was standing in daylight with ruins all around. Now then, Guinevere, I know you set little store by my dreams, yet this was so vivid I can still picture every detail. What do you make of that?"

Guinevere scooped up some of the tiny wedges of fruit on the blade of her knife and delicately licked them off with her long tongue. Slowly and with a great show of unconcern she then turned to Arthur. "I'm sorry, my dear. What was that?"

* * *

". . . almost as if I could let it go and yet it would remain suspended in the air." Lancelot cupped his hands gently around the base of the bowl, his eyes wide with wonder and disbelief.

"Be that as it may," I said, gesturing toward Carbonek, "there is time for no more magic."

The defenders, having at last rallied themselves, had begun to issue from the gate in great numbers and, to judge from the noise that reached us across the valley, in great wrath also. Hastily we mounted and fled the place while men afoot and in swift chariots pursued us with thoughts of vengeance in their minds and screams of rage in their throats.

We rode past our campsite without stopping. "What about the wagon?" I called. But Lancelot merely shook his head, and glancing back I could see the chariot ponies were already gaining on our weary destriers.

They might have caught up with us, but they did not. I believe they still feared our prowess and would not assail us without their men on foot also. No doubt it grieved them sorely to lose both their chieftain and the Grail, but this much consolation they could enjoy: they had our provisions and stores, and at the last they had sent us packing.

The loss of the wagon troubled me greatly; if we should have avoided gentle society whilst in search of the Grail, how much more must we do so now that it was in our keeping? Lancelot, however, was not concerned about this, and soon I learned why.

Later that day, when he judged it safe enough for us to rest, he passed me the empty cauldron and bade me drink from it. Partly to humor him and partly too in order to satisfy my curiosity (for many stranger things had happened that day) I put it to my lips — and lo, a colorless, lukewarm liquid ran thickly into my mouth! There was the merest hint of sweetness, like water that is very lightly honeyed; otherwise it was tasteless. But it was nourishing also — for a whole day I wanted nothing more of food or drink, and thereafter when any of us did we simply took it from the Grail.

The journey back was uneventful — did the Grail have a role in this, too? — and for this reason quite pleasurable. On a fine spring day, three months and seven days after our departure thence, we came again to Camelot.

PART THREE

16

THE DAIS HAD BEEN CARVED IN MARBLE TAKEN from the quarries at Purbeck. The height and girth of a man and many times heavier, it rested on a platform of elm planks, which in turn rode on the thick wooden rods that on certain ceremonial occasions were used to carry King Arthur's throne. Six hapless servants sweated and cursed as they staggered about the Great Hall with this burden. But Arthur did not mind. "What do you think?" he asked his companion when they had set it down in a different place for the fourth time and stood drooping and panting like men saved from drowning.

Merlin said, "I am not sure, sire. It is rather a dark corner, don't you think? And when those doors are open, they will quite obscure it."

"Quite right, Merlin." Arthur nodded briskly to the servants who, with resigned looks and sighs, took up their burden once more.

He bade them set it down beneath the east window, so that the rays of the rising sun might catch the Grail. But when they had done so, he put one hand to his beard and another to his ear and said, "I am sorry, lads," for he had realized that in such a position he and the knights on that side of the Round Table would not be able to see the Grail without turning in their seats. "Try the west window."

As they staggered forth, he took up the Grail again

from the table beside his throne, cradling it to his chest as if it were alive and he could feel its warmth. He fell to examining again the panels of beaten silver, his fingers thrilling to their texture, his eyes twin silver orbs of possession and delight as they contemplated the elongated and elegant figures that stared out with blank, concentrated expressions. "What is represented here?" he asked for the fourth or fifth time, pointing at another place, and Merlin patiently explained that the scene in question depicted Manawyddan ab Llyr and his fortress of human bones in Gower. "And does this marvel really exist?" Arthur asked.

"Assuredly, sire, and it may be visited by anyone who is careless of his life."

"Remarkable," Arthur muttered. "I must tell that to the Table. Some of them will surely want to hazard such an adventure. And this panel?"

"That, sire, is Pwyll, lord of the underworld. All those figures groaning so piteously as they are ground beneath his merciless chariot wheels are the souls of dead warriors, now his subjects."

So realistic did this scene seem to Arthur that he put down the Grail with a shudder and turned again to his footmen, who were taking a brief respite beside the west window. "No, I'm sorry," he said with a sigh. "That's not quite right, either."

Arthur was in a good humor. The servants might grumble, and with good reason, but at least they had not felt the edge of his tongue nor experienced one of his terrible fits of rage. Since the Grail had come to Camelot, he and Merlin had been behaving much like children — only Merlin, as the elder, was better able to contain his excitement.

In the end the dais was placed in the most obvious place — in the center of the hall, with the circle of tables around it. Then King Arthur pronounced himself satisfied and called the three Grail knights unto him. As they knelt before him he said, "Truly, sirs, you have done the most worship that ever did knights in this world."

Lancelot, who was the least shy, replied promptly. "Such as we did was for love of thee, King Arthur."

Arthur then took the Grail and reverently placed it on the dais, but straight away he felt the lack of it so he took it down again and began explaining to them the stories of the various panels. "This one here, this is Morrigan the war goddess. An ugly bitch, isn't she?"

But not so ugly as the frown that knit his brow when Lancelot bent forward to touch the tracery. It was the briefest of scowls, and Arthur immediately regretted it, but Lancelot stepped back and did not attempt again to touch the precious cauldron.

Arthur felt ashamed, and also a little afraid. He was beginning to suspect that the Grail was not wholly a power for good. With some effort he passed it to Merlin, who replaced it on the dais. "There let it rest until we have need of it," he said.

Then, turning to the three knights with forced cheerfulness, he presented each with a torc of solid gold, far more rich and beautiful than those they already wore. "Just a small token of my gratitude," he said, adding, "And I have let cry a tourney in your honor. The best knights in all Albion will try their prowess in striving for the prize." He clapped his hands. "I tell you, it will be a marvelous occasion. I can hardly wait. Though I suppose"— he turned to Lancelot, frowning good-naturedly —"the result is a foregone conclusion."

Lancelot shook his head. He had thought to resume his carefree ways and dandified manner on returning to the court, but that had not happened. When the bored and beautiful ladies of Camelot had pressed him to recount his adventures, he had dutifully obliged, but his heart was no longer in it; the storytelling skill had left him. Instead he told them of betrayal and hardship, of fear and freezing nights in the open. He told them about the squalid and wasted lives that many of Arthur's subjects patiently endured, and one by one the ladies of the court drifted away in search of more entertaining discourse. Except for Guinevere, of course. Now the thought of a tournament, where he would be expected to joust with a lot of armored young fools and send them and their silly hopes rolling in the dust, made his heart ache. "I beg that you will excuse me, sire, but I think I should hie home, for I have left there many pressing concerns long unattended." He smiled wanly. "Besides, we should give the young folk a chance."

Arthur tried to look disappointed, though he was not. At least now it would be a real contest. "I cry you mercy, Lancelot. It is true that I have kept you too long from your business. And"— he became briefly grave —"you must not think this tourney is some idle amusement I carelessly devised, for we are in your debt and mean to repay you. We shall be making use of the occasion to announce our schemes and issue our commands. Isn't that right, Merlin?"

"You can rely on us, Sir Lancelot," said the Druid.

Lancelot was glad that the king would keep his promise, but he still meant to hurry home.

* * *

When they were alone Merlin said, "What may we not do, sire, eh?" He rubbed his hands with uncharacteristic glee. "Why, may we not bestride the world with our arms?"

Arthur was looking thoughtfully at the doorway. "I hope I did not offend him. He seemed rather reserved. That is not like him."

Merlin waved a dismissive hand. "Lancelot? Remember he is a Gaul, sire. They are all like that. Moody fellows." He was worried about Arthur. The king's enthusiasm seemed tinged with unease. Most times when he looked at the Grail, it was almost with reluctance, as if he were confronting a powerful adversary.

This time Arthur stared at the Grail for a long time, his sharp, clear breathing the only sound in the grey hall. When he eventually tore his gaze away, a silver light still gleamed in his eyes. This made Merlin very glad.

"Yes," he murmured dreamily. "There is so much to be done. Where to begin?" The question hung suspended for a moment, and then Arthur snapped upright in his throne. "Merlin, how old am I?"

"You are forty-seven, sire."

The king sprang to his feet. "I feel I am at the height of my powers. As if everything has been leading up to this. Do you understand what I mean?"

Merlin did not feel he was at the height of his powers; that had happened a long time ago, in King Uther's day. But he could remember what it had felt like.

"I used to dread going to my bed at night, Merlin, because when I awoke I would be gripped by a nameless terror."

"You have told me of this, sire." Merlin too had been forced to come to terms with the fear of growing old.

"Well, I shan't complain to you any more about it. But we must be careful, mustn't we, Merlin? We must not overreach ourselves."

Must we? thought Merlin.

Arthur was looking puzzled. "You see, I also feel . . ." The king's voice trailed off, but the silver light in his eyes was burning so fiercely now that for a moment Merlin was aware of nothing else. Had he been, or had either of them turned around, they would have seen the Grail as Mordred had first seen it — an angry, swirling cloud of darkness, evilly pulsing in the heart of Camelot. But instead Merlin was watching Arthur and thinking, What does he see — Oh, what does he see? Then the moment passed; the Grail returned to normal, and Arthur was shaking his head as if clearing a minor disturbance. He turned to Merlin and smiled slowly, somewhat vacantly.

"Sire, you must consider what you are going to say to the assembly. The tourney is but a few weeks away." Merlin thought it best to keep the king busy.

"There is so much that whirls about in my head, it is making me dizzy." Arthur fell back into his seat. "Help me to order my thoughts, there's a good fellow."

Merlin was delighted. So rarely was his advice invited in this way, without qualification. "Well, sire, you have always wanted a capital like the Latins have. I think Glastonbury would be an ideal place, don't you? There is the tor, and your academy."

"It's five feet under water."

"We will have it drained. This realm is full of idle layabouts. All those beggars who daily cluster at the gates — let us give them some honest toil." He paused before adding shrewdly, "Any king may build a city on a hill. Who but a puissant king would build it on water?"

An idiot king, that's who, is what Arthur should have replied, but the Grail had shown him some disturbing sights as well as tantalizing ones, and he was eager for diversion. He nodded, only a little doubtfully. "You may have something there. . . ."

"And what about your majesty's summer palace?"

"Cadras? Yes, I suppose I shall finish it one day."

"Why not now? You know how gloomy the queen finds life here."

"Ah, yes, it would be good for her to get away," Arthur said. He did not yet suspect Lancelot, but he suspected someone.

"It would be good for both of you."

Too late for that, I am afraid, thought Arthur. "You know, Merlin, for years I have been promising her I would rebuild the old place. She has never reproached me for not doing so."

"Then her patience deserves reward."

"And it would provide more work for the poor, would it not? Work brings dignity as well as bread."

Merlin nodded briskly.

That subject seeming to be settled, the king went on to another. "I have had some interesting conversations with Mordred since his return. You know, Merlin," he said as he shook his head in self-reproach, "there was a time when I did not greatly care for the boy."

Merlin was silent.

"This quest seems to have changed him. Or me. Anyway, it has been an education talking to him. He tells me that many of my subjects in the north lead truly pitiful lives, broken by poverty and wasted by privation and disease. Something must be done about that."

"Indeed it should." But Merlin knew better. He knew that a king may command many things, but not the natural ordering of men and their estates. Gently he added, "But, sire, I must remind you that before a ruler may be wise and dispense justice and give succor and the like, he must first be puissant and feared."

Arthur, who liked to be both of those things, said, "I suppose you are right."

"We are beset by enemies, and whether we like it or not they must be dealt with sooner or later, together or separately."

"I know, I know. There is the King of Northgales and of the Brigantes—"

"And Brittany. And the Latins. Don't forget, you have as good as promised Lancelot."

"I know all this, Merlin," said Arthur uncomfortably. "And I do not shrink from it. I feel we could take on the world and win. It's just that sometimes — only sometimes, mind — I wish there were other ways of settling matters."

Merlin was quite lost for a reply.

Then Arthur seemed to rouse himself. His initial enthusiasm may have vanished, but he was quite prepared to maintain a passable semblance of it. "You are right, Merlin. A promise is a promise, and I mean to discharge it to the full. We shall drive the perfidious Latins back over the Alps and liberate our Celtic brethren who groan beneath their yoke." He shook his head again, though he could not completely dislodge the cloud that had settled within. "No, by Bran, we shall march on Rome itself!"

Merlin's eyes briefly closed in quiet satisfaction.

"And when we have done all these things," Arthur said, "we shall have peace at last in Albion."

* * *

It had been a long time since my father had let cry a tourney, and the news brought people flocking from every part of the kingdom; from Wales and Scotland and the Out-Isles as well. During the days before the lists opened, the fields and meadows around Camelot became a vast tented city, and the baileys of the castle became so crowded with pedlars and gaping sightseers that for us ordinary inhabitants it was like being under siege.

In the past Arthur had objected to tournaments, denouncing them as futile displays of vanity, wealth, and bravado. Seven years before he had permitted one in Camelot. After only two days, it had degenerated into a vulgar brawl between rival squires, and in the ensuing confusion a number of spectators had been fatally injured. Afterward Arthur issued a proclamation suspending all tournaments, declaring that a knight's first duty was to succor widows and orphans and to bring recreant knights to justice, not to indulge in swaggering displays.

Alas, only the best of his knights were prepared to follow these admirable precepts. Most of the members of the Round Table were little more than armored thugs — a restless, violent, and impetuous crowd for whom fighting was as essential as meat and drink. They did not take kindly to the king's edict and responded to it by holding "secret" tournaments in the privacy of their own castles.

Arthur was gravely displeased at this, but there was little he could do. He needed a large body of armored knights, and, the times being what they were, he could not afford to be too particular. So he made occasional examples of those whose disobedience was intolerably flagrant, but to the rest he had no choice but to turn a blind eye.

Now it seemed he was prepared to go even further in the other direction, much to the dismay of those knights who had long supported his campaign for chivalric reform. Not that the thugs had things all their own way. Arthur changed the rules so that all combats were to be between individuals with arms blunted. This angered many for whom the melee, or miniature battle, whether as spectacle or means of settling old scores, represented the climax of a tournament. Still less popular, especially among the poorer knights, was the ruling that no ransom or other forfeit might be demanded of a fallen opponent. The only material reward the king himself would offer was a circlet of oak leaves.

"What each of you will be fighting for," he told the assembled knights and their retinues when they had all gathered at Camelot for the days of feasting that would precede the tournament proper, "is the honor of your respective ladies, and whoever carries the prize away, then his lady will be acknowledged to be of most virtue in all the land." With a disarming smile he added, "Of course, should you not win, it does not mean that your ladies are therefore lacking in virtue."

It was all very well for Arthur to try to boost the flagging ideal of chivalry in this novel way, but his scheme placed me in a quandary. Hitherto it had never greatly concerned me that I had formed no attachment, but as the king's son and a Grail knight to boot, I would be under heavy scrutiny in this tourney, and even ere it began everyone would want to know about the lady for whose honor I professed to fight.

On the evening before the lists opened, there was yet another noisy feast in the Great Hall. The Grail had been removed to Merlin's workshop for safekeeping (and because Merlin wished to discover its magic), and many extra tables had been brought in so that there were several Round Tables instead of one. I had contrived to sit next to Guinevere, and amid the shouting and cursing and general bad manners of the guests we attempted some sort of conversation.

"What's that?" she shouted, leaning her head so closely that I could see the flame-colored strands of her hair stirred gently by my hot breath. I repeated myself, and this time she heard. "No, Mordred, I do not have a champion. Your father is getting a little too old for that sort of thing. And Lancelot has left us."

I did not hear her sigh. I saw her lips part for a moment, and the briefest of wistful looks came over her visage. Then she turned to me with a girlish smile. "Why do you ask? Does my virtue need a champion?"

In spite of Lancelot's sudden departure, she was in a cheerful mood. Arthur had told her that he was finally going to restore her father's old castle at Cadras, which had been destroyed during the early wars of Arthur's reign. It was the place where she had spent her childhood, and so, I suppose, she had many happy memories of it. It was at Cadras also that Arthur, barely a king then, had first met and later paid court to her.

"The queen should have a champion," I replied, swallowing my embarrassment. "I will be your champion if you like."

She touched her long, white throat and gently smiled. I avoided her eyes and looked elsewhere while waiting for my answer. I saw several men looking at her hopefully, each no doubt thinking that her gesture had been meant for him. Men were always looking at Guinevere.

"Oh, Mordred," she said after an interminable few seconds, "wouldn't you rather have someone who is nearer your own age?" She must have seen me frown slightly then, for she dropped her humorous tone, reached out and touched my cheek and added warmly, "My dear boy, I should be honored to be your lady."

I had not frowned at Guinevere, but at a careless guest at an adjoining table who had spilled his beer. The brown puddle had begun to creep across the floor toward us. As a servant arrived to clean up the mess and I sat wondering if anyone else could see the imprint of Guinevere's hand burning on my cheek, she said, "I do hope you win, though. If you do not, I dread to think what people will say of me."

* * *

To be the victor of a joust, a knight has to achieve one of three things: he must either unhorse his opponent, break three spears squarely on his shield, or strike off his foe's helm without causing undue injury. Sometimes, according to the usual rules, the issue was decided on foot, but Arthur had forbidden this also, as too often it led to frayed tempers and bad feelings. During the three days of the tourney I unhorsed seven opponents, broke forty-three spears, and struck off three helms. I also struck spear tip to spear tip with Sir Bedivere, which was deemed so rare a feat as to deserve a prize in itself.

Next came the Passage of Arms, where those knights who had fared best in the jousts would set up their pavilions about the field, declaring it their intention to defend that spot for the space of a day against anyone who cared to challenge them.

Eight knights hammered on the shield that I placed outside my pavilion, and of these I defeated seven. I deem it no shame that the last, Sir Bors, unhorsed me, for he was a redoubtable knight and brother to Lancelot.

That I took the prize is, I admit, due in some measure to the fact that many of Arthur's best knights were either away succoring widows and orphans or had declined to take part in what Sir Gawaine, for one, dismissed as "playfighting." But I defeated some formidable adversaries as well as many mediocre ones, and for that I thank my skill in the saddle, a steady aim, and a strong right arm — as, no doubt, did Guinevere.

I thought of her as we sat that final evening across the crowded hall from each other (for I was seated in a place of honor opposite the king and queen). I watched her constantly, and she would occasionally reward me with a glance and a brief smile. Yet afterward, when the feasting was done and the revelers had staggered drunkenly to their beds, it was not Guinevere who came to my chamber but another.

I cannot remember her name (if she told it to me) nor can I recall many of her features, save that she had dark hair and was passing comely. We must have spoken, yet I cannot remember the words that passed between us. Sometimes I wonder if she was real at all; perhaps she was a fairy or a clever illusion devised by Merlin. But fairies were rarely beautiful, and anyway Merlin was not so skilled as that. But when she entered she was carrying a candle, and in its dim, trembling glow she certainly seemed unreal.

About her neck was a fine silver chain that glistened so that when she removed her clothes and only the chain remained, I fancied that moonbeams were woven about her throat. I sat up in my bed, and she sat next to me and began kissing me — gently at first, then (as with practice I improved) more firmly, so that within a short time I was doing things with my mouth and hers that I never before had known about.

Then she knelt before me, her head level with my thigh, and as she bent forward with her mouth open and her eyes fixed on mine, a sigh of release filled the room. I started and looked about me in alarm before I realized that the voice was my own.

Firm hands pushed me back onto the bed, and then she was above me, her hips joined to mine in an embrace of such intensity that for a while I knew not whether it was pleasure or pain that I felt. *This is what my Father's knights boast of in their wild carousings,* I thought. *Well, I shall not boast about this. I shall tell no one about this.*

Oh, that it were possible to relive such sensations! That exquisite closeness of damp, beating flesh; the mingling of warm breath and tongues; the many incidental kisses and caresses. Though I am lucky, I suppose, to recall so much after such a passage of years. All these I still can remember: her arms like thin white columns, supporting her gently swaying body; looking down and watching my hips trembling involuntarily beneath hers, as if they did not belong to me but to some other; the pain as I bit my tongue to stifle my mounting cries; turning my eyes up to see a face lost in concentration and the simple silver chain swinging gently between her small, firm breasts. I reached up and grasped the chain in my hands, and she looked down at me and whispered something I could not hear.

When the noises in the courtyard woke me the following morning she was gone, but the broken chain lay on the floor.

* * *

Later Mordred went to find Merlin in his cavernous workshop. For once the Druid was not puzzling over the Grail, which stood gleaming and unattended on a shelf, but was instead busy with his latest invention — a siege engine that could fire a projectile over an enemy's ramparts. It appeared to be a simple enough device, a thick iron tube mounted on a wooden platform. But it was immensely heavy. Twelve men had maneuvered it down the narrow staircase into the workshop, and one of them would not be around to take it out again, for it had fallen on his hands.

Merlin was on his knees, tapping the iron gently in several places with a small hammer so that a series of dull rings reverberated about the room. "I trust you slept well, Mordred," he said without looking up.

"Gramercy, Master Merlin. What are you doing?"

For once Merlin did not resent the interruption. Despite the troubles he was having with his siege engine, despite the secret of the Grail still having eluded him, he was in a remarkably good temper. Since the Grail had been brought to Camelot, he had not suffered a single fit. His mind felt clearer and more lucid than it had for years; the rottenness at its core had — for the moment, anyway — abated. He felt safe, and all his problems wanted was but a little time.

"It will be a marvelous thing when it works," he explained. "But there is a flaw somewhere that I have not discovered yet." He had black rings around his eyes, and his beard was filthy, for he had been searching the barrel inside as well as out. "What happens is"— there was another dull ring as he lightly touched the metal with his hammer —"every time the projectile reaches here the tube bursts, sometimes with fatal results. This is the fourth casting we have made. I have lost count of how many Druids have been killed or injured." He looked up at Mordred, and his face creased in an ugly, knowing smile. "Are you sure you slept well? You look rather tired to me."

Mordred, who had heard many times the thunderous explosions behind the castle and had seen the bloodstained stretchers as they hurried to and from the infirmary, bent forward for a closer look. "Why is the tube bent so, Master Merlin?"

And Merlin, who was usually impatient of ignorant and inattentive laymen, replied, "So that when the projectile leaves the tube it will follow a trajectory that will take it over the walls of an enemy's fortifications."

"With what purpose?"

"When it hits the earth, the projectile makes an enormous hole. The defenders will think that demons, summoned by our dreadful magic, are burrowing out from the underworld." He folded his arms. "They will surrender immediately."

Mordred bent down, nodding. "What is this hole for?"

"That is the chamber for the firepowder. We set a taper to it, and"— he clapped his hands close to Mordred's ear —"bang!"

Mordred thought the Druid's playful manner ill became his age and status. He mulled over the problem for a moment. "Why not a straight tube?" he asked.

"Eh?"

"Why not cast a straight tube and set it at an angle?"

In spite of his good mood Merlin almost said, That's a silly idea if ever I heard one. But something made him pause, and instead he gave a noncommittal grunt, went over to his bench, and began turning over sheets of parchment. "What did you want with me, anyway?" he said absently.

"There are knights gathered in the courtyard outside, and a great many soldiers and wagons. What does it all mean?"

"They are tourneyers returning home." Merlin took up a quill and a rule, and with a patient, steady hand began plotting angles and trajectories.

"That cannot be, for they are my father's knights. I thought I would ask you before approaching him."

Slowly Merlin put down his instruments. A year ago he might have sent the young man packing, but Mordred was a Grail knight now, and even Merlin had to show him some respect. "We are going to bring the turbulent north finally to heel. Your father plans to lead the expedition himself."

"With the Grail, I suppose?"

"We know so little about its powers"— both of them turned for a moment to the shelf where it stood, as if in brief homage —"but we really need to try it out in the field, as it were."

Mordred began pacing the narrow spaces between shelves and benches cluttered with instruments and vessels and papers. A small, angry cloud of dust clung to his heels. "When I spoke with my father about the peoples of the north, of the great hardship suffered there, I thought he agreed with me."

"He does. He still does." Merlin watched the young man uneasily.

"Then what does he intend with fifty knights and more than a hundred men of foot?"

"Forty knights, actually."

"I see what this is." Mordred's face and body showed anger. "It is a punitive expedition. My father intends to burn and plunder and rob these poor folk of the little they have. Then he will return in triumph after laying waste his own kingdom."

"That is not it at all." Against such youthful passion, Merlin's defenses suddenly seemed to him weak. He was concerned, too, lest Mordred inadvertently do some damage with his wildly gesticulating arms. He wanted to get back to his calculations. The young man, he grudgingly conceded, had possibly hit on something. But, of course, that did not mean he was right about those other things as well. "You must understand, Mordred. Your father is a mighty king. This country will see none greater. People must be made to realize that."

Mordred's arms now hung limply at his sides, and he was shaking his head sadly. "I don't know, Merlin. I can remember when my father was loath to take up arms lightly."

"And that was one reason for all his troubles."

Then Mordred, angered by such glibness, said without thinking, "It seems to me the Grail has poisoned his mind just as surely as it has cleansed yours."

Even considering Mordred's new status, that was a bold and dreadful thing for him to say, and for a moment a shocked silence persisted during which neither man seemed to know what to say or do. Merlin, who felt that a display of justified wrath was called for, could only mutter inaudibly to himself as he gazed with crimson-faced concentration at his instruments and papers. Mordred's eyes alit on the cause of their quarrel, and for a moment they rested there. Presently he said, "I cry you mercy, Master Merlin. That was unforgivable."

Merlin was so relieved that he failed to notice the shrewdness that lay behind Mordred's shamefaced expression. "Think nothing of it, my boy," he answered eagerly. Then, to hide his own shame and embarrassment — for if Mordred knew about his malady, then who had he told? — he buried his head again in the cannon's mouth. "I will consider well what you have said — about the tube." His disembodied, muffled voice sounded almost mournful. "It seems to me a sound notion."

But Mordred was already gone, having stopped briefly to snatch up the Grail on his way out.

17

MORDRED GALLOPED ALONG THE NARROW ROAD through the forest, the Grail in its canvas bag bouncing crazily against the palfrey's flanks. He was thinking, *I have heard of fathers driven so mad by wrath that they have even slain their sons.* He remembered that, after the incident at the academy, poor Agravaine had been beaten within an inch of his life when he returned in disgrace to Northumberland.

But whether it was just the temper of the times, or whether men had always been like this, he did not know.

He did know that he was probably safe from pursuit for a while — there was more than one path through the Forest Sauvage — but this did not stop him from turning frequently to peer through the cloud of dust slowly settling in his wake.

He had been four years old when last he had traveled this path, in the company of Palomides. But not for a moment did he consider that he might have difficulty finding the way. As he approached a certain sharp bend in the road, he slowed almost without thinking. Then he dismounted and tied his sweat-stained animal to a fallen branch. He turned slowly several times in his tracks, wondering how he could know which direction to take when all the trees looked the same and when any of those gaps could have led to pathways, but somehow he did know.

He hoisted the bag over one shoulder and with his sword began hacking a slow passage through the thick undergrowth. No one has been this way for years, he thought. But a path through the wood might have existed here. . . .

The voice came unbidden, sounding not through his ears but directly inside his head, talking to him with the speed of thought: Indeed it did, the voice said. This is where your father came the night you were born, yet without leaving his bed. This is the place where we buried him, you and I.

Mordred spun around, sword upraised, but no one was there. In the distance he could still hear the patient shufflings of the tired palfrey and he could feel the lightest of cool breezes on his cheek. He lowered the sword and continued on his way.

When he reached the clearing — he knew straight away that it was the right one — he realized how unprepared he was for this moment. Of course he had expected to find a neglected wilderness and to feel a certain pang. But surely that would pass after a minute or two. She had been dead for twenty years, after all. But as he gazed across the expanse of dead bramble, so brown and seared that it looked as if winter might never have left this place, he was thinking, *There must be something here, something I remember.* And when he was halfway across he forgot entirely for a moment the purpose of his journey and began hacking instead at the tangled, brittle archways in a futile search for some tangible remnant — surely at least the postholes must still remain. But though he raised a choking cloud of ancient dust and dead thorns, he found nothing to attest to that uniquely lonely childhood. Eventually, exhausted, he fell to his knees and wept silently for several minutes.

He must still have been tired when he picked himself up again and hoisted the Grail to his shoulder, for it suddenly felt much heavier.

He was a long way from the road now, but still he had no difficulty finding his way. Sometimes he would hesitate and raise his head before forking one way rather than another, almost as if he was smelling his way.

And yet he did not feel at home amid the gloomy silence of the forest. It was not comforting as it had been then. Once this had been a vast playground in which he had always felt safe. *But that was because Mother made it so.* He told himself that if the trees seemed suffocatingly close, it was only because he was much larger now. And if he felt cold, it was because the sun could not easily penetrate their thick crowns.

But the feeling that he was surrounded by the hostility of inanimate things would not leave him, even when more and more of the trees he encountered were dead or dying. Their spindly branches plucked at his shoulders like brittle fingers and broke with dull, lifeless cracks as he brushed them away. So great did his aversion become that he would bend almost double or wield his great sword against tiny twigs rather than feel their touch. *Is the forest dying?* he thought. *And from the center outward?* He was not going to the center of the forest — he could walk for months and never find that — but to its heart. What would he find there?

He wrinkled his nose in distaste as the smell of rotting vegetation grew stronger, more pungent. It seemed to be coming from below his feet; the ground felt soft and spongy, but it did not have the springiness of healthy woodland decay. Instead he had the feeling of stepping across a rotting carcass, and every time he trod on a concealed twig or root he would recoil as if those were dry bones cracking beneath him. He began to step more carefully, just in case the ground should swallow him up.

It was quite late in the afternoon when he came to the lake. Though few trees grew in the clearing, those about its edge were crowded so closely that their dead branches formed a roof against the light, making it seem almost like dusk. Mordred stood blinking for several seconds before his eyes could make out a number of shadowy, motionless figures. They crouched on the ground or in the thicker branches of the trees silently, like expectant apes. As he walked farther in and peered closer, he recognized their different species: a shrouded banshee, some hobgoblins, a boggart, but no individuals that he could name . . . none of his friends. But then, thanks to Finn, he knew where they were.

They all looked so dreadfully old. He knew they were not immortal, but according to all the stories they were not supposed to age. All he could see was desiccated flesh and hollow, pathetic faces.

They recognized him. As he passed through their thin ranks there was a stirring like leaves, and cracked, toneless voices whispered among themselves.

"Who's this, then?"

"It's only the bastard."

"He took his time, didn't he?"

The lake was as black and dreadful as he remembered it, but ever so much smaller too. He could have bridged it with his body had he wanted to. Of course he would not.

When he turned again, the Fomor had hardly moved. So far he had counted fourteen. "Is this all of you?" he asked, half to them and half to himself. In the old country they had numbered in the thousands. Even the remnant that had fled to Albion years before had been more than a hundred strong.

No one answered him. Perhaps in the gloom one or two heads nodded slowly; he could not be sure. Mordred removed the bag from his shoulder, took out the cauldron, and held it aloft. For a moment it burned with a pulsing yellow glow, illuminating some of those ghostly faces and causing them to look up. But the light quickly faded, and with it their interest.

"I have brought you the Sangrail," he persisted. "That

the son of Balor was commissioned to bring you. Well, here it is." He thought, *It is like declaiming to blocks of stone.* "Look here, I have gone to a lot of trouble to bring you this." He raised it again above his head, but it felt so heavy that his arms ached, and he quickly lowered it again. "It is your salvation."

The Fomor shuffled uncomfortably and muttered to themselves. Some turned their backs on him. A spirit of fatalistic gloom had settled about them; they had gathered at the lakeside to await not salvation but death. Some of the bodies that Mordred had counted were as good as dead already, judging by their faces. Apathy and resignation had become their settled choice, and those others that bothered to think about it at all resented Mordred's intrusive presence.

He sensed the resentment and was hurt by it, but he would not give up. Crouching before an aging sprite with a face like cracked parchment and a beard tapered and twisted like a goat's, he held the Grail to stubborn, closed lips. "Come on," he said gently. "It will do you a power of good. Just you see." The little man kept his head averted like a determined baby but after a while, realizing that his tormentor was not going to go away, he gave a sigh of exasperation and, snatching the cauldron with his crabbed and bony hands, lifted it to his lips.

"Not too much," cautioned Mordred, mindful of Finn's wordless prophecy on the ramparts of Carbonek. "It is a very powerful medicine." He took back the Grail, and the sprite returned to his sullen vigil.

After that it was easier; the others too decided it would be best to humor this interloper. There were even a few whose minds seemed to grasp the significance of what they were being offered, for their eyes seemed to light up briefly as they drank, and they blessed Mordred in quiet, hoarse voices when they had finished.

But on the whole the result was rather disappointing. Some of the Fomor found the energy to rise to their feet and drag themselves to another part of the clearing, like ruminants leisurely searching for fresh pastureland. But once there they simply settled themselves into new attitudes of patient melancholy. *Perhaps I was too sparing,* he thought.

He was debating whether to risk a further draught for those who would have it when a noise in the undergrowth made him turn. Through the trees he saw a flash of silver. Then six or seven giants, their armor palely glowing, trampled into the clearing, their steps clumsy but horribly purposeful. Behind them a smaller figure, white-bearded and dressed in a grey cloak, was struggling to keep up and to make himself heard above the noise of groaning armor and trampling feet.

The knights, cursing and sweating inside their closed helms, could not hear Merlin. Even had they done so, they would have paid him little heed, for they were very angry. They had armored themselves in expectation of meeting a foe who was formidable and possibly even magical as well. Instead, he was simply ugly. They stumbled across the clearing, swords weaving terrible patterns above their heads, their muffled, inaudible cries sounding like the trumpetings of distant beasts, determined that someone should pay for so much discomfort needlessly endured.

This second interruption stirred the Fomor more effectively than Mordred's had done. They rose uncertainly to their feet and began looking nervously about them for avenues of escape. Alas, for most of them, too late.

So while Mordred watched, dismayed and helpless — for though brave enough, he was also prudent and knew that without armor he could not meaningfully intervene against so many — and while Merlin rushed about the clearing with much useless energy shouting, "Stop! Stop this at once!" the last faeries of Albion were being briskly and bloodily consigned to legend.

Merlin's protests faded as he, suddenly aware of his

own imminent danger, tried to extricate himself from the confusion. The knights, after the roar of their initial onslaught, settled down to their butcher's work with grim, remorseless relish. The only sounds — groans and poor whimpers mostly — came from the Fomor themselves as they were variously decapitated, disemboweled, and thoroughly dismembered. Somehow the knights had got hold of the absurd idea that unless they made a thorough job of it, the Fomor would piece themselves together again. So even when their victims were dead the knights, with a seemingly inexhaustible ferocity, continued to madly hack at their bodies until the ground all about was stained and strewn with shapeless pieces of flesh.

Some of the Fomor were larger than their assailants and in former times might have dealt with them easily, but none resisted and few attempted to escape. Some of them, however, survived the bloodletting. Perhaps they had drunk a little more of the Grail's sweet liquid than their fellows, for they managed to avoid the sword blows with a marvelous dexterity and vanished into the forest where the knights, hampered by their armor, could not easily follow. But these too died later, mainly from grief and loneliness. They were not a very attractive body of creatures. At times they had been downright evil. But then, the same can be said of many humans.

Mordred watched an ungainly boggart lumber with little grace but prodigious speed in the direction of the protecting trees. Then he turned to Merlin. He thought as he slowly rose to his feet, *If I may not save these poor wretches, I can at least stop my father's fool from getting himself killed.* Dodging the clumsily flailing knights, whose blows were becoming wilder as their victims decreased in number, he guided the anxious and shaking Druid to the relative safety of a grassy bank on the edge of the clearing. "You should have known better," he softly chided. "Those men are half blind with their visors down, and in their present mood they would cut down Arthur himself and not realize what they had done."

Merlin was looking aghast at the bloody mess that lay all around him. Save for a small pile of heads that had been neatly stacked to one side, almost everything had been hacked beyond recognition. Gingerly he picked up a piece of white flesh spotted with coarse hairs, from which a colorless particle of cloth fluttered like a tiny banner. He turned it over in absent, puzzled fingers for a while, then threw it away. "All gone," he said.

Their exertions had evidently improved the knights' tempers, for they were grinning hugely as they now unlaced their helms. At last Mordred could see their faces — pink, glistening and brutal. He recognized most of them. The fat knight leaning on his sword as he gasped raggedly for breath was Sir Garad le Breuse; his brother Sir Arnold was also there. The two knights who were scattering remains about the clearing with their feet — just for good measure — were Sir Petipace and Sir Brandiles. Mordred knew all of them to be among the least regarded of Arthur's court; knights who had bought their places at the prestigious Round Table by means of calculated acts of generosity toward the king, or by bribing another member to overpraise their worth. "Really, Merlin," Mordred said. "These are men of no worship."

Merlin watched glumly as with a gleeful shout Sir Brandiles lifted the head of an elf from the pile and sent it sailing across to Sir Petipace. Because it was almost spherical it rolled quite easily when Petipace kicked it back, but as they continued to batter it back and forth between them it rapidly began to disintegrate — to the loudly voiced concern of some of the others, who objected to seeing their trophies thus abused. Merlin said, "I had no time to be particular. I was concerned about what you might do. I thought you were going to give them the Grail."

"That was not my intention. You do not understand."

There was another loud groan from the onlooking knights as Sir Brandiles, carried away by boyish excitement, gave the mud-begrimed and by now almost shapeless head such a hefty kick with his mailed foot that it finally burst altogether, showering a couple of bystanding knights with a thick, noisome brown liquid. Then Brandiles lifted up his foot, with a pointed ear still attached to it, and their dismay turned to laughter. No one noticed the few dripping fragments that fell into the pool or the brief, angry stirring of the water that followed.

Merlin's shoulders rose and fell, and he sighed heavily. "They promised to follow my counsel. I made them promise. How could they behave like this?"

"It is their nature." Mordred stood up. "You of all people should know that." When he lifted the Grail this time it did not feel heavy at all, and when he threw it toward the pool it sailed effortlessly over the heads of the capering knights and landed with a dull splash in the very center.

Merlin sprang to his feet in time to see the cauldron vanish beneath the black water, then bob up again to float as easily as any boat. The knights turned around with mouths agape. Merlin did not know whether to be shocked or relieved. "That was lucky," was all he could think to say. Brushing his hands on his cloak, he hurried over to the lake while Mordred, who had no more ideas, slumped to the ground, dejected and beaten.

Merlin was halfway across the glade, and one of the knights was already leaning over to retrieve the Grail, when the dark waters stirred again. Mordred looked up in time to see a delicate white hand rise swiftly from the depths and grip the astonished knight by the throat before jerking him forward. He was off balance, so he could not resist, and because he went in head first he could not call out either, but he made a great deal of noise for all that, kicking his iron legs like a huge protesting insect as he slowly disappeared beneath a surface that seemed to possess the texture of thick mud rather than still water. When his feet, noisily clicking to the last, finally vanished, the black water closed over again, leaving neither a trace nor a ripple. No one in that stunned company could speak. Even when an arm, draped in blue samite, rose again and this time continued to rise, they could only stare in silent amazement.

Mordred leaped down from his grassy platform shouting, "Come away now! Do not look! For your lives, do not look!"

More from instinct than sense, the knights sprang back and averted their eyes. Only Merlin would not turn away. *Old fool,* Mordred thought, even as he too felt sorely tempted to behold Nimue once more.

But his common sense prevailed, and he continued to gaze steadfastly at the ground. Though in the dread moments that followed he could hear nothing save the anxious breathing of the others in attendance, he could feel her presence and her quietly seething disdain as she contemplated her disordered realm.

Then she said, in a voice like ice, "I never had much time for those wretches. They were a loathsome and shiftless breed and have been going to seed for years now. All the same, Merlin, this is my sacred ground, and your friends here have made a dreadful mess of it."

Merlin's reply, when he was at last able to voice it, began with a painful, hesitant stammer. "I— I—"

Don't say I didn't warn you, Mordred thought.

Then the old man found his composure. "Forgive us, dear lady," he said. "It is the fault of these knaves. They did not do as I bade them."

Mordred snatched up the polished helm of a knight who cowered trembling beside him. In the reflection on its dented surface he perceived two distorted figures — a fragile ghost that hovered above the lake like a pall of blue smoke, and a prostrate old man with arms outstretched in supplication or yearning.

"I see," she said in a tone of affected hurt. "The Flower of Chivalry is too good for me. You brought these rank growths instead." Then she glanced away from Merlin and said, "That's a good idea, Mordred."

He dropped the helm in fright, and it rolled on its side at his feet. "But even if you were to turn around," she added coaxingly, "you would be perfectly safe. You have a certain immunity to my charms, you know." Bending cautiously, he retrieved the helm. "Besides, for your mother's sake I would not harm you. Not that we were friends exactly, but we might have become implacable enemies had she wished. Instead, though we lived so close together, we kept to our separate realms — she the queen of air and I of darkness — and neither challenged the other."

Mordred almost believed her. He dearly wanted to see her face more clearly. But he still would not turn around.

"I see you are a prudent young man." She did not sound offended. "Now you must tell me what shall I do with all these people? I am inclined to forgive the old goat, for he could be very useful to me." Mordred saw a wraithlike arm extend and brush Merlin's face, and a violent tremor briefly seized the old man's body. "But these others, they have offended me greatly, and I do not think your father would greatly miss them, do you? What do you think, shall I bake them in their tins?"

There was the faintest whisper of silk as the Lady of the Lake raised her arms, followed by a terrible cry from Sir Petipace, who, unable to endure any more, sprang to his feet and, throwing down his sword, ran screaming toward the edge of the clearing. He made a ludicrous sight as he waddled heavily in the direction of the trees, for the top half of his body was moving too fast for his stiff iron legs and he looked as if he might overbalance at any moment.

But there was nothing remotely amusing about the

horrible bubbling sound that his scream turned into only seconds after he disappeared into the forest. It did not even sound human. No one could see anything, but all the knights began cautiously sniffing the air.

Mordred said quickly, "No more — I beg thee, Lady. Let this be punishment enough."

He heard a gentle laugh. "Very well, Mordred. For your sake I will stay my hand. But they would do well to avoid this place in the future."

"I think they have learned their lesson, Lady."

"Tell them to take their picnics elsewhere."

"I will tell them." For the briefest of moments the flawed image in the helm became perfectly clear. A cold, ageless beauty stared into his eyes. The face that riveted his gaze, though he tried to turn away, knew nothing of human time or human error. It smiled on him with kindness and yet with scorn also. And behind the mask was a mind composed and tranquil, utterly indifferent to human good and human evil.

As the vision faded, Mordred felt something roll up against his foot. "That toss of yours was a nice gesture," Nimue said. "Idealistic, thoughtful. That sort of thing would make your mother very proud. But really I have no use for the thing."

He picked up the Grail and briefly examined its delicate contours with his eyes and fingers. Considering what it had been through lately, it should have sustained at least a dent or two. But of course it was perfect. "Why did it not work?" he wondered aloud.

"It is just like my medicine," Nimue explained. "Marvelously effective when applied at the right time, but useless otherwise. Those wretches were too far gone. And the few that escaped will not last long." She laughed again, and it was as if a cold breeze wafted through the clearing. "And of course the Grail does not help just anyone. It is potent but fickle. A bit like me."

Then, in a harsh, toneless whisper, Merlin spoke

again at last. "Take these men and go, Mordred. Wait for me at the path, and I will attend thee later."

Mordred took up his mirror once more. The Druid was standing now, though not very steadily. He was like a drunkard or a sleepwalker. His body largely obscured Nimue's. All he could see of her was the faint outline of her blue gown, like an aura around Merlin as he rocked slowly on his heels.

Throwing down the helm, he called to the others to follow closely. Because he knew only the one path out of the clearing, he had to first lead them around the pool while Nimue's teasing laughter rang in their ears. But then, they were a ridiculous sight. With their heads stiffly averted as they tried not to look around while at the same time trying not to slip on the blood-soaked ground, they stole away in a slow, crablike shuffle like exotic but ungainly dancers.

As he stepped out of the clearing, Mordred heard the Lady speak again. "You see, Merlin, I did not tell him — though I was sorely tempted. He will find out for himself anyway."

He did not dare linger, though he wanted to, and he was out of earshot before Merlin made any reply to that. He puzzled over this remark for a long time as he led the knights back through the forest, and while he dutifully trod the path he wished that he had taken a chance on eavesdropping after all.

Behind him the knights bickered among themselves; each taxed the others' pusillanimity and each vowed to return and wreak vengeance. Presently Mordred stopped and turned and said quietly, "Should you not first retrieve your two comrades whom you have left behind? I shall wait here while you go and fetch them." After that they sulked in silence until they reached the road and the waiting horses.

Merlin did not appear for nearly an hour; during this time there was a brief but heavy shower that the knights complained about even though the trees provided ample shelter. It did not improve their tempers when Merlin came bounding out of the forest with a spring in his step and a foolish smile on his face. Without a word of apology, he climbed into his wet saddle and bade the others do likewise. He seemed blind to their reproachful looks and deaf to their impatient sighs. He was young and in love — what cared he for the convenience of others?

The knights rode back in a sullen, disaffected silence broken only by an occasional grumble about the weather or their discomfort. Later they would have to agree on a more or less credible version of events, for Arthur loved to hear all about the knights' adventures and would let them omit no details.

Mordred was curious to know what had passed between the Lady and the Druid, but to all his questions Merlin would only smile vacantly or mumble into his beard, and so he gave up.

* * *

I was considerably more anxious to learn what sort of reception awaited me, for my failure had left me quite drained of courage. Now the best I could do was to try to fashion some barely plausible account that might incline the king to leniency.

"What will you say to my father?"

"What's that, my boy?"

"He will want an explanation surely. What will you tell him?"

Merlin raised his hand listlessly and let it fall. "Oh, you mustn't worry about that. Everything will be all right."

No doubt everything was all right in the golden avenues where his mind now wandered, but I could still remember my father's eyes when he had first beheld the Grail, and I had long known about his terrible temper.

"What if I say it was the Fomor who stole the Grail, and you followed me to help retrieve it?"

Merlin smiled but did not turn his head. "If that is what you wish."

Arthur was waiting outside the gates when we arrived, his expedition drawn up in patient array behind him; the silver knights with banners furled, the bored men-at-arms leaning on their axes and shields, and at the rear a dozen or so covered wagons for provisions and booty. At the procession's head was a small, open cart and in this, behind the driver, sat a Druid Ovate, small and white-robed, his head bent in prayer or meditation. I watched as the king whipped his grey palfrey into a gallop toward us and wondered how long he had been waiting there.

He was bareheaded, and over his mail he wore a red cloak that streamed magnificently behind him. It was a long time since I had seen him accoutred for war. On horseback he cut a splendid figure, stern and straight-backed, his grey hair flowing behind him. "Where have you been?" he called above the pounding hooves. His eyes, narrowed against the rushing air, were unreadable slits. He jerked his horse to a halt beside me and struck me painfully on the shoulder. "We have been waiting for you."

Though I had an answer of sorts prepared, I could not reply out of sheer astonishment, for his face had broken into a huge grin. He slapped me again and cast a swift, speculative eye over my companions. "Following some adventure of your own, I see. Well, when I return you must tell me all about it, but I cannot tarry now. I only stayed this long to wish you good-bye."

"Where are you going, Father?"

We both knew the question was unnecessary, but if I could not alter his purpose I might at least try to stir his conscience a little.

"I shall be gone several weeks, possibly months." He

started to pick absently at the palfrey's mane. This was my father as I remembered him of old; clumsily evasive as he tried to avoid my gaze. "I have considered well all those things we talked about, Mordred. The grievances of my subjects and so forth. Merlin and I have spent a long time discussing what should be done. Haven't we, Merlin?"

"Indeed, sire."

"Are you all right?"

Merlin, who was leaning dangerously in the saddle but seemed to be unaware of it, replied, "I never felt better, sire."

Why do you need a small army if your purpose is to extend aid and succor? That is perhaps what I should have asked. Instead, I looked over to the innocuous little cart that would go before everything else. "What is in that?"

"Why, the Grail, of course." Arthur turned his restless mount around. "Keep well my kingdom while I am away — I have never left you in charge before, that is why I wanted to speak to you before I left. Look after your mother. She didn't want me to go on this trip, you know." He winked at me slyly. "And heed Merlin's advice, for he knows more about good governance than anyone. . . . Are you sure you're all right, Merlin?" But the palfrey whipped him away before the Druid could mouth a reply, and with a final wave he rejoined his waiting knights.

As we watched the expedition slowly move off, Merlin, whose mind was clearly still elsewhere for the most part, muttered, "I told you not to worry."

18

MERLIN, IN SPITE OF MORDRED'S IMPATIENT questions, would not explain matters straight away. Instead he led the way into the Tower Bedegraine. They did not go down to the gloomy cellar but ascended the dark, winding staircase. It was a slow climb; Merlin's brief interval of renewed vigor had been just a cruel illusion after all, and now that it was gone he felt older than ever. As his crabbed fingers groped for precious handholds in the smooth, damp stone, he cursed his folly under his breath. Now, he thought, I shall never again be my own master. . . .

* * *

"I may come again, then, Lady?"

"Yes, Merlin, you may come again. But not in such clamorous company. Come alone next time."

"This parting seems to me such a terrible wrench."

She sighed. "That is because you are out of practice, dear." She bent forward and lightly brushed his cheeks, and he thought for a moment that he would swoon.

* * *

At the top of the staircase they came to a long, white room with tall windows that looked out upon the endless forest far below. "I need the light for my more intricate work," Merlin muttered as he carefully bolted the door behind them. There were workbenches against the walls and shelves that reached to the ceiling and were full of instruments and containers and various arcana. But though the room was crowded, it was much better ordered than the chaotic, unswept workshop where Merlin felt most at home. There was an air of purpose and efficiency about the room. It was the sort of place where things got done.

But for the moment they were its only occupants. Merlin had banished the Druids who usually worked here to other parts of the castle. "This is to be our secret only," he said, gently tapping the side of his nose.

He told Mordred to remove the Grail from the sack he was carrying. Then, going over to one of the packed shelves, he lifted down an object that was covered in a piece of coarse brown cloth. With a flourish he whipped this away and then said in a tone of gentle amusement, "Now, are you sure you have the real one?"

Mordred could not speak. He was dazzled by the light that shone from the Druid's hands, and by shock; he had really thought that nothing else could surprise him that day. With an expression of foolish, dumb amazement he took the cauldron Merlin had revealed into his almost trembling hands. Then he examined each in turn, peering closely inside and out, sniffing gingerly at the dark pool of liquid that lay at the bottom of each; finally, at Merlin's behest, taking a few cautious sips. But he could not tell which was which.

Merlin, who was pleased with both his handiwork and the impression he had just made, said, "The other one, the one I gave to your father, is a much better likeness, I think. Still, this one too does pass muster, does it not?" He, of course, could tell the difference, but though he had wanted to show Mordred his craft — it would be dull indeed if he could tell no one — he was not anxious to trust him further, and so would not reveal the secret marks he had made on his cunning forgery.

As he handed back the cauldrons Mordred said, "It did not shine like this when first I beheld it." He was gazing at both as he spoke, for he was no longer sure which was the real Grail. "The Caledonians had to keep it in a dark pit, for it devoured all the light around it."

"Of course. It was not meant for them." Merlin placed the Grail and its twin on the shelf and covered both with the brown cloth. Later he would find a more secure hiding place, but for the moment he considered they were safe enough. Mordred, he believed, would not attempt to repeat his theft. "You see, your father was right in a way. The Sangrail is far too precious to be taken into battle — the king may one day encounter an enemy as cunning as you, and then it would be lost again. I could not allow such a thing." He shook his head firmly several times. "No, no." Then he looked at his hands, old and twisted but marvelously dexterous still. "And I wanted to see if I still had my old skills."

"And do you?" Mordred asked. "Will the likeness you have given my father make him invincible?"

"If he thinks so, that is probably enough. It is faith, not magic, that moves mountains. Anyway"— he stroked his beard thoughtfully —"I have managed to make it self-replenishing, like the original, so who knows? At any rate, you must not worry about your father. He is a naturally cautious man and will take no undue risks."

Mordred did worry, but his well-meaning folly had left him deeply implicated in the old man's schemes, and he could do little save keep silent and hope that Merlin did, after all, know what he was doing.

* * *

"Tomorrow, then?"

Her laughter was like tiny bells. "You are insatiable,

aren't you? Very well, Merlin. I do not mind if you return tomorrow."

He heaved a sigh of gratitude that was like a dying man's last breath, but as she slowly faded Nimue waved a slender warning finger. "Ah, but I did not say that I would be here, did I?"

* * *

Mordred felt almost sorry for the old Druid. As he left him to wrestle alone with his terrible, conflicting passions — the consciousness of his folly and the desperate urge to sink deeper into it — he said, "I pray you, Merlin, do not fashion any more of these. I do not think I could keep quiet about so many, and people might think that there is something amiss."

He hurried away, fervently wishing that there was no such thing as magic in all the world.

* * *

Yesterday the fleet sailed from Dover. Guinevere and I stood on the cliffs and watched. They made a pretty sight, the tiny ships bobbing like a necklace on the flat, shimmering sea. Guinevere cried a little. "I don't know what's come over your father lately. This is his second expedition in a year. Why can he not stay at home like other men his age?"

I put my arms around her, and after a while she stopped. I suppose they will be gone for years. The king is determined to march to the very gates of Rome in order to turn back what everyone now calls "The Latin Tide." Personally, I think the physical obstacles are too great, though, as Merlin has reminded me, armies have crossed the Alps before.

I do not welcome this stewardship. I have many responsibilities but little power. Besides Merlin, the king left me his three chiefest counselors — Sir Kay, old Uncle Ector, and King Pellinore. They began trying to bully me almost right away. Now they are anxious for me to lead another expedition to the north. The first, though adjudged a great success, did not find the Hyperboreans, and Carbonek was a dismal ruin, apparently abandoned many months before. They tell me that the knights who have been left behind must have something to occupy them, but I know it is their own reputations they seek to inflate. I am determined not to be ruled by the counsels of these bellicose dotards. If I cannot have my own way, then they shall not have theirs.

There shall be no villages burned while I am in charge.

Merlin is neither help nor hindrance. He takes no interest in affairs of state, but spends his time in the forest or the Tower Bedegraine. Nobody sees him for days at a time. He has been like this for many months now, and though it may seem a curious admission, I really do miss him. He is the only person with whom I can have a real conversation, and in matters of day-to-day practicality his advice is truly indispensable.

No one knows what he is about, closeted in that dark tower, but I am even more anxious to know what passes between him and the Lady of the Lake. This is not prurience on my part. For over a year now I have been haunted by those words that I am sure she intended me to hear. I have a horrible feeling it all has something to do with Mother and I sense that nothing good will come of it, and so I have been loath to follow Merlin to his trysting place. But I cannot put this off forever. I have ever been a seeker after truth, and even if my discovery should prove painful, I cannot avoid it on that account.

Perhaps tomorrow, then.

Or the day after.